Rose's Ghost
a novel by Theresa Dale

First published in November, 2019 by Paper Doll Publishing.

This is a work of fiction. Any similarities between real life and the characters and/or events within is purely coincidental.

ISBN: 978-1999277321
ISBN: 978-1999277352 (eBook)

*For my Aunt Bobbi, a faithful and kind supporter
who read the first, flawed version and still cheered me on.*

Also by Theresa Dale

Bird With A Broken Wing

That Summer

Prologue – Charis

She was woken by something.

Adrenaline sparked in her brain and shot liquid lightning down her arms and legs. She had the presence of mind to take note of her tingling fingers and toes, her every cell on alert.

In the seconds since she'd come awake, her eyes had worked to adjust to the pale streetlight that shone through a gap in her curtains, her ears straining for any sound. She had not taken a breath. Every muscle was buzzing, at the ready, but she was frozen.

She waited.

But there was no sound, nothing visibly wrong. She allowed herself a controlled breath.

She ticked through the most logical possibilities first. The kids were with their father, so it wasn't a voice calling for her, and the cats rarely scratched at the bedroom door anymore, knowing its futility.

But there was something. She opened up, just a little. And there it was; a warm heaviness in the room. A presence, but different than that of a living person. Ah. At the realization she would most likely escape being raped, murdered, or otherwise violated, she let her fear transform into determination. She'd done this before, and she had rules.

Rule number one: don't intrude while I'm sleeping.

I know you're here; I can see you, and I know you have something to say, but NOT while I'm sleeping.

1

She remembered how life-changing it had been to discover that she had a *choice* when it came to seeing the dead.

Well, that wasn't entirely true.

But she had a choice when it came to acknowledging them, and she'd worked hard to learn how to control that. As a single mother of three boys, who also had a stressful full-time job and no family close by to help out, she needed her sleep. Equally relevant was her penchant for catastrophic thinking; it was an inconvenient and unshakeable affliction, one she had developed young, when the fear set in. When she'd realized she was different but didn't yet understand.

Consequently, being woken in the middle of the night was not only inconvenient; it was also a guaranteed trip down 'what's the absolute worst thing that could have woken me up?' lane.

And Charis had an exceptionally well-developed imagination.

Now, to lower her blood pressure. She took a deep breath, envisioning the air inflating her lungs, infusing her body with calm. With oxygen. With strength. Then she breathed out, letting the tension flow out of her on a stream of spent breath.

She mindfully relaxed her muscles, letting her body absorb the warm comfort of her bed again.

She felt much better. She also felt wide awake, and she needed to go back to sleep if she was going to be of any use at work in the morning. She sighed, connecting to the energy in the room. Sometimes she needed to reinforce rule number one.

I'm trying to sleep. Leave me be.

She felt the excitement at her acknowledgement and the eagerness to engage. Ah, that explained it. It was a child.

I'm sleeping.

She shut the connection down, purposefully blocking it with her own energy, making it heavy and strong.

She rolled over, satisfied, though she was undeniably wide awake. Even worse, she quickly realized she wouldn't be going back to sleep before she made a trip to the bathroom.

Defeated by the effects that gestating and birthing three babies could have on one's bladder, she rose. She recalled somewhat wistfully the days of her youth when she could wake in the night and simply go back to sleep, putting off any bladder-related urges until the morning light woke her, or the alarm did.

"Not anymore," she said aloud.

As she left her room, she stubbornly ignored the heat of the presence, which she discovered was in the right-hand corner.

She rested her chin in her palms, her elbows on her knees as she sat on the toilet. Her eyes were heavy, her body coming down from her adrenaline rush, wanting, thank God, to rest.

Her mind on nothing but the warm cocoon of her bed, she unconsciously dropped her guard as she re-entered her bedroom and consequently was startled by movement to the left of her, in the very corner she'd ignored on the way out. Just a peripheral hint but undeniable, nonetheless.

A ghost.

Instantly choosing to accept and be calm, despite her newly racing heart, she closed the door and made her way to the bed. There

3

was an audible shuffle in the corner now, a more precocious effort, and she gave in. She'd messed up and let her guard down, after all. She connected, instantly realizing there were not one, but two ghosts. Two children, desperate to make peace with how they'd passed on.

Sitting in the corner, focused on her. Aware of her attention, and happy for it.

Girl.

Boy.

It was always the first information that came.

She saw their faces in her mind, knew their deaths. Suffered with them. For them.

And in that one instant of openness, she sensed the dark man, too – the one who had always been there, who didn't bother her, and whom she ignored, as long as he let her sleep. But this night, he felt glad for the recognition.

Hello. Yes. But not now.

She focused again on the children.

Sweet ones, it's time.

She offered love.

Offered options.

Offered peace.

And, relieved, they let go and became free.

Charis was flooded, then, with their gratitude. It was the most fulfilling perk of her gift. She let it fill her completely, her cares –

including the devastation of experiencing the deaths of the two children she'd just met - disintegrating in a torrent of pure bliss meant only for her.

Though she'd never felt the need to take drugs or even drink, she was quite sure that this was the greatest high that any human could experience.

She wrapped herself in her covers.

Smiled dreamily as she floated.

And slept.

Chapter 1 – Maggie

Jack's filthy coveralls, draped over the foot of the bed, were her first target. She scooped them up, then bent down to grab his (equally filthy) socks off the carpeted floor. She sang loudly as she worked.

She couldn't help but think of the wood floors underneath as she moved about the room, tossing dirty laundry into her basket. Such a beautiful old house. Surely there would be gorgeous natural wood floors beneath this old carpet.

She allowed herself to fantasize about small renovations; allowed herself to feel excited about their new home. Well, new to her. It had been in Jack's family forever. His grandfather had built it more than sixty years earlier, and it had been occupied only by family since. Jack's mother, in her eighties and fading in the grips of dementia, had moved to the senior's home in Wolfville six months ago, and Zoe, his older sister, had been trying to keep it up while the family decided what to do.

She and Jack, living in Sackville at the time to be close to the construction opportunities that Halifax, Dartmouth and Bedford offered him, had been reluctant to move, though they loved the old house in Greenwood Square. Maggie's work was portable; she was a writer and editor for a small magazine. The money was mediocre, but she loved her work and did most of it from home. It was Jack's opportunities in construction that were fewer and far-between away from the big cities of Nova Scotia.

In the end, convinced by the fact that the house came mortgage-free and without surprises, and that the move would bring them closer to family (not to mention Zoe's frequent and often agonizing calls pleading for help), they left their busy but satisfying life in Sackville and moved to Jack's childhood home.

The immediate effects of this had been wonderful. Zoe had relaxed again into her pleasant nature, buzzing around helpfully and showing her relief and gratitude by helping Maggie paint the outdated living room and master bedroom (taupe and slate blue, respectively). And, despite the drop in work for Jack, he was happy with his new crew, which was affiliated with the Halifax main office and happened to employ an old school friend of his.

And Maggie had her own office, finally, in the third-floor loft. It was drafty, the ceilings were angled to the roof, and she loved it. She felt it was hers from the start, eagerly setting to work filling it with her overfull bookshelves, desk and computer. It was a large space, so even fitting her bulky fax machine/scanner/printer in was satisfyingly easy. She'd laid a rug on the gorgeous dark-stained oak floors, fit an old but comfortable couch and chair in the opposite end of the long room, and was more than content with her space.

The immediate effects of the move, yes, had been good; had reassured them that they had chosen well.

But in the months since, some of the longer-term consequences of the decision were making themselves apparent, positioning Maggie in a state of transition that she hadn't expected.

It was no longer so simple to walk to the nearest coffee place, set up the laptop and work. The slower pace, the distance, the feeling of being cut off - all of that added new challenges to her days. Before, she'd had everyday experiences to draw from - the group of kids at the table next to her loudly exclaiming over the latest movie, small talk at the Lower Deck - just the feeling of being in touch with people. It was harder here in little Greenwood, with fewer people, more trees and farms, and no major theatre, book chain, or entertainment venue to speak of.

If you lived in Greenwood and wanted fun, you went to Halifax.

She shook her head, snickering over her thoughts as she made her way to the main floor to grab damp dishtowels and the bathroom's hand towels before heading to the basement – the one part of the house she had zero desire to be in.

Sixty years ago, the basement had apparently been nothing more than a crawl space. When Jack's parents had taken over, they'd hired a good crew to come in and make it functional, at least. Apparently, it had cost them plenty; support pillars were installed, and cement floors were poured, all much easier tasks when completed *before* a house stands built above you. The challenges were nearly insurmountable, she'd been told, but the end result had met their expectations, as basic as they were.

Maggie, however, wondered whether the cost had been worth it. The space had been divided into two small rooms, one for laundry and the other for storage. Despite that, while the washer and dryer found their home in the dark, dank basement, not much else did. While it had pleased her in-laws just to be able to walk fully upright in the space, they did not account for any other sort of luxury. The walls were still exposed insulation, the ceiling unfinished, and the lighting pathetic - it never seemed to reach the corners - and it was always cold.

Though a sturdy table had been set up for folding clothes directly from the dryer, warm and fragrant, she never lingered. She hated the way the hairs stood up on the back of her neck when she stood at that table.

But just now, her thoughts were focused elsewhere. The slower pace, the feeling of being cut-off – she was sure she could adjust to that. It would just take time.

Being closer to family was something else she wasn't used to. Well, closer to Jack's family, anyway. Her immediate family still lived in Ottawa, except for her brother Max and his wife Kathy, who lived nearby in Greenwood. But most of Jack's family was very close. Besides his mother in Wolfville, Zoe lived in Kingston, and she and her husband Sam's twenty-nine-year-old twin daughters, Chelsea and Ophelia, were in Middleton running a small pizza place. Their son John (named after Jack's father) was living in Wolfville and doing his Masters in Education at Acadia.

Jack's younger brother, Martin, lived in Waterville, but he was something of a recluse. Maggie had only met him a handful of times; he wasn't the type to pop in for a visit, like Zoe.

She found herself enjoying the closeness of family, especially being able to see Max and Kathy more often. It just took some getting used to. Jack was the middle child, born seven years after Zoe, meaning Zoe was in her early fifties and Martin was forty. Getting past the age difference had been so easy with Zoe; they had a relaxed, enjoyable relationship.

It was the visits to Jack's mom that were hard. Wolfville was a beautiful university town, populated by students and retirees for the most part, boasting close proximity to the dykes and the Minas Basin, not to mention quaint little coffee shops and a few excellent restaurants. The glorious Victorian inns and historic sites were icing on the cake.

So, she tried to look forward to the beauty of the town during the visits to the home where Alice now dwelt, but the unavoidably depressing ambiance and obvious decline in Alice's health were hard to ignore.

As she surrendered further to her dementia, it became harder for her to hide it as she'd been inclined to do. Her countenance gave her away. Her eyes. Maggie thought she resented that. Her mother-in-law had been through much in her life, but she had always taken pride in giving the impression of strength and confidence. That everyone saw her that way, even if it had been an illusion, had been important to her.

Now, it was slipping through her grasp like water, Alice forgetting, sometimes, that there was anything to hold on to. And Jack was coming with her less and less on the weekly trips to the home, despite his increased availability.

Maggie descended the basement stairs, lit overhead by a bald 100-watt bulb. The chill hit her halfway down. Suppressing a shudder, she tried to let her thoughts carry her.

Jack had been worried about the decrease in work, and rightly so. The opportunities were fewer, as he'd feared. But he'd filled his time with work around the house – replacing the cabinet doors in the kitchen, re-shelving the pantry, even building a little bridge over the charming trickle of a brook in the back, which led to a trail in the woods. Where the trail led, they hadn't yet explored. The bridge had been the last of Jack's projects before the cold had hit, after which he chose to work inside at home when he could. He had no choice but to work outside with the crew, so he took his breaks from the finger-numbing bite of the Canadian wind when he had the luxury to do so.

Aside from fixing up the home he'd grown up in, Jack had been spending time with old friends, refound. Adam, the old friend on Jack's new crew, was a frequent companion. Sometimes helping out at the house and sometimes taking Jack out for a drink or three (*"I won't have him out too late, Maggie!"*), Adam quickly became a familiar presence. But it was odd for Maggie, Jack's new pastime. She knew he was easily bored, but in the past, he'd fill his time with books, TV, board games or heading out to a movie or to dinner with Maggie. Strangely, Maggie was feeling lonely for her husband now, despite his leaner work schedule.

Feeling a bit shocked at this revelation, she opened the washer with one hand, the other poised to toss in the first handful of laundry. Glancing inside, she froze. She closed her eyes, then opened them, and instantly jumped back as if she had touched a hot burner, laundry spilling onto the floor. Her heel stuck on a rough part of the concrete, and she tumbled down, the bony part of her butt striking the unforgiving cement floor. She cried out in pain. Behind her came a sound like an exhale and then a cold breath of air grazed her shoulder and right ear.

Her heart hammering painfully against her ribcage, she launched herself up and bolted to the stairs. She heard another sound and was terrified to realize it was her own voice making a whimpering noise she'd never have recognized as her own in other circumstances. She tripped over the first step, jamming her knee into the edge of the third with a yelp. She scrambled up the rest of the stairs, using all four limbs for speed.

Crawling out onto the linoleum of the kitchen floor, she turned and sat hard, panting. As soon as she got her wits about her, she shot an arm out to slam the door shut, a few tears trickling down her cheeks.

She sat gulping for air for what seemed like a long time until she realized she was holding her left forearm with her right hand. Coming out of her shock, she pushed herself backward to lean against the cupboards beneath the kitchen sink. The solidity of them was a relief.

Working to gather herself, she took her hand away from her arm, peering cautiously at the place she had unconsciously been covering. A long, deep scrape was showing faint lines of blood, worse here and there, and pierced at one end by a large splinter.

Must have been from the stairs.

Remembering her feverish, terrified climb, her heart began pounding again, her breath catching in her throat.

What the hell happened down there?

She didn't let the answer come, didn't let the memory of what she'd seen crystallize.

She moved to get up, her knee and back protesting. Slowly, she rose to standing, her eyes compulsively fixed on the basement door. She wanted to go fix her scrape, put some Polysporin on it, a Band-Aid, maybe. She wanted to take some Ibuprophen for the dull, throbbing pain in her knee and the sharper, more insistent pain in her back.

She wanted to call Jack.

She wanted to stand there and look at that door to make sure it stayed just as it was, closed. Quiet.

But in the end, she wanted to get the laundry done!

She thought of the mess of it on the floor – Jack's overalls, her jeans, her much-worn fleece nightshirt - and shook her head. She raised her hand to her mouth, suddenly feeling a little bit silly.

She'd always been scared of the basement. She couldn't have seen - *no*.

She shook her head in an effort to deny it.

And the sound, like someone exhaling behind her, the cold brush of air… Imagined. She'd gotten carried away.

She almost believed it.

But –

But she'd been completely lost in her thoughts, not consciously worried at all about being down there. And nothing could have prompted what she saw… *Oh, God.*

Unable to escape the truth, she was left with one question: what was she supposed to do with it?

Chapter 2 – Alice

It's never quiet here.

I know I hate that, but I can't tell you why.

I can't even tell you why I can't tell you.

I don't remember where I want to be, but it's not here.

And, where is she? When does she come again? She reminds me of Marla, isn't that strange? And isn't it strange I remember Marla's name, but not this other girl?

Oh, she's Jack's wife, I think. And Jack is my son. One of them.

Sometimes I get this fearful desperation. When I realize I've just remembered a vital piece of information like that. Like the fact that the girl whose company I'm longing for is my daughter-in-law. Remembering that I can't remember - it's so frightening, but I don't know how to say it out loud. This torment…

This desperate confusion.

What is her name?

Ah, I can't remember.

I remember Rose, though. She showed me things. I don't know if she showed anyone else. I don't know. But she showed me, and sometimes, now, when I'm confused or sleeping, the things get mixed up with what's real, and I get even more confused.

I get scared, too, because the things she shows me aren't nice.

And sometimes I feel like I can talk to that girl about it. I don't know why, but I feel like she'd understand. And maybe she could help me understand?

I'm so tired.

Maybe she won't come today.

Oh yes.

Maggie.

Chapter 3 – The Boy

Maggie's dreams had always been strange. She'd often wake in a sweat, breathing hard, trying to grasp the last tenuous threads as they faded away.

By breakfast, she rarely remembered enough to tell Jack. Just enough to say, "I had another strange dream last night." But even that was rare, now, the statement having grown old when there was nothing to follow it up with, so she spared her husband and kept her troubled nights to herself.

Jack read the paper as he absently scooped scrambled eggs onto his toast. Folding the corner of the paper down, he eyed her and smiled.

"You OK?"

"Hm?"

She grasped her coffee between her palms, savouring its warmth, as the big, old house did not hold heat well.

"Are you alright, Magpie? You're so quiet lately."

His pet name for her made her smile.

"Yeah, I just, well I guess it's taking time to adjust, you know? I miss my old routines a bit."

He lowered his paper to give her his full attention. "Getting stuck in your ways, hm?"

She grimaced and threw a corner of toast at him. He had taken to poking fun at their respective ages lately; she figured it was an effort to add some humour to his trepidation about turning 45 soon.

Fortunately, she didn't feel insulted; she had turned 35 before the move and was confident that age had a lot more to do with chronology than it had to do with who a person was. But she let him make his little jokes. If it made him feel better, she was all for it.

"Are you making a comment about my age, mister?"

He grinned and threw her toast back at her. "You know what they say about old dogs and new tricks!"

"Ugh! Now I'm a dog, too?" She rose, carrying the abused toast to the counter. Jack only laughed. She smiled back at him over her shoulder.

She stood over the sink, craving the warmth of her coffee but unable to let the dishes sit. As she rinsed and then fed them into the dishwasher, she tried to name the anxiety that lived beneath this playful surface. This strange feeling of unease. Outwardly, she and Jack were as comfortable with each other as always, but she'd never kept secrets from him, and now she was. Maybe that was it.

Jack startled her out of her thoughts.

"Well!" He stretched in his chair and stood, then brought his plate to the sink. "I'd best be off, babe. We're in Coldbrook today, and I'm picking up Adam and Marty on the way."

She kissed him and pinched his butt for good measure.

"Hey, now!" He looked down into her eyes, his arms still warmly around her. "Hey, I know I haven't been around as much. I think I'm just getting used to this new life of ours, too. Being back in the old house…" He gave a low chuckle, glancing toward the window, "It's weird sometimes." At her puzzled look, he perked up. "But with you here, it's great!"

She opened her mouth, inhaling as she gathered a thought into words, but he'd already let go of her, taking his warmth with him. She hugged herself in the absence of his embrace.

"I love you, Jack."

"I love you too, Magpie. See you later tonight."

He opened the door, pausing halfway out, the cold air snaking in through the kitchen and finding her bare legs. He turned.

"What are you doing today?"

She chuckled, hoping it hid her flicker of annoyance. "I'm working, Jack."

He raised his hands, palms out, in the classic sign of surrender. "Right! Sorry, hon. Just because you don't go to the office every day doesn't mean you don't work, and all that. I know. But I also know you do twice the work of the average person in half the time."

The charm worked as always; she couldn't help but smile. "No plans for after yet, but we do need groceries."

He looked satisfied. "OK. Love you." He winked and was off, hopping a bit in the cold as he dug his gloves out of his pockets.

She headed to her bedroom for some warm clothes. The loft would be cold this morning. She stopped in front of the full-length mirror, eyeing herself and thinking about Jack's jokes about age. She needed to get back to her yoga; it had been tough to keep it up since the move, and she missed it, already feeling a bit softer, a bit tighter in her movement. Lifting her nightshirt off, she observed her reflection.

She looked good. Her legs, as always, could use some work.

Damn thunder thighs.

But she was proud of the way she looked, especially now that her bruises had faded to almost nothing.

It had been easy enough to explain to Jack. She'd fallen while doing laundry. She made sure he didn't see the bruise on her knee; the two injuries would be too hard to explain with one fall. But the bruised scrape on her arm proved believable as part of it.

She had planned to tell him right up until he caught her off-guard changing for bed and surprised herself by making up the story on the spot, quickly pulling up the pyjama bottoms she rarely wore to bed so he didn't see her mottled knee.

She still couldn't explain why she didn't just tell him what had happened. Maybe because it was too crazy, but probably because of the distance growing between them, even without her starting to go crazy and believing there was something going on in the house.

Admittedly, though, she'd been paying more attention to rogue shadows or odd noises since that morning in the basement. And an old house has many. But besides the dreams (which she supposed she could chalk up to her unease), nothing out of the ordinary had happened since that day. Since she'd seen the horrible thing in the washer.

She'd even done the laundry by herself once, but felt on edge the whole time, deliberately taking her time until she was heading for the stairs and then running up them two at a time.

She felt silly after, but still found herself reasoning that there was no rule saying she had to do laundry when Jack wasn't home. She could do it in the evening. If Jack thought the small change was odd, he hadn't said it. Rather, he helped her fold on the floor of the living room while they watched tv.

Maggie quickly pulled on a t-shirt, her purple plaid fleece pants and a sweater. Her moment of naked reflection had been enough time to chill her, and she shook her head at herself. Although she didn't consider herself beautiful, she had always liked the way she looked. Her dark, curly hair was easy to take care of, as only one style worked for her: no style. She cut it herself when it got too long, keeping it just to her shoulders. Her pale skin and blue eyes gave her a striking look, in her mind compensating for her sharpish nose and a mouth she'd always considered too big but which Jack proclaimed his love for regularly.

Dressed, she turned sideways in the mirror, standing tall and sucking in her tummy theatrically, and then exhaling slowly as she stared at her profile, allowing herself one moment to wonder how her body would have been changed by children. She saw her face hardening, her reflection displaying her unconscious effort to block the thought, and turned quickly to go to her loft, feeling lighter already with the thought of her work.

She turned the heat up a bit and was comforted by the sound of the furnace in the basement groaning to life. Sitting at her desk, she gazed momentarily out the window at the grey and white visage of the back yard and the forest beyond, then began the regular tasks of going through her papers, turning her computer on and planning her morning.

Two hours later, she had stripped off her sweater and edited two pieces. She pushed send on her email to the office, stretched, and contemplated a snack. Definitely coffee. Looking around her space, she thought of picking up a cheap coffee maker and setting it up on her side table and smiled.

Just then, she saw a movement from the corner of her eye, making her turn to look out the window.

There was a boy standing in the middle of her yard, with his hands hanging loosely (and mittenless, she noted) by his sides and his head cocked up to her window.

Is he looking at me?

An uncomfortable chill ran up her spine. Floundering, she found herself at a loss for what to do.

Tentatively, she raised her hand in a sort of greeting. No wave. Just... *hello.*

The boy instantly raised his hand in return, then reached up to his cap - what were those called? - pulled the brim down in a farewell, she guessed, and looked back toward the footbridge that led to the woods.

It all only took a few seconds, she was sure, but during that time she saw nothing but the boy. Maybe six or seven years old. Little guy, with his brown trousers - *those were old-fashioned* - plaid button-up shirt under a brown corduroy jacket, and that hat.

Pageboy? Yes.

Then, as she was still puzzling over his clothes, he had given her that little nod and started to turn, and she suddenly didn't want him to go. Whose kid was this? Where had he come from? Why the hell was he in her back yard, and why was he staring up at her third-floor window, at her?

But he was already walking toward Jack's little bridge, and though she fully intended to run downstairs and outside to talk to him, she seemed momentarily frozen. Mesmerized by his calmness. He'd pushed his hands into his pockets, and no wonder. His jacket was far too thin for this weather.

Knock knock knock!

She jumped, startled by the sound of a visitor at her front door. It was Zoe, who looked her up and down and laughed.

"Ahhhh, working from home. Sure saves on the clothes budget, eh?"

Maggie shook her head, still feeling stunned, and laughed. She turned once and posed for her heckler, who clapped and laughed.

Then, looking more concerned than entertained, "What's up? You look as if you've seen a ghost!"

The chill ran up Maggie's spine again as she thought of the boy walking toward the little bridge. Suddenly in a hurry, she ran past Zoe onto the front porch and to the edge of the deck, where she peered around the house.

"What the -!"

"I can't see far enough. Come to the back!"

"What?"

"There's a boy!"

"*What?*"

Maggie kept running, feeling the bite of the frosty air on her bare arms and the cold, hard ground through her slippers.

She stopped at the spot where she'd seen him only minutes ago. Zoe was quickly beside her, breathing hard and giving her a questioning look.

"Where'd he go?" Maggie breathed.

"Where'd *who* go, you crazy woman?"

Maggie couldn't help but laugh, though she was more perplexed than amused.

"The boy -"

She continued across the lawn, which was lightly dusted in snow.

And stopped in her tracks.

Not only was there no boy walking toward the bridge or on the bridge but the blanket of snow on the lawn was pristine. Perfect.

Unmarred by footprints, save her fresh ones.

She turned back to look at Zoe, incredulous, and Zoe gazed back, confused. She raised her arms by her sides, palms to the sky.

"Maggie, what in God's name is going on?"

Maggie felt flustered and not a little embarrassed. She turned toward the bridge, then back to look at Zoe.

"Zoe, I was working up in my loft -" she pointed up to the window, and let out a yell. There was someone in her window!

Zoe turned and gazed up, then slowly looked back at Maggie.

"Mags, are you OK?"

Maggie moved a bit, left to right, and the shadow moved with her.

A reflection.

"Oh, God." She bent over, palms on her thighs, and laughed. Standing back up, she rubbed her arms. "I think I'm losing it, Zo. Let's go inside."

Exasperated, Zoe followed her in and watched her get the coffee maker going.

"So, Mags. What in the name of sweet baby Jesus just happened out there?

Maggie laughed. Zoe could always be counted on to add some humour into the mix when called for.

"Zoe -" she bowed her head, leaning on the counter, "I saw a boy in the back yard from the window of my loft. He waved at me."

Zoe's reaction was puzzling. She seemed to make an effort to appear unimpressed, but the flicker of interest in her eyes was unmistakable. "OK, and?"

"And - well this is going to sound crazy, but the kid was really young. Maybe six or seven. My first thought was 'Who do you belong to?'"

She poured the steaming coffee into their cups and offered milk and sugar, both declined by her company.

"But the fact that he was alone sort of pales in comparison to how he was dressed." She looked away, took a breath, and shook her head in disbelief at her own story. "I mean that little boy looked like he was straight out of the sixties! Seventies, maybe? I don't know, I'm not good with fashion through the years..." she trailed off.

Zoe cocked her head, looking accusingly at Maggie's current outfit.

"Uh, present year included," Maggie added, giggling lightly as she looked down at herself. "Zoe, I know how it sounds, but I swear, just as you knocked, I was about to run downstairs and go after him. Find out where he belonged."

"But Maggie, where'd he go?"

"Good question."

"And why'd you freak out when you looked up at your loft?"

She chuckled again, wrapping her palms around her coffee cup, then looking at Zoe. "I guess I was spooked. I thought I saw something that wasn't there."

Zoe paused, then smiled.

"Jack said you were lonely."

"What -"

"Don't be mad. Jack called. Said you're home all day here by yourself, and maybe I could stop in. Hey, don't be upset!"

Maggie had crossed her arms and taken a breath to protest, but Zoe carried on.

"He's right, you know. You're used to being in a much livelier place, doing much livelier things. It must be hard going from that to - quiet!"

Maggie shut her mouth. She couldn't argue with that. Then, wanting to reassure her sister-in-law and herself at the same time, she said, "Oh, I'm fine, really. I love the loft, and work is fine. The house is fine, too. I guess it really is a lot slower around here than I'm used to, though."

Zoe looked at her knowingly. "You said 'fine' three times in that statement, you know that? You need to get out of here. C'mon. I know you need groceries."

Jack is going to hear about this.

"Let's go shopping. But let's go to the mall first. I need pantyhose. What do you need?"

I need to know who that boy was! And why he didn't leave any footprints.

"OK!" She threw her hands up in defeat. "You've got me. I'm done work for the day, anyway. And," she gestured to her attire, "I guess I could use a new ensemble."

Zoe laughed.

"Oh, yoga pants. I need yoga pants!"

Zoe laughed again. "I was hoping you meant actual clothes that you wear outside the house!"

"Meh. Who needs 'em?"

Chapter 4 – Walter

Walter Stack felt most content at this time of day. Closing time. The office grew dim, and from his desk he was able to hear colleagues talking about their evenings, sharing their plans with those who cared to listen. In contrast to the mornings and afternoons at the station, it was usually quiet at this time of day. Other parts of the station were still brightly lit and carrying on slow business - the holding cells, called the "drunk tank" by the locals, for instance, always had at least a skeleton crew, and the lab geeks never kept regular hours. He marvelled at their odd work habits and odd brains, but despite his fuzzy understanding of them, he never denied their crucial contribution to the work of the squad.

And then there were the main office stragglers like himself, finishing paperwork, or an obsessed detective feverishly doing research for a case, and always the chief! But the general hustle and chaos of the day had retreated.

Walter was sixty-four, well past typical retirement age for police officers, and mostly a desk jockey these days, which didn't bother him much. Before Nola had died, his age had not affected his eagerness to be out in the field, interacting with the locals and doing active work rather than paperwork.

When Nola was so suddenly taken, though, he'd been filled with regret. How ironic that he'd denied her more time while she was alive, and now that she was gone, he found his nights at home lonely and ever-long. Now he struggled with the fieldwork that she'd been so anxious about all those years, especially as he grew slower and more plagued by the aches and pains that came with age.

She'd rarely nagged; she presented her wishes both logically and lovingly. *You need to slow down, Wally. You know I wouldn't mind having you around more.* Her smile sweet, her eyes betraying her anxious heart. She'd known what she was getting into when they married, and over the years he'd trusted she'd allow him to control his schedule and consequently his proximity to danger as he wished. But then there'd been no children - just many, many failed pregnancies. Her heart slowly broke as they grew older and she remained lonely.

He waved goodnight to Mason as he passed his desk. A young cop, perhaps a touch too dedicated, and working on something "big" as always. He returned Walter's wave hurriedly, muttering a gruff, "Have a good one, Stack."

Walter carried on, giving a quiet knock on the chief's door and saying, "'Night, Chief," as Mandy Carlisle glanced up from paperwork of her own. She nodded and bent back down to it, looking harried.

He drove home slowly, deciding to make his rounds, checking out the outer neighbourhoods en route. He'd taken a quick run home to Pilot, his adopted police dog, at lunch. He'd walked him and fed him before leaving again. Pilot had stood on the couch to watch him from the window, his tongue lolling from his open mouth just as it had when he was a pup. Walter felt a twinge of guilt here, too, for Pilot used to be his constant companion, on or off duty. Quiet little Kingston and Greenwood were usually quite tame compared to police work in the city, but the dog still loved any job he was tasked with, even if it was just to lie at Walter's feet while he nodded off on the couch.

With Walter's transition to his quieter desk job, Pilot had been staying at home more these days. If Walter knew he'd be spending some of his day outside the office, he'd bring the old German Shepherd to work, but it was often a comedic failure. The office brought back memories for Pilot, it seemed, unfailingly causing his instincts to kick in. Eager to walk the familiar streets or go on stakeouts, he'd wag his tail and jump at any movement toward the door while Walter tried hard to ignore him and get through the work on his desk. The poor dog just didn't get that those days were over.

Kingston was quiet. He drove toward Auburn, watching sidewalks and houses. Just before Auburn, he made a right on Old Notch Road and decided to do the quick drive around Greenwood Square.

Nothing out of the ordinary. Sleepy houses, kitchen lights ablaze. Families inside. Together.

He drove up toward the old farm, then to the grown-over gate at the dead-end of the street. He parked, peering into the woods toward the long-abandoned Maplestone homestead. The driveway was barely discernible from the rest of the darkened area. The house sat far back from the road, surrounded by forest, and as the neighbourhood had aged and the elderly had moved or fallen into dementia, the place had been forgotten. The last time he'd gone there, it had been in bad shape, the second floor having finally given up and fallen into the first. He made a note to get out there before the snow really flew, then headed back out to his home in Greenwood.

Pilot greeted him, his tail wagging. Nola's absence hit him as it always did when he walked through the front door.

She was never there. She never would be.

But he was disappointed, anyway.

Always.

Chapter 5 – The Dream

She'd had a dream.

And this time, Maggie woke suddenly, with its details fresh and all too clear. She replayed it in her mind, hoping it would make more sense looking at it from a different level of consciousness.

She'd gone to bed exhausted. She and Jack had gone for seafood in Wolfville after visiting Alice, and then to see a movie in New Minas. Though she knew it wasn't possible, she seemed to have fallen into the dream immediately, only waking from it just now.

Is it possible to have a...

She picked up her phone and glanced at the time: 6:04.

...six-and-a-half-hour dream?

She shook her head gently, wanting to preserve whatever quiet and stillness she had left before Jack woke in six minutes.

In her dream, it was twilight. The house had been uncharacteristically quiet and dark. She remembered wondering where Jack was, then realizing she was dreaming.

She went around the house flicking light switches, which seemed to have multiplied exponentially. But even when she'd flipped them all on she remained frustrated at the continuing dimness. She just couldn't make it bright.

She'd ended up inside the rear entryway off the kitchen, spotting one last switch beside the door and flipping that one, too. Immediately, she was stricken by the power of its glow, reflexively shielding her eyes as she stepped out onto the stairs. But just before she'd been temporarily blinded, she'd seen something at the edge of the back lawn; something on the footbridge.

She gave her eyes time to adjust, yelling, "Jack?" She frowned at the continuing silence. Maybe she'd been mistaken. Maybe she was just hoping for someone's company and his was best.

"Anyone?"

She let herself chuckle a bit at her sad calls. She knew nobody was there and that she'd come to a decision point. Continue, or not?

Continue.

She opened her eyes slowly and allowed them to further adjust. The back yard was lit by the little porch light as though it had taken energy from all the defunct lights inside the house. *Ah, no snow. And it's mild. Spring?* She looked down at herself, reflecting on her clothing. *A sweater over a flowery dress. Not my style at all.* Everything was greyish, like colours drowned out in an overexposed photo. But something else was off, too.

She breathed, observed. She could see the wall of forest, way at the back of the yard. The little bridge that Jack built and yes, something on it. And she could see the darkening sky above, with the first stars shining through like a backlit blanket poked through with holes.

That was it. Or part of it, anyway; there was a distinct line between light and dark. A cube of light contained solidly in her back yard.

She stepped down to the lawn, not bothering with shoes, or to close the door. In her dreams, these things were of small consequence. Positively ensconced in the light now, she felt as though it were pressing into her on all sides. Her head pounded as her eyes struggled with the brightness.

"I'm here now. I'm here. It doesn't have to be so bright."

Instantly the yard dimmed, her eyes rejoicing.

"Thank you."

She had no idea who she was talking to. Maybe herself?

She set her path toward the small footbridge with the dark lump on it. She kept her eyes on that target for fear it would disappear if she looked away.

It moved.

She fought against the fight or flight instinct (*flight, flight!*). Muscles tensed, she neared the bridge, becoming aware of the sound of the air in the trees. The woods, tall and dark, seemed to be watching her approach. And she'd been wrong – the light did not stop in her yard; it snaked gently past the bridge and down the overgrown path as far as she could see.

She stopped before stepping onto the bridge.

She knew it was a baby before a tiny hand popped out of the dark material it was bundled in.

"Baby," she said out loud in barely more than a whisper, without expecting to say anything at all.

The baby sat up. Far too small to sit, yes, but sitting nonetheless, resting its palms on its still-covered knees.

Her gut coiled within her, hot, as it regarded her. She put her hands to her stomach and stepped back. Everything was still.

Then, it spoke.

"Maggie."

The infant had said her name. She saw its mouth move, but the voice that came out was that of a grown man. And - familiar?

"What the fuck?" A whisper from her, and again she was surprised by her unexpected words.

She took another reflexive step back.

"It's OK, Maggie. Follow me."

The baby flipped onto its hands and knees and crawled to the other end of the bridge, the blanket trailing behind. Compelled only by curiosity (and the knowledge that she was dreaming), she stepped gingerly after it but simultaneously planned her escape should it be necessary.

The baby stood, then. So tiny. Legs pudgy and still slightly bowed from his stay in the womb, he turned and looked at her, his face changing, his body growing. The material he'd been swaddled in wrapped itself around him in a toga of sorts, and his peach-fuzz soft head became covered with reddish-brown hair. Before she could scream, he turned again and said, "Come." The man's voice again, unchanged.

Her body clenched, her muscles tightening in preparation to run, her fists balling up as they readied to fight, her pelvic muscles squeezing to prevent her from peeing her pants.

He was about forty feet ahead of her by the time she kicked herself into gear and walked forward with determination.

She watched the figure in front of her. It seemed... the only word she could think of was *un*solid. His body continually twitched and changed. The question, *is this happening, or is this my eyes playing tricks on me?* hammered around in her head.

It's OK.

It's OK.

She breathed in the pine bark and damp earth smell of the forest, then glanced back at her house, now lit invitingly. The yard's light was fading, though, as she propelled herself forward. Turning to the path ahead of her once more, she was shocked to see the child had grown again. He looked back, laughing a bit in that deep voice. It was him. The boy from the yard that day.

Her fear was tempered with curiosity now.

"Who are you?"

He kept walking forward, turning once to beckon her onward, his arm flickering a bit like a trick of the light. She thought of Star Trek and holograms, and even then, cursed her nerdy streak with a blush.

"I saw you from my window. You know *my* name." And then, "Where are we going? Please!"

The now young man who stopped and turned around looked familiar, but his face moved sluggishly, twisting a bit as it changed.

She felt her face reflect her confusion (and revulsion?) as she worked to solve the puzzle.

"Who -?"

"Shhh." He stepped aside and gestured further up the trail. She walked forward and saw a large, dark shape in a clearing ahead.

She gasped, her legs carrying her toward it, seemingly of their own accord. A building. Dark in the weakening light and stood amidst the grasses and purple heather growing wild and tall. She walked faster now, burning with the need to know what the building was and why it was there. Why *she* was there.

She did not recall passing him, but when his voice came again, it was from behind her.

"You must come here."

Turning, she began, "I *am* he -"

The young man was gone. Jack's brother Martin stood in his place. The voice was the same, though.

Has it been Martin all along?

His face flickered as the boy's arm had. Like bad reception on an old tv.

"I am here."

He smiled.

"Martin, I'm confused."

He laughed.

"Yes, you are." His smile lingered.

"I haven't seen you in so long!"

"I see you, though."

Her skin tingled as the hairs on the back of her neck stood up at his words.

"Martin -"

He shook his head.

She frowned. "No?"

He turned and moved away, the unnatural speed at which he retreated back up the path filling her again with adrenaline. She focused her gaze on his feet, and yes, they moved at a leisurely pace, but somehow, he retreated soundlessly and so quickly he became small in her vision in seconds. And the light was fading with him.

Her feet were cold and hurting on the hard trail strewn with sticks and pinecones. She had lost all track of time. She rubbed her arms in the evening chill, breathed quickly the damp air.

His voice again, so distant now, so quiet, and yet somehow as though it came from the woods around her: "You need to come here, Maggie."

"What -? I *am* here!"

She turned around, darkness engulfing her.

"Martin!"

No answer.

"*Martin!*"

Seemingly in answer to her scream came the low moan of a woman. In her disorientation, Maggie felt panic rise in her. She couldn't remember which direction she'd come from. Had no idea whether that sound, filled with anguish, had come from the direction of the small building she'd spotted or from her own house.

Again, with more urgency, came the moan, elongating into an unnatural yell that she feared would go on forever. It seemed to reach into her chest and grip her heart.

She turned again on the spot, slowly, looking for anything that could act as a navigation point. Her hands splayed out at her sides like starfish, searching for – what? Anything. Help.

Finally, a small square of light in front of her, maybe a hundred and fifty feet in the distance. Without thinking, she moved toward it, and the scream came again, loud and shrill now.

She found herself in a crouch, her hands over her ears, her skin tingling and her mind racing, desperate to know what to do. And then a wave of realization came over her and tears of relief filled her eyes.

This is a dream.

This is a dream!

I need to wake up...now!

And she had.

And now she'd gone over it again in her mind, her heart pounding and her stomach roiling unpleasantly.

The alarm blared.

Jack's arm arched lazily to the bedside table to slap the thing silent, then he rolled over, reaching for her, but she was already gone. Bolting to the bathroom off the hallway and barely making it to the toilet, she fell to her knees and heaved the contents of her stomach, then retched some more, her eyes streaming.

"Babe? Babe are you OK?"

"I need to call Max," she said to herself, and then to Jack, "It must have been the mussels."

Chapter 6 – Max

Max realized he was awake, and was instantly glad it was before the alarm did the job. He loathed the shrill, incessant bleeping of the alarm, but Kathy couldn't wake up quickly any other way. Thankfully, the alarm slept on, and he relished the warmth of his bed, the soft darkness of the early morning, and, utterly content, wrapped himself around his soft, warm wife.

Drifting again, he remembered bits of the dream he'd woken from. A young boy. A lost baby. A dead woman. *And his oldest sister?*

From drowsy comfort, he shuddered himself alert.

He couldn't remember how it had all fit together, but he remembered the discomfort of it. He'd always been able to wake from dreams he didn't like. He, Maggie and Kaia had talked about it as kids and bragged about successes in the morning. Kaia, two years his senior and two Maggie's junior, was the best at controlling her dreams. He was never able to fly as she could in her dreams, or decide what would happen next, but he was glad he'd been able to teach himself to wake from dreams he found unpleasant.

He tried to sink back down into the bed, but then the alarm did go off and Kathy moaned quietly, turning to face him. It was beyond him how that noise didn't knock her out of bed, but no, it only roused her enough to turn her over. He shook his head and reached across her, breaking the rule, and turned the damn thing off.

"Mmmhey. Yer no s'posed to do that. You have to let me do't or I won' wake up."

He kissed her cheek and her neck and her forehead, pressing her head into his lips with his palm at the back of her head. Her hair was smooth beneath his hands. Oh, he loved this woman.

"I've gotta get up, darlin', so you'd better too, before you're back to sleep."

"I'm awake," she smiled up at him, her hazel eyes at half-mast, her leg moving languorously over his hip. And with that, he knew they were both doomed to be late for work.

But he didn't care.

In the shower after, she talked about her upcoming shift as she shampooed his hair and washed herself. He surrendered to her attentions, enjoying her words and her hands on him, sending thanks to God or the Universe or whoever (whatever?) it was out there taking care of him. Them.

They kissed at the door, he in a rush to make the next bus and she more casual about her lateness. As long as she did her hours, she was safe. Working in a lab doing mostly research rather than time-dependent experiments, like some of her colleagues, afforded her that convenience.

En route to his stop, Max thought again about Maggie. He'd have to call her today when he got a break between classes. His schedule was stricter than Kathy's, as he taught science and math classes at the local high school. He'd still make his first class but miss the only sort-of mandatory teacher's scrum before classes.

It was worth it.

While he was qualified to teach at university (and had been offered positions at two, including Dalhousie in Halifax), Max preferred the pace of the high school and the openness of the younger students' minds. Besides, he wasn't ready for the much more substantial responsibility the university positions represented. In fact, he struggled with his choice of vocation in general. Certainly, he was a scientist, but he detested the outdated (and admittedly waning, as time wore on) tendency of scientists to hold to the posture that scientists could not be spiritual, or intuitive. There was such a perceived divide between science and "the not understood" that Max was often conflicted.

He was terribly spiritual, despite not holding to any specific religion.

Which is why quantum physics attracted him so. Some could not see it, but the link between the unknown - the forces bigger than us - and the known was so apparent to him in this field of study. He studied and researched it on his own and taught experimental physics at school.

He got a disapproving look or two from his colleagues and one high-five from Shane, the history teacher, when he stumbled over excuses as to why he was late. The day was cake after that. Easy classes, the students attentive for the most part, and at the end of the day an hour spent marking labs. Just as he was packing up to leave, he noticed his cell phone blinking red in his satchel.

He'd forgotten to turn the ringer on after classes again.

Sighing at himself and opening the phone, he hoped he hadn't missed Kathy, wanting to meet for dinner.

He nearly dropped the phone when it rang in his hand, reacting fast to grip it hard and push the answer button at the same time.

"Hello?"

Maggie's laugh was unmistakable. "Hi, brother! Did I catch you running to the car or something?"

Maggie. He exhaled and sat on the edge of his desk. "Mags. I nearly dropped the phone. It rang in my hand."

"I've got good timing like that. Actually, I called earlier and left a message but figured you'd probably forgotten to turn your ringer back on after your classes."

He couldn't muster any annoyance at her uncanny accuracy. Though she knew his absentmindedness well, he knew she didn't hold it against him.

"Hmm. Yeah sorry about that. It's funny you called, actually. You were in my dream last night." He left out the part about how strange the bits he remembered were and how it had made him so upset that he'd had to wake himself up.

"Oh yeah? You'll have to tell me about it. I've been having some crazy dreams myself lately." She paused. "Actually, some things have been happening that have got me jumping out of my skin every time there's a strange noise." She laughed feebly.

"Aaaaah, it's that house! I never liked that house, Mags. It's got ghosts."

Max had always said that. He'd been to the house rarely, but on the couple of family events she'd gotten him to attend, he'd unfailingly regarded the house with caution.

It's got some bad memories, he'd say.

"Yeah, you have said that, haven't you?"

"Mmm-hmm. What's going on with you?"

"Well, I don't know. Lots. Or nothing, maybe." She chuckled. "But God, I've got to tell someone, and I think it's you, bro. Congratulations!"

He laughed. "What about Jack?" He had no problem listening to Maggie's woes but was surprised she needed him for that. Unless it was about family; something only he or Kaia would understand. Maggie and Jack seemed to be each other's support systems entire. It was something he'd always admired.

"I can't tell Jack, Max. Something – well, I feel as if it would push him away. I don't know; I can't explain -"

"OK. OK, Mags. I've got classes until Friday, and then probably only a couple hours of marking to do. I'll come late morning?"

"Fridays off, huh? Must be nice."

"Don't start, Miss Work-From-Home-and-Done-by-Lunchtime!"

Maggie made a sound of annoyance, and Max smiled. He knew she didn't let his teasing bother her. What the magazine expected from her rarely presented a challenge, and her theory was why work extra when the pay remained the same?

"Blah, blah, blah. OK, see you Friday then? I'll get some cinnamon rolls or something yummy."

"Pie!"

"Haha! Pie in the morning is never a bad thing. See you then."

"Yep!"

He hung up, feeling elated. He always enjoyed time with Maggie. Well - that wasn't entirely true. There had been times when he'd just wanted her to shut up - when she acted as though she knew something he didn't, for example. Sometimes she did, but he just didn't want to see. Still - pushing him hadn't helped.

In any case, that was years ago, now. He supposed they'd both gained some wisdom along the way, the innate need to be right fading in the process. But even through those times, they'd shared the undeniable bond siblings can. Similar in so many fundamental ways but individual in their decisions and the paths life took them on.

Max dialled Kathy and, finding she was home already, said he'd get home within the hour. He suggested going to their favourite pub for fish and chips. No protests from her, so he hung up, looking forward to the evening and to his Friday visit with Maggie.

But he was a bit anxious, too. Strange that he'd woken up with the thought of her in that dream, and now she was talking of dreams and strange happenings at that house.

Maggie's usually the one with advice, but now it's she who needs help. That's why this feels off.

He stamped his feet at the bus stop and waited in the cold.

Chapter 7 – Max's Visit

Maggie worked quietly on Friday morning, feeling warm and contented in her loft. The coffee maker she and Zoe had picked up on their shopping trip gurgled pleasantly on the side table, and she sailed easily through her opinion piece. Now she was deeply into editing the first of two articles she had deadlines for but paused to look out the window at the snow-covered scene below.

No boy today.

After her conversation with Max earlier in the week, she'd been relieved to feel a sense of calm settle over her. She even began to wonder whether she had overreacted by calling him. Nothing out of the ordinary had happened since that dream; in fact, her nights were generally uneventful now, save some trips to the bathroom in the early morning hours, which she attributed to the extra coffee she'd been drinking. She made a mental note to limit herself. Just having a new and more convenient coffee maker didn't mean she needed to take advantage of it to the point of abuse!

She smiled.

Then there was the sickness. While she first thought the mussels had been the culprit, Jack seemed perfectly fine (though the man rarely got sick; he had an enviable constitution), and she ended up chalking it up to a virus as she'd felt ill off and on all week. Stress did that to her, always, and she was thankful she couldn't detect a sign of it, today.

Still, it would be good to have a visit from Max. At least she wouldn't feel silly confessing her recent stresses. Max would make her feel better, as he always had the knack of doing, with his knowledge and/or happy acceptance of the unknown.

She was in the kitchen when he knocked on the front door. She skipped through the living room and let him into the entryway with a hug and a smile.

"Hi, brother!"

Max grinned and patted her arm. "How are you, Maggie? Any more crazy stuff this week?"

She laughed. "Nope! In fact, I'm thinking I've just been stressed trying to get used to my new life here. After I talked to you and knew you were coming, I started to feel much better; the rest of the week's been great!"

He puffed out his chest. "Aha! See what a sense of calm and contentment I bring to the world!" He spread his arms, palms up, and exclaimed to the ceiling, "I've done it again, Universe! You're welcome!"

Maggie laughed and rolled her eyes and, grabbing his arm, led Max to the kitchen. "Come on, you gigantic weirdo. I have something for you!"

Max rubbed his hands together. Maggie laughed; she always produced confectionary delights for her brother for precisely this reason.

She'd set the table for them, with Christmas plates and napkins, but the star was in the center of the table: a homemade apple pie, just waiting to be served. Max threw his arm around her shoulders, and she smiled delightedly.

"Woo! You're the best, Mags!"

She took a pot of boiling water off the stove and poured it into each mug until it was about two-thirds full. Chocolate powder swirled in each as she stirred, then she topped off the mugs with hot milk. Her eyes twinkling, she indicated a bowl of little marshmallows. "Indulge, brother." Max paused, taking in the bounty and looking a bit giddy.

Together they plopped the marshmallows into their hot chocolate and stirred slowly, watching them melt.

"Mags, you're amazing. You know you didn't have to make me a pie." He smiled. "A store-bought one would've done!"

She smiled back, reaching for the pie server. "Hey, it's not just for you!" She served them both a generous slice, offering him some whipped cream, which he eagerly accepted.

They fell into comfortable conversation: work, family (*have you heard from Kaia? Yes, she's on a new medication for her migraines*), Christmas.

"It's just two weeks away," said Maggie, watching his eyes for the surprise she knew would be reflected there. Max was as scatterbrained as he was brilliant, which was an oft-entertaining contradiction.

There it was. "*What?*"

She burst out laughing. "You'd best get shopping, my man."

He brightened. "I've got a great idea for Kathy. You heard of that blanket with the sleeves?"

Maggie pictured Kathy scrapbooking in their chilly apartment. "Ah Max, that's perfect!"

As Maggie began to clear the table, her gaze drifted out the window and into the back yard. She was aware, peripherally, of Max twisting in his chair, trying to see what she saw. But it was all just -

white. The majesty of the woods beyond the blanketed lawn. Closer, the barbeque, covered in its protective blanket.

"Maggie?"

She continued to look out the window. "Hm?"

"What made you call me earlier this week?"

She paused, considering the option of not telling him at all. Just letting this be a nice visit, uneventful and pleasant.

"Mags?"

She turned to face him, sure that her face displayed her reluctance, but the words spilled from her mouth. She told him about being so terrified in the basement that she'd fallen and hurt herself, about the boy in the back yard, and about the dream and of being sick afterward. She told him that she never felt alone in the house and that she found herself staring at the bridge at the edge of the woods, having no idea how long she'd been looking. As if she'd been in a trance.

She told him how worried she'd been that she wouldn't be able to transition to this new, quieter life in Greenwood Square, and how she felt a growing distance between her and Jack.

Max listened intently, asking questions here and there and nodding. He squirmed noticeably in his seat, goosebumps on his arms. When she was done, he shook his head, muttering, "Wow."

She gave a low chuckle. "Maybe I'm just crazy. That last bit was just a dream, after all, and God knows we've seen our share of crazy dreams. Remember that one Kaia had about the Stay-Puft Marshmallow Man? The nightmare?" She laughed again. "It terrified her, but in the end, it was just a dream."

"Mags, remember? Kaia told you about that dream the day after she had it, after she learned that you'd given me that big Stay-Puft figurine as a birthday gift."

Her eyes widened. "Oh, yeah! On your birthday."

"Yes. There's something to be said about her dreaming of such a random thing and then your giving me that same random thing."

"Yeah! And I had only gone out and shopped for you that day. I picked that up on a whim."

He looked at her. "Listen, Maggie, I'm not saying your dream is real. I'm just suggesting *elements* of it might be, like Kaia's crazy Marshmallow Man dream. Maybe it's worth some exploration."

"What kind of exploration?"

He looked thoughtful. "Maybe you need to follow Martin's advice."

She gasped. He managed a smile. "I'll go with you. We'll think of it as research."

Maggie nodded.

"And you know, you could do some other research, too. You could find out more about this place. Where does that path lead?"

She shrugged. "Looks like it hasn't been used in years."

"Right, but the only people who have lived here have been family. Jack's family. Whoever used that path was a relative, sis."

She nodded again, her gaze distant, then turned to look outside again. "Thank you, Max. It's a relief, not feeling so alone in the mystery of what lies beyond the backyard!" She met his eyes. "Feels good to get someone else's perspective, you know?"

He studied her for a moment. "Which brings me to a question: why aren't you telling Jack?"

She remained quiet, unsure of her answer.

"Come on; you tell each other everything."

"I don't know, Max. He's actually not even around much. And when he is, it feels like he's not, if that makes any sense."

He made a face but nodded.

"I feel like he's having a hard time being back here, and I don't want to make it worse by complaining and suggesting there's something not quite right in this place."

"OK, I get that, but Mags -"

"I know. I have to tell him, and I will. Just – I need to figure some things out first. Let's take that walk, and I'm going to talk to Zoe, too. Fish for information. She's ten years older than Jack, I think. Maybe she'll have more memories of this house and its surroundings."

"Good idea. And remember you're not alone in this, eh? I want to help, and I want you to keep talking to me about it."

Maggie stepped around the table to bend down and hug him, grateful tears springing to her eyes. "Thanks so much."

"Of course." He met her eyes as she pulled away. "I wish you'd told me sooner! And you should tell Kaia, too."

She considered, then shook her head. "I don't know. I'd love to talk to her about it, but you know she's been having a hard time lately.

I really don't want to add to that. Let's just keep it to ourselves for now, OK?"

"OK." He stood and reached for his coat.

"Are you leaving already?"

"Nope. Let's go." He gestured to the back yard.

"Now?" He looked at her quizzically. "I guess when you said, 'I'll come with you,' I thought you meant 'I'll come with you *someday*.' Like, in the future."

He laughed but didn't pause in putting on his coat and boots. "Come on, Mags."

Maggie hesitated, but determination surged within her in seconds. "OK, OK. I've gotten you over here, fed you my crazy story. I guess I owe it to you to follow through on your suggestion!"

He led her to the door, smiling.

At the base of the little bridge, they paused, both wrapped in not just their coats but scarves, hats and mittens that Maggie had dug out of the hall closet and insisted they wore.

Max shook his head, regarding the woollen scarf draped around his neck. "It hurts my heart a little," he said quietly. When she sent him a questioning look, he gestured to his hat and scarf. "You would have been a wonderful mother."

It was such an unexpected statement that it filled her eyes with tears. "Thank you, Max."

"I'm sorry I've never said it," he muttered, then looked toward the path on the other side of the bridge. "It's just ironic, your wanting children so badly and being unable, and my being so scared to parent that I went as far as getting a vasectomy to ensure it wouldn't happen."

She took his hand and squeezed it. He met her eyes. "I'm so sorry."

She laughed quietly. "Jesus, Max. I've never been angry – or resentful! - over it. It's just – life, you know?"

He nodded.

Big flakes of snow fell silently around them.

They stood facing each other, but now both of them looked warily into the woods. When she brought her gaze back to his face, she laughed, brushing fluffy clumps of snowflakes out of his slightly-bushier-than-average eyebrows.

"What?" He self-consciously pulled his hand out of his mitten and smoothed his eyebrows.

"Nothing. You just had a snow unibrow."

They laughed together, a bit nervously, then looked again at the path into the trees.

"It's really overgrown," she said.

"Yeah." He walked over the bridge, shielding his glasses from the falling snow. He looked along the path as far as he could see.

"See anything?"

"Come here."

She crossed the bridge, shivering when she stepped over the point where the strange, morphing baby had been, and squinted into the woods. The trail was crowded in closely with branches all covered in snow.

"Look further; do you see it?" He pointed down the path.

She leaned forward, finally discerning a large tree trunk across the path. "Ah. Well, we can get past that."

"Yeah, for sure, but maybe you're right. Maybe we should wait a bit, 'til the trail isn't so covered. There might be ice under the snow – you could slip – and getting past that trunk won't be fun in this cold."

She frowned at him, puzzled at his change of heart. "Is this you being worried about me? Since when have I been a delicate flower?"

He didn't smile. "I dunno, Mags. It just doesn't feel right. It feels - weird."

His phone rang. He looked at her, reaching for his phone, and she nodded. "Answer it!"

She listened to his side of the conversation, which, judging by the way his voice had softened, was with Kathy.

His appeared moderately distressed when he hung up. "Kath got called in early. Her shift wasn't supposed to start 'til four."

"Go get your wife. Take her to work. I thought she didn't do those late shifts anymore?"

He sighed. "Once a month, and when she's called in. Which she often is." He shook his head as he peered into the trees again. "It's so quiet."

"I know. You're right, though. I don't want to go, either."

"We will."

"Just not today."

"I feel like a loser."

She punched him lightly on the arm, laughing. "Hey, things happen when they're supposed to, yeah?"

He smiled. "Yeah."

They turned and made their way toward the house.

"Oh, wait!"

He started at the urgency in her voice.

"Pie! I'll give you some to take home for you and Kathy! It'll only take a sec!"

He happily followed her into the house and watched her place two big slices into a container. "Enjoy. And give Kathy a hug for me. I miss her!"

"You'll see her on Christmas, if not before then."

"OK. Thanks for today." She hugged him again.

"You have to get back there, Maggie. I'll come back."

Her brother had always had an overblown sense of guilt, even over little things like this. She squeezed his arm. "Don't worry! I'm going to do a bunch of research on this place and the history of the area, just as we talked about."

Max nodded. "OK. I'm going to check up on you, though. And I want you to let me know if there's anything I can do."

She nodded in return, then followed him out through the back porch. He turned back as they rounded the corner of the house.

"Hey. What was it?" he asked, and she instantly knew what he meant.

"What I saw in the washer?

He nodded, once.

She swallowed hard. "An umbilical cord, I think. Wrapped around the agitator."

Max's eyes widened.

Maggie grimaced before continuing. "And at the bottom, when I opened my eyes again, well, I think it was a -" She was unable to bring herself to say it.

"A placenta?" he asked, seemingly knowing the answer.

"Yes. How -?"

"I don't know. Remember I had that dream? I don't really remember it, but what you're saying sounds familiar." He rubbed his forehead. "Oh, man. What the hell?"

"And there was a bunch more cord, in a little heap. And – and it was all *writhing*, Max."

He winced.

"But I can't be sure. I mean, I've never seen a real one. And I only looked for those quick seconds!"

"Don't worry, sis. We'll figure this out." He turned again. "Ugh. In the washer. *What the hell?*"

She called after him, suddenly. "Don't tell Kaia! And hey, maybe you don't need to tell Kathy, either."

He looked back at her as he opened the door to his old Mazda. "Don't worry, Mags. Until we find out more, I think that particular little tidbit should remain between us."

"Yeah. Ha." She smiled.

He stood quietly for a moment. "Love you, sis. Don't worry, 'K?"

"'K."

She waved as he backed down the driveway, and suddenly eager to put the past thirty minutes aside for a while, she headed back to the kitchen, her mind on a second piece of pie.

Chapter 8 – Gaining Insight

Breakfast on Monday morning was a sombre affair. Neither had felt well on the weekend – Jack with a cold and Maggie continuing to feel anxious and, consequently, sick. She hadn't objected when Jack had suggested putting off their visit to his mother. She felt guilty about missing their time together but didn't want to make her sick, either.

Part of her wondered whether they'd even been missed. Alice had barely spoken on their last visit, and Jack had stood up to leave early, obviously upset about his mother's continuing decline. He'd refused to talk about it as they had driven to the pub.

This morning, they'd both reported feeling better. Maggie hugged Jack extra-long before he left, secretly thankful for the extra time they'd had together on the weekend, despite the fact that they hadn't felt well enough to go out, even to take Zoe and Sam up on an invitation to dinner. She had enjoyed making chicken soup and snuggling in front of the TV together. She felt shamefully needy as he went out the door.

Max's visit had done wonders for her; she felt less crazy, for certain, and was glad for an ally. But now that someone else knew what had been going on, she also felt more anxious when she was alone in the house.

Her loft brought her little comfort. She turned on some music, hoping for something to fill the quiet and loneliness, but all that did was distract her from her work. Making coffee, she thought of Alice and Zoe and felt sad for having missed visits with both of them on the weekend, especially now that she had a mission. She had promised Max she'd start digging for information, and Zoe was a good place to start. Then again, she wouldn't have brought anything up with Jack present.

But he wasn't around today.

Maggie returned to her desk, coffee still brewing loudly on the side table, and picked up the phone. As she dialled Zoe, her mood elevated. She could look forward to something and maybe gain some information about the house that could help her.

"Hello?"

"Zoe, it's Maggie."

"Hey, Maggie. I've got Ophie on the other line, can I put you on hold for a sec?"

"Sure. Tell her I said hi, and hi to Chels, too."

Maggie tapped her foot impatiently while she waited for Zoe to come back on. She gazed outside, mesmerized by the stillness of the scene.

"Mag? Sorry! Ophie's got a new boyfriend, and she wanted to tell me all about him. Twice."

Maggie laughed. "Young love!"

"Yeah, let's just hope this one's different than the last." There was no humour in her voice.

Maggie remembered the devastation of Ophelia's last breakup, followed by a depression. Her twin and the business had been critical in her healing, but it had been a long road, and Zoe was worse for wear.

Zoe sighed. "Hey, how are you guys feeling?"

"Better. Jack's back at work, and I'm craving company. What are you up to today?"

"Actually, I was thinking of going to see Mom. Is everything OK?"

Maggie hesitated, as she had with Max, and considered what she wanted to share with Zoe. She'd be looking for information from her, so knew she'd have to share *something*, but how just much was tricky. Zoe wasn't just her friend and a potential source of information – she was Jack's sister.

"Um, yes, I think so. Well sort of. I mean, well, I've been a little stressed lately, to be honest with you. Some things have been happening."

"What kinds of things?" Zoe's voice plainly illustrated her concern.

"Nothing to worry about. Nothing about Jack. Just - it's this house. Maybe I've just got cabin fever, being here by myself most of the time, you know? My imagination might be playing tricks on me."

There was a long pause, and Maggie felt her heart speed up a bit. Oh God, had she already said too much? The last thing she needed was Zoe going to Jack with concern. But Zoe's eventual reply surprised her.

"I want to hear everything that's happened. Come with me to visit Mom. If she's having a good day, she might want to hear it, too."

"Really?"

"Yeah. Maggie, it wasn't always happy times in that house. Mom went through a very rough patch, in fact, that really troubled Jack."

"Why didn't anyone tell me this?

"I guess nobody ever thought it would matter. I imagined Jack still doesn't like thinking about that time, and honestly, it didn't even occur to me to tell you. Except -"

Maggie perked up. "What?"

"I'll explain why later, but when Jack started building that little bridge over the brook at the end of your yard, I thought it was odd, considering. But then maybe he was just being sentimental -"

"Zoe, you're not making any sense."

Zoe sounded frustrated. "Sorry. Tell you what: get yourself ready, and I'll come pick you up. We can talk on the way to see Mom, OK?"

Maggie hung up, reminding herself that Zoe was in her fifties. Her girlish voice, wicked sense of humour, and good looks would never betray her age to a stranger.

She picked the phone up again and dialled Jack's cell.

"Hey, baby."

"Hey; how's work?"

"Going good, but I don't feel as well as I thought I did this morning. I'm going to try and knock off early if I can. What's up with you?"

"Poor babe. I might not be home if you do get to leave early; Zoe invited me to go see your Mom with her, and I figured since we missed it yesterday -"

"Oh, good. I've been feeling bad about her not having visitors on the weekend. Yeah, that's great, babe. Don't worry about me; I'll eat the leftover soup."

"Good. Maybe on the way back home I'll stop at the farmer's market and get some of those cheese biscuits, too."

"You are a wonderful woman."

"I know."

Jack laughed, and she heard how his sore throat was affecting his voice. As if in confirmation, his laughter turned into hoarse coughing.

"Aw, you don't sound good, hon."

"I don't feel good, either. Have a good time in Wolfville, Magpie. I'm going to try to get finished here."

"Love you."

"You, too."

They hung up, and she saved the editorial piece she'd been working on, glad her deadline was days away. Just before she shut down, a meeting request popped up from her boss: staff meeting at head office in Halifax next week. Excellent. An excuse for a trip to the city and a chance to catch up with some of the magazine staff. She smiled. She could finish up her Christmas shopping, too.

Zoe was at the door before Maggie was ready but waited quietly in the entryway as Maggie turned off the lights, turned down the heat, and checked the stove. "Good. I'm not the only obsessive person in this family."

Laughing, Maggie put on her coat and boots, and they were off.

Zoe's SUV was comfortably warm. They were soon on their way to the highway, the radio playing quietly.

Maggie felt awkward in Zoe's rare silence but was at a loss for how to start. She was grateful when her sister-in-law spoke first.

"Tell me what's been happening, Mags. I want to know."

"I've been seeing... things have been happening at the house. Er - and outside, too."

"Does this have anything to do with that day you thought you saw the boy?"

"Yeah. And I *did* see a boy, Zoe. I dreamt of him, too."

Zoe looked resolutely forward, her hands gripping the steering wheel.

"And there was something else. I saw something in the basement."

"What was it?"

"I don't want to say, Zo. It was enough to knock me backwards onto my ass, though."

Zoe pursed her lips, inhaling through her nose. "Sweetie, I understand your not wanting to upset me, so I won't push. I'll just ask you this: did it have anything to do with a baby?"

Maggie simultaneously experienced the desire to vomit and urinate. "Ugh." She clutched her stomach.

"What's wrong?" Zoe's reaction was a maternal one, her eyes anxious and glancing over to her passenger several quick times in a row.

"I guess I'm still not feeling well. And all this - the stress of it – seems to be affecting me physically." She moaned. "Pull over, Zo. Now!"

She stumbled out as soon as the car was safely stopped on the shoulder of the road. Using one hand on the car to balance her and another to clutch her roiling gut, she bent at the waist, waiting for it to come.

Zoe was at her side in seconds, her hand on her back. "It's OK, honey. Just breathe."

Maggie closed her eyes and followed orders.

In.

Out.

In.

Out.

She felt better. Breathed a few more times, slowly, slowly, and opened her eyes. Stood.

Zoe looked at her quizzically. "What's up? What's not up?" Her hand was on Maggie's shoulder, holding her at arm's length. "You alright?"

Maggie took a shaky breath and then a deeper, steadier one. Relief flooded her as her nausea faded. "Yes. Thanks, Zoe."

She drew the cold air into her nostrils and focused on how it felt as it travelled to her lungs, filling them up, cooling her down.

"Let's turn around." Zoe opened Maggie's door for her.

"No, no. It's all good. Really, I think it's talking about this that's bothering me. And I tend to get car sick now and then when I'm not driving." Maggie didn't want to turn back; she felt that she had to see Alice. And she'd told Zoe her secrets without the quid pro quo she'd hoped for.

"Mags, if you are sick, you shouldn't be around Mom."

"I'm sure it's just the stress. This has happened to me in the past…" She recalled that devastating conversation with the obstetrician when she learned she'd most likely never have children.

It's nothing in particular, Maggie. You have healthy eggs, and you do ovulate, just not in any dependable way, even with medication. Your hormone levels are a bit off, yes, and your uterus is positioned a little irregularly. But I wouldn't say any of those things were reason enough for you to not have gotten pregnant in six years of trying. And we've tried nearly everything. In-vitro is the next step, but I tell everyone who ventures down that road to prepare for the worst – no baby and a lot less money.

He'd put his hand on hers across the desk, making sure he had her full attention. She, in turn, had grabbed Jack's knee with her free hand to prepare for what the doctor would say next. *Maggie, sometimes there is just no clear reason to explain why a couple can't have kids.* She had appreciated his including Jack in that sentiment, though there had proven to be no problem with Jack's inner workings. It was somehow her fault, even though the reason was unclear.

"… so I'm not surprised. The first time it happened recently was right after that dream about the boy. It was a strange dream, Zo,

63

and you mentioned a baby. My answer is yes, what I saw in the basement did have to do with a baby, and the dream did, too."

Zoe gently took her arm and led her into the car, closing the door, also gently, then walked quickly around to the driver's side.

Maggie was pleased that Zoe got back on the road and continued toward Wolfville.

"Thanks, Zoe. And sorry about this."

"Just don't puke in my car."

They laughed together.

"Maggie, wait. There was a baby in your dream, too? I thought the dream was about the boy?"

"It was, but he started out as a baby. He led me down that trail – you know, the overgrown one past Jack's bridge and into the woods?"

Zoe pursed her lips again and nodded.

"What does that mean to you, Zoe? You mentioned the bridge on the phone, too!"

"I'll tell you everything; just tell me the rest of your dream."

Maggie complied; she was feeling too queasy to argue. "There was a baby on the bridge. I approached it, and it sat up and talked to me. It had a man's voice."

"Oh, wow."

"It was - it was *freaky*, Zo. He stood up and started changing. He told me to follow him, and as he led me down the trail, he continued to change until we got to a point where we could see an ancient building at the end of the trail. When I looked at him next, he was gone, and Martin was standing there!"

Zoe gasped involuntarily.

"What, Zoe? Tell me!"

"What else, Maggie? Why did he lead you down the path?"

"Ugh, Zoe."

Zoe was resolutely silent.

"I don't know. But he disappeared, and there was the scream of a woman. It was terrifying, and I have no idea what it means. I woke myself up when I remembered it was a dream."

"Wow, I wish I could do that. Just give me a sec here, Mags. The road is kinda slippery, and I need to absorb what you just told me."

"I know it's pretty nuts. Actually, it's pretty *fucking* nuts. But I know you know something."

Her sister-in-law sighed but said nothing.

Zoe drove for a while, and Maggie, again feeling her anxiety churning in her stomach, took the opportunity to fix her eyes on the horizon as her often-carsick mother had taught her when Maggie was just a little girl.

She must have dozed because, before she knew it, they were turning off the highway and onto the main street between New Minas and Wolfville. She sat up and straightened her coat, then patted her hair.

"What the hell, how did I fall asleep?"

"You really do take stress hard, hm?" Zoe laughed. "You need a vacation. Maybe after Christmas? Sam and I are thinking of going down South to an all-inclusive." She brightened. "Oh, you and Jack should join us!"

"Yeah. Yeah, maybe we should," Maggie replied without enthusiasm. "Send me the details, and I'll mention it to him." She yawned, looking around to get her bearings. They were very close to the home, now. She felt strangely rested. Sharing these recent troubles really did ease the mind, but she couldn't help but feel annoyed that Zoe hadn't reciprocated. Without an obvious alternative, she decided to accept that, for now. There was only so far you could push a person; she'd learned that the hard way.

Within minutes, Zoe was pulling into the home. She parked, but made no move to get out, turning toward Maggie instead, her seatbelt tightening at the new position. Zoe grunted, annoyed, and undid the clasp. Maggie remained quiet, barely breathing, for fear Zoe would change her mind about whatever it was she was about to say.

"Maggie -" Zoe took a breath, seemingly working to gather her thoughts. "Mom had her babies late. She and Dad were just busy with life; Dad was in construction like Jack, and as you know, he had drinking as a constant preoccupation."

Maggie only nodded, waiting for Zoe to continue.

"For a while, they thought I'd be an only child. It was fine with Mom. It was hard for her, having a husband who was rarely around and drunk when he was. But then along came Jack, and Mom was overjoyed! So was I. I was a little mommy." She smiled, remembering. "I guess I've always had a maternal streak. Mom and I had wonderful days together, taking care of Jack. I have a lot of good memories of that time."

Maggie couldn't help but smile. Jack had told her about his happy childhood with Zoe. She'd been bossy, but Jack hadn't cared. He adored his older sister and forgave her everything.

"Then Mom got pregnant again when Jack was barely five. It was unexpected, but though Mom was terribly sick for the first few months, she tried her best to be positive. We were living off Dad's construction salary then, which was, of course, compromised by his habit, so Mom worried. Dad shrugged off her anxieties and was as positive as he could be. I have to say he did an amazingly good job at carrying on with life, even with his addiction." Zoe gazed out the window, caught up in memory again.

"Jack has referred to him as a high-functioning alcoholic," Maggie said quietly, not wanting to break the spell but hoping to rouse Zoe enough to continue. She had never heard this story.

Zoe turned back to her. "Yes. That's an appropriate term for him. But then they found out they were having twins. They were ecstatic!"

"Wait. What? Martin's a *twin?*"

"Yes!"

"Why -" The question was so obvious she didn't finish it.

"We don't talk about it, Mags, because of what happened."

Maggie settled into her seat and looked expectantly at Zoe.

"Maggie, I hope you'll understand by the time I'm done, and I'll try and make it quick so we don't have to sit in the cold much longer. Besides, I'm starving."

Maggie's stomach lurched in response to Zoe's words, but not in a bad way. She was surprised to discover that she was hungry, too.

67

"Listen, things changed when they discovered it was twins. No history on either side of the family, and Mom and Dad were convinced it was some sort of miracle or message from God. They're not even religious! But life had been a bit of a struggle for them both, and they took the news as a sign that their new happiness would continue. And for a while, it did." Zoe paused, a faraway look in her eyes as she remembered. "Dad was home more often. It was good. I remember it was good. Then, when Mom was about six months pregnant, they learned there were problems. Mom was way too big. I mean, of course she was bigger than with Jack and me; she was carrying twins! But by then, there was no denying it. There was something wrong. The doctor said she had too much fluid, but the really devastating news was that the babies were significantly different in size."

"Oh my God," said Maggie, "Twin-to-Twin Transfusion syndrome!"

Zoe recoiled a bit. "How the heck do you know about that?"

"My sister, Kaia. She knows everything about pregnancy; she was studying to be a midwife."

"Ah. Well yes, you're right, and it was very late to be diagnosed, though I guess it was a good thing that symptoms didn't show up until later in the pregnancy. As it was, the boys had to be delivered early, and care for premature babies wasn't even close to what it is today." She looked out the front windshield, her efforts at holding her grief at bay obvious, even in her profile.

"I'm so sorry, Zo."

She shook her head, waving the sentiment away. "It was so long ago, now, but I don't think I ever really came to grips with it, you know?"

"I don't think that's unusual; in fact, given his neglect to fill me in, I'm sure Jack feels the same."

Zoe nodded, sniffling. "Anyway, at just under two months early, the twins were both fighting to survive, and the smaller baby just didn't have the strength. He died two days later." She wiped at her nose with the back of a finger, her eyes fixed on the seniors' home. "They think – thought - from heart failure."

Tears sprang to Maggie's eyes. "Oh, Zoe. How awful. I had no idea."

"Martin had problems, too. He had high blood pressure when he was born that took a really long time to resolve. They weren't even sure *he* was going to make it! And the problems just kept plaguing him as he grew. He was developmentally delayed - and the poor boy -" Zoe hung her head now, a tear rolling down her cheek. "God, Mags, he just didn't get a whole lot of love."

"I don't understand."

Zoe met her eyes again. "Remember I said Mom went through a hard time? That was an understatement. She had a nervous breakdown. Martin was taken care of by Dad, who, incidentally, quit drinking when they found out there was a problem with the twins."

Maggie's jaw dropped. This, too, was news.

"Yeah. I told you, they thought these babies were a miracle. Dad took it seriously. The liquor had already done its damage, but we didn't find that out until much later. Anyway, when they were born, they both went into intensive care. Dad and Mom spent a lot of time there while Martin grew and eventually got strong enough to come home."

"Jack told me your dad quit drinking. I had no idea what the reason was."

Zoe nodded. "But after Martin came home and reality set in – well, that's when Mom went downhill. The loss of the baby was like - it was as if Martin was the consolation prize. One baby when there were supposed to have been two." She looked thoughtful. "I heard her talking to Grandma, once, about how part of her was still sure she'd lose Martin, too, and because of that, she didn't know how to let herself care for him. It was something that, at that age, I couldn't make sense of. Anyway, Dad's newfound sobriety was wonderful, but it didn't make up for an absent mother."

"Of course not." Maggie shook her head.

"Dad had to work. Dad's mom - my grandmother, Marla - helped as much as she could, but most of her attention went to Mom. We kids were often left to fend for ourselves. I took care of the baby by myself for hours at a time, and I resented him, Maggie, for taking our happy times away. And Jack - poor Jack! Mom and Grandma went on these long walks in the woods; they *made* that trail past the brook!" She shook her head. "Jack begged to go with them, cried and pleaded, but they denied him. Said Mom needed time away."

Maggie was crying now, imagining this time in Jack's life. And poor Martin, unloved when he *needed* love to thrive. She imagined how bewildering it must be for an infant so new to the world without his mother to comfort him. And the absence of the soul you grew with in the womb. It must be devastating, that loss, even as a baby.

"God, Zoe. Oh, God. I have to talk to Jack about this."

"You can try, Maggie, but don't set your expectations high."

Maggie nodded, sniffling and feeling miserable for her husband and his siblings. She threw her arms around Zoe, to Zoe's apparent surprise and gratitude. "I'm so sorry you went through that."

"You know, it was a relatively short time in our lives, all things considered. But at that age, even an hour of sadness can feel like forever, right?"

Maggie nodded and took Zoe's hand, holding it between both of hers.

"But there's something else, Maggie." She grasped Maggie's hands, now, holding her gaze. "Mom saw her dead baby in that house."

Maggie's skin grew cold even as her belly twisted hot inside of her. "*What?*"

"Not literally. Or – well, I don't know, now. It's like she was haunted by the ghost of him. Or in so much misery over him, so guilt-ridden over something she had no control of, that she saw him everywhere - in the bathtub, the toilet. Ugh, she even saw blood in the washer -"

Maggie gasped.

"She'd wake in the night screaming. The nightmares must have been terrible. And something, I don't know what, compelled her to that path in the woods."

"Well, it seems I need to find out what. Because now I'm being asked to go down that same path."

Zoe wiped at her tears, nodding. "Yes, I agree, and I'm hoping against hope that Mom's having a good day. Maybe she can help you out with that and finally solve the mystery for me, too."

"But, Zo, if she went through a nervous breakdown when this happened, and nobody talks about it – Jack never breathed a word of it to me – maybe bringing it up isn't a good idea?"

Zoe shook her head. "No. I've been wanting to bring it up for more years than you've been alive, my dear. I need this, too."

"Wow. Now that's perspective."

Zoe smiled, and the tension was broken. "Let's go in; I'm freezing!"

They got out of the car and slowly made their way to the building, both lost in thought.

Maggie paused before they opened the door. "So, is it him I saw in my dream, then? I thought it was Martin, but was it his twin? Am I seeing him, like Alice did?"

"I don't know, Maggie. Maybe it was him – Sebastian was his name." Zoe stopped, too, looking pensively at her sister-in-law. "Maybe." Her brows furrowed. "But one thing I do know is that it's been too long since I've talked to Martin. I'm going to call him tonight. I don't know if I'll ever be able to make it up to him, his being so lonely in his own family." She dropped her head and seemed to study her boots in the slushy snow.

Maggie, desperate to lift her out of the guilt and sadness of those memories, linked her arm with Zoe's and gave it a squeeze as she opened the door to the home. "You were – what - *twelve*, Zoe? You were scared and often alone with a five-year-old and a baby to watch when your father wasn't around. God. I'd say you did a pretty awesome job."

Zoe sniffed, wiped a stray tear from her cheek, and squeezed Maggie's arm in return, though Maggie knew that truly, nothing could erase that time.

Chapter 9 – A Conversation with Alice

Alice was sitting by the window in the common room, her hands resting in her lap. As Zoe and Maggie approached, she turned and saw them, her face lighting up.

"Girls! Isn't it a lovely day?"

Zoe and Maggie shared a questioning look. *Good day or is she really confused? Girls?* The nurse who showed them to the common room had said Alice was quiet but seemed content that day.

Zoe hugged her mother. "Hi, Mom. It is nice out; very clear. Very cold too, though!"

Alice gently grasped Zoe's arms as she bent over her. "Too cold to walk?"

They hadn't taken Alice out since the weather had turned cold. "Yes, I think so Mom, though maybe we can bundle you up and sit outside in the sun for a bit? On the patio?"

Alice let go of Zoe's arms, shaking her head. "No, that's alright, dear. I don't want to get cold. My circulation, you know." She held her hands in front of her, observing her fingers as she flexed them slowly.

"Good thinking, Alice," Maggie said as she swooped down to hug her, too.

Alice put her hand on Maggie's arm as she pulled away, not quite as intensely as she'd gripped Zoe but more to catch her eye as she prepared to say something. It took Alice some time to form thoughts into words now, and Maggie stood patiently, smiling at her mother-in-law.

"You've never called me 'Mom'."

Maggie chuckled and patted Alice's hand. "That's true. It's always been Alice for me. Is that OK?"

Alice released Maggie and opened her palms, shrugging. "Of course it is, dear. I love you just the same." She patted Maggie's knee as Maggie pulled a chair over and sat close to her, Zoe following suit.

Alice vacillated between being cold and distant on her bad days and overly expressive on days like to today when she was feeling better but still confused. It was as if she was present enough to be herself but also cognizant of her illness, and she felt the need to make up for it.

Apologizing with love.

Zoe launched into the regular updates, mostly about the twins and John, and Alice smiled brightly, enjoying the news.

"You know your John came to visit me last week?"

"Yes, he told me the two of you played rummy for a while."

"We did. I won three times. He won too, I think, but not as much as I did. We had a lovely time, Zoe. He's really a very good boy."

Zoe smiled. "I know Mom. We're so proud of him. He'll be a wonderful teacher, I think."

"Yes. I'm hungry."

"Would you like me to get you a snack?"

"That would be lovely, dear."

Zoe left to find the nurse.

Alice turned to Maggie and took both of her hands. "How are you, dear?"

"I'm alright, Alice. It's been a bit hard transitioning to living in the house." Seeing Alice's disappointment, she quickly went on, "It's really a pretty area, and the house is perfect."

"A bit drafty, I know." Alice smiled apologetically.

"That's fine; nothing a good pair of socks doesn't fix! It's not that. I've been having some dreams…" Maggie simplified the events into "dreams" for the sake of preserving Alice's pleasant mood.

Alice's face dropped, and her eyes clouded. Maggie instantly regretted her words.

"About her?"

"Her? No, Alice, not about a woman. About a boy, mostly. And the path in the woods."

Alice's grip on Maggie's hands tightened. "She stayed back there when she was being punished."

Alice paused, and Maggie tried to smile. "It's OK, really, Alice! They're just dreams. I'm fine, don't worry! I love the house!"

"She stopped. She stayed away. I needed her to leave me alone so I could be a mother." Alice began to cry.

"Oh, I'm sorry Alice, I didn't mean to upset you."

Zoe returned and, seeing her mother's tears, put the crackers and tea she was carrying on the table beside them, then sat down in front of her. Alice looked at her daughter.

"When my Zoe got pregnant with twins, I was so scared." She shook her head. "So scared."

Zoe's hand flew to her mouth. Maggie imagined her shock was in reaction both to having her mother talk to her as though she was someone else and to hearing her mother refer to her fear over Zoe's own twins, a sad consequence of what had happened to her own.

Zoe's hand stayed at her mouth, and her eyes brimmed with tears.

Alice looked confused at Zoe's reaction and turned to Maggie.

"Have you lost a baby, darling?"

Maggie couldn't help but physically recoil from the question. "No, I've never been pregnant."

"I used to see my baby everywhere -"

A chill ran over Maggie's skin, but the moment passed quickly as Alice turned to her snack. "Oh, thank you, dear!" She looked at Zoe, apparently recognizing her now. "I *am* hungry. Would you girls like some crackers?"

Chapter 10 – The Woman in the Woods

The remainder of their visit had been quiet. Zoe and Maggie had chatted about their holiday preparations and arranging with the home for Alice to spend Christmas Eve, Christmas Day and Boxing Day at Zoe and Sam's house in Kingston.

Maggie was glad Alice wouldn't be staying with her and Jack; she feared her presence in the house might worsen her own situation. *How selfish*, she thought to herself.

But she was still glad.

The visit with Alice had raised more questions than it answered.

"What woman? Who is she talking about?" asked Zoe on the drive home. Maggie had filled her in on the part of the conversation with Alice that she'd missed. "'*She stayed there when she was being punished?*' What does that mean?"

"I don't know. But in my dream, there was an old, broken-down building in a clearing at the end of the path and that woman screaming."

Zoe looked sideways at Maggie.

"I can't believe I didn't think of that 'til now."

"I think it's safe to say we don't *know* anything yet."

They were silent for a long time. Maggie noted she was feeling excellent: no nausea, and her exhaustion had faded. She was getting better.

"Maggie, I'm sorry about my reaction when Mom talked about my being pregnant with the twins."

"Zo, don't be ridiculous. It must have been hard having your mother look into your eyes and talk about you as though you weren't there."

"Yeah, that was weird, sure. But really it was what she said about being scared when I found out I was having twins."

Maggie frowned. "Well of course she was –"

Zoe interrupted. "Yes, of course she was, but that was the first time she's ever said anything about being scared."

"Really?"

"Yeah. I figured she didn't want to make me worry. She always acted happy and excited when we talked about the babies." Suddenly her eyes lit up and she inhaled slowly, her mouth open and eyes wide.

"What?"

"She was *so* happy when we learned they were girls. She never even asked if they were identical or fraternal."

"TTTS can only affect identical twins that share one pla -"

Maggie stopped, a realization overwhelming her. The washing machine with the cord wrapped around the agitator, and what she thought was more of the same cord in the bottom of the drum. But maybe it was another cord entirely. And the one placenta.

As that piece of the puzzle fit into place, she felt a sense of elation.

"Maggie?"

"Huh?" She realized she was smiling and tried to tone down her joy.

"Where'd you go?"

"I just - something just made more sense to me. Now that I know about Sebastian and what happened."

"You mean you understand the woman?"

"No. Not at all, actually." Some of her elation faded. "No, just what I saw in the basement. It makes sense now."

Zoe slid her a look again and nodded. "OK. Good."

She pulled into Maggie's driveway, turned the car off and faced her. "Maggie, listen. I'm going to suggest something. But don't think I'm a freak, don't judge and *don't* say 'no' until you hear me out."

Maggie laughed. "That was a mouthful. What the heck are you talking about?"

"I know this girl who knows a girl. They're both in Ottawa, actually. I met them on a work trip years ago when I was with the pharmacy. You must miss Ottawa. Anyway -"

"Zoe, spit it out!"

Zoe laughed and took a breath. "Let me start again. Maybe you need some perspective here, from someone who deals with this sort of thing."

"Like what? Like someone who's been through something similar?"

"Sort of. I mean, someone who *deals with this sort of thing.*"

Maggie laughed. "You already said that Zoe. Wait. Are you talking about a *psychic?*"

Zoe spoke in a rush, "Yes! But, well, sort of. More like a reluctantly gifted energy worker. That's what Libby calls her. See, Libby owns a business consulting company, and they hired this girl – ugh, I can't remember her name - to do energy work sessions with the staff. And then that turned into classes; the staff learned how to connect, read energy and teach some techniques to clients." Zoe looked at Maggie hopefully. "She's the real deal, Mags."

Maggie's reaction, after giggling some more at Zoe's bumbling explanation, made Zoe light up. "Yes. Call her. Today."

"Yeah?"

"At this point, I'm willing to try anything. And besides, I totally believe in all that stuff."

"Oh!"

Maggie started telling Zoe about Kaia and Max and their childhood experiences. Suddenly Zoe grabbed her wrist, saying, "Maggie!" and looking toward the woods.

Maggie froze, and she whispered, "What?" hoping that Zoe would say, '*A deer!*'

"*Look!*"

Maggie turned her head slowly. Maybe it *was* a deer.

But no.

At the edge of the woods, standing on the far side of Jack's little bridge, was a woman.

She was dressed in a sleeveless white gown that reached mid-calf, her legs bare in the cold. Her tangled hair was dark and long, a stark contrast to her pale skin. She was some distance away, but Maggie got the distinct impression of large dark eyes in her pallid face.

Regarding them.

"Oh, my God," Maggie whispered. She noticed blood was streaming from the woman's arm onto the snow. *"Oh, my God! Zoe! She's hurt!"*

The woman held something in her other hand, though it was hard to see what it was. She wavered a bit where she stood and slouched as though she might fall.

Maggie jumped out of the car and ran toward the bridge. She slipped on the ice and fell to her knees. In a panic, she looked up, and the woman was gone.

Zoe appeared at her side and started to help her up, looking past the bridge in confusion.

Maggie turned to her. "Please say you saw her! Please tell me you saw that woman!"

Zoe grasped Maggie's shoulder. "I saw her, Mags. Come on."

They walked quickly to the bridge and then over it, not speaking. Maggie stopped where she'd seen the woman.

"Where did she go?"

Zoe was dialing a number on her cell.

"Who are you calling? *Zoe!*"

Zoe waved her off. "Shh!"

Maggie folded her arms and waited.

"Hello. I'm on 121 Greenwood Square."

Maggie jumped up and down in her eagerness to correct Zoe.

"What?"

"Everyone calls it Greenwood Square, but that road actually leads off *this* road!"

Zoe's face cleared with the memory of that change, which happened after she'd moved out. "Right! Well what is *this* road called?

"Old Barn Road, after the Brown farm."

But Zoe was already giving the information to whoever she'd dialled. Maggie presumed the police. 911.

She looked around. If Zoe'd called the cops, someone was going to come out here, and what evidence would they see? Her own footprints. That was all. No others, aside from Zoe's, which stopped at the end of the bridge.

She frowned. No blood, either. She had seen blood! Lots of it, flowing from the woman's left hand. And she'd been holding something in her right; what if she'd hurt herself?

Zoe hung up. "C'mon. We should leave this area so whoever comes to check it out can see it as clean as possible. But I have to say I don't see any footprints but our own. And I *saw* her turn and walk down that trail."

"You did?"

"Yeah; you didn't?"

"No. I fell. When I looked up, she was gone!"

"Right. You OK?"

"Yeah. It wasn't a hard fall, just a clumsy one."

"Good. Let's get back to the house; they said an officer would be out in a couple of hours."

"Hours?"

Zoe looked at Maggie and smirked. "Hey, we have crime in small towns too, city girl!"

Maggie was reluctant to leave the spot with nothing solved, but she was freezing. She managed a laugh as she walked over the bridge. "Sackville's not exactly the city, Zo."

"OK, outer-city girl! Also, they probably don't have as much staff at the station during the holiday season."

With a final look back at the trees, they went inside. Maggie put coffee on, though more out of habit than desire. She felt jumpy enough as it was without caffeine coursing through her veins. Just the thought of it made her stomach churn.

She turned to Zoe, who was checking her messages in the back entryway, appearing calm.

"I can't stop thinking about her - who was that? She must have been freezing -!"

"Mags, you didn't see footprints either. And I don't know about you, but from what I saw, there should have been some blood in that snow."

"Yes, I thought the same. It doesn't make sense, but we both saw her. We both *saw* her there!" Maggie struggled to breathe deeply as a wave of dizziness rolled over her.

"Maybe she's who Mom saw." Zoe's quiet statement hit her like a fist in the stomach, and she bolted to the bathroom.

Zoe, startled, followed. "Mags? Oh, God."

Maggie knelt before the toilet and let her body do what it had been threatening, off and on, all day. After, she flushed the toilet and backed up, settling her back against the cold porcelain of the tub. Zoe closed the lid on the toilet and sat, crossing her arms. "Maggie, how long has this been going on?"

Maggie pinched the top of her nose with her thumb and forefinger. "The first time I actually got sick was after that dream, just a week ago. But I felt sick before that. I remember it on the morning after the basement - Jesus. What is going *on*?" She took a deep breath but felt better now, the nausea gone. She thought she could even stand and return to the kitchen but stayed put, just to make sure the dizziness was gone, too. What would she make for dinner?

"What the hell – I'm thinking of what to have for dinner now!"

Zoe chuckled. "I think we'd better get you a pregnancy test."

Maggie was sure the look she sent her sister in-law was insulting. "No, that's impossible. You know that, Zoe. You know how hard we tried!"

Zoe shrugged, and Maggie found her hand inquisitively exploring her abdomen through her shirt. She looked at Zoe. "We tried for six years, everything short of in-vitro, and then we forgot it. It was ruining us. Driving us crazy."

"I know, sweetie." She squatted on the floor in front of Maggie. "Maybe I'm wrong. It just seems so obvious, now." She laughed, and Maggie found herself laughing, too, and feeling a tiny glimmer of hope deep inside. It couldn't be. But it couldn't hurt to make sure, either.

"When was your last period?"

Maggie thought. "A couple weeks after the move, I guess. But I'm so irregular -"

"So just under three months ago. Ten or eleven weeks ago." Zoe shrugged.

Maggie studied the linoleum tile, stunned. "It would make sense of a lot of things." She met Zoe's eyes and allowed herself to be helped up.

They walked slowly back to the kitchen, Maggie touched by Zoe's hand on her elbow, her arm across her back. "Thanks, Zo. I'm good."

Zoe laughed nervously. "You sure? You've said that a few times today!"

"Yeah. Let's make a snack."

Zoe laughed loudly now and sat Maggie down at the table before making them sandwiches, moving easily in the kitchen she knew so well.

"Thanks."

"Stop thanking me, silly. I like taking care."

Maggie smiled. That was true, and thank goodness. She ran the events of the day through her mind. It had been a long one already, and they still had the visit from the police to look forward to. She suddenly wanted a nap.

Zoe served the sandwiches and sat, making small talk and answering a quick phone call (John) to talk about holiday plans while Maggie scarfed down her sandwich and the handful of chips Zoe that thoughtfully provided on the side. When they were both finished, they sat back in their chairs and regarded each other.

"Interesting day. I'm so glad you called me this morning." Zoe smiled. Then, looking outside, "Oh, no. Look." Seeing Maggie's fearful expression, she added, "No, nothing bad. It's just snowing. It'll be hard to make out anything back there now."

Maggie looked out into the yard and beyond, nodding and feeling defeated. "Not that there was much to see, though."

"Like that day you saw the boy."

Maggie looked at Zoe. The way she'd changed the subject, Maggie had been sure Zoe hadn't even believed her that day. "Exactly. Ugh, what's going on? I just want to live a happy life here with my husband!"

Zoe stood and gathered the plates. "How's that sandwich sitting?"

Maggie patted her stomach. "Excellent, thank you very much!"

"Hm, a happy life here with your husband. And maybe…"

"Don't say it. I'll check it out. But don't say it, especially to Jack, OK?"

Chapter 11 – Meeting Sergeant Stack

There was an authoritative knock at the front door. Maggie got up to get it, but Zoe was ahead of her. She greeted the cop who stood on the deck. "You're early; good."

"Hello, Ma'am. He tipped his hat to Zoe and nodded to Maggie beside her. Who is the owner of the residence?"

"Me. Maggie Ridgewood."

"Ah. Hello, Miss – uh, Mrs.?"

"Mrs." Maggie accepted his extended hand and shook it.

"Mrs. Ridgewood. This has always been a Ridgewood house, right?"

Maggie and Zoe nodded.

"This is Zoe Armiston, my husband's sister."

He shook Zoe's hand.

"I'm Sergeant Stack. Please feel free to call me Walter."

He motioned to the patrol car, where a German Shepherd eagerly observed them through the backseat window. "I was on the way to my place, close to here, to feed Pilot, the old guy you see in my back seat there. I heard the call over the radio, and after I'd fed him, I called in to see if anyone had responded yet. Pilot likes to get out, see, so I took the opportunity to bring him along. Do you mind if I tie him to your porch, Ma'am, while I get your statement?"

Maggie couldn't help but smile at the explanation of both his early arrival and the dog's presence. While he'd spoken, she'd wondered how old he was and guessed late fifties or early sixties. She observed a too-loose shirt and pants cinched with a belt so that they folded in on themselves at the waist. She wondered why he'd lost so much weight. But mostly, she was glad for his friendly nature.

"Do you think he'd rather come inside?" she asked.

"Well, yes ma'am, but I couldn't impose."

"No imposition. Go ahead and get him, and please come in, both of you. It's freezing!" She and Jack had talked about getting a dog over the years, but for one reason or another, it had never happened.

"Ain't that the truth!" he said, his back to her as he went down the stairs and toward the patrol car.

"Zoe, could you -"

"Coffee. Yep." She was walking back toward the kitchen before Maggie could finish her sentence.

Then the Sergeant and his dog were in her entryway, the dog sitting instantly and looking up at her with obvious curiosity.

"He looks so smart. Pilot, you said?" She went to pat him but paused and looked to Walter for permission first.

"Go ahead; it's OK." Walter took his big boots off and stood awkwardly as Maggie and Pilot made friends.

"Come to the kitchen; Zoe's making coffee."

The next forty-five minutes were spent filling the sergeant in on what they'd seen. Despite looking at them questioningly and shaking his head a couple times, he took meticulous notes and treated them with kindness and respect. Pilot snoozed happily in the corner of the kitchen where Zoe had placed a bowl of water for him.

"Sergeant, I know how it sounds," Maggie started.

"But we both saw her. We know she was there," Zoe finished.

He leaned toward them. "Well it's an odd story, especially considering the absence of blood, but I've heard and seen stranger, trust me. Let's go take a look."

Pilot rose from the floor and stretched, finally sitting and looking eagerly at his master.

"Come on, old boy," said Walter as they stepped outside, and the dog made his way down the stairs with careful determination.

Zoe was already halfway across the lawn, so they made haste to follow her.

"These are your footprints here?" inquired Walter, kneeling, his knees popping.

"Yes. It's snowed a bit, since."

Walter stood. "Yep. That's OK. Just making sure these are from you."

"Yes."

They continued toward the bridge. "Nice property you've got here. Very big yard. Do you know where it ends?"

"The property?" Maggie asked.

"Yes."

Zoe answered this time. "I think it's the edge of the woods, if I remember correctly, but Dad used to say the woods were ours, too."

"He's partially right. You own another acre back, and the property beyond belongs to the old farm."

Maggie and Zoe shared a surprised glance. "I didn't know that," Maggie said, looking into the trees with renewed curiosity. This was all theirs.

They'd reached the bridge, and Walter asked the women and the dog to stay on the yard side of it but to explain again what they'd seen and exactly where they thought they'd seen it. At the end of their explanation, he studied the footprints in the snow, which were just indents now, partially filled in with the fresh snowfall. He crossed, then, to the other side of the little bridge, commenting, "Good work," as he bounced a bit in the middle.

"Thanks," said Maggie, feeling nervous as he neared the spot where *she*'d been. "Jack built it." And at his questioning look, "My husband."

"Right. Well, he did a great job. Solid."

Her anxiety grew at the continued small talk.

He knelt again as he studied the ground. "Whose are these?" He motioned to the mess of Maggie's boot prints where she'd spun on the spot, turning in a desperate circle to find the woman.

"Those are mine," she admitted sheepishly.

"Then yours stopped there?" He pointed to the end of the bridge while looking at Zoe.

"Yes."

"OK. And this?" He motioned slightly past Maggie's prints.

"What?"

"I'm guessing you didn't see this, then. No, stay there for a sec, please!" Maggie and Zoe had instantly started moving forward to see what he was talking about. Maggie noted that the dog hadn't flinched.

"What is it?" they chorused.

"Another print. Bare. Just one. And new. It's not got any of the new snowfall in it. You sure you two didn't see anyone after you went inside? Maybe through the kitchen window?"

"No!" Zoe exclaimed, but Maggie touched her arm.

"We weren't in the kitchen the whole time."

Zoe remembered Maggie's urgent dash to the bathroom and set her mouth in a line, nodding.

"Well. This makes me think it was someone playing a trick on you. I only see the one print of a bare foot, but there could be more within your prints, Mrs. Ridgewood."

"Maggie."

"Maggie. Anyhow, the one print makes no sense. Unless someone is trying to scare you. You know, they have those print-makers at the Dollar Store: rubber prints of all sorts at the end of a stick. The deer prints are never in stock this time of year, though. Maybe someone thought it'd be funny to pick up a 'human' print, too."

Maggie shook her head. "Who would do that?"

Walter shrugged. "I don't know. And I don't know if I'm right, either. Just a thought."

They were all silent until Zoe said, "OK. But we saw a woman. And she was bleeding."

"Oh yes, the blood. That could have been a trick, too, somehow." He looked doubtful. "Let's see…" He knelt again, surveying the area, then removed his baton from his belt and used it to move the snow around carefully. "No blood here. But are you sure she was standing all the way at the back of the bridge? Not on it?"

Maggie saw where he was going. If she'd been standing on the bridge, the blood could have gone into the still-trickling brook, partially covered by a thin layer of ice, below. She looked at Zoe, who shrugged.

"I don't know. I thought she was past the bridge."

"Me too, but - it was confusing," said Maggie, her head swimming again and her ham sandwich suddenly heavy in her belly.

Not now.

Walter walked back on the bridge, to the middle, and peered over the edge. "You can see a small place here, where the ice doesn't cover the water." He motioned them forward, and both women were with him in seconds. "It's possible," he said, straightening and grunting a bit, bracing his lower back with his hands. "I'll let Pilot sniff around now."

At the sound of his name, Pilot stood up and panted eagerly, his tongue lolling and tail wagging slowly.

"Wait! Can we look first?" Maggie implored.

"Oh, yes. But don't put too much thought into that stray print there, ladies."

Maggie and Zoe walked to Maggie's prints and easily found the stray bare one, about four feet back from them, in the direction of the overgrown path into the woods. They shared a look but no words.

"OK?" asked Walter, and at their nods, he must have made some motion the women didn't see, for the dog was up and sniffing across the bridge, his tail wagging wildly.

"Hey, don't you want to get pictures first?" asked Zoe, and Walter laughed a bit.

"I wouldn't call this a case yet, with all due respect. But don't worry, it's all going in my notes. I wouldn't be too upset. You know there are teenagers nearby who love to pull a good prank. And you're very close to the big corn farm where I've been called to expel those teenagers from the barn or the corn more times than I can recall." He shook his head. "That poor family's had more corn stolen than…" he trailed off, looking in the direction of the farm and the road's dead-end.

By then, Pilot was at Zoe and Maggie's feet, sniffing and blowing snow alternately, absolutely focused on his work. It would have been comical if Maggie could have stopped glancing at the footprint, delicately shaped, the toe prints slightly separated from the sole. Pilot looked up at them, sniffed the prints around them again and, apparently satisfied at having found the source of the smells he was examining, stepped outside the circle of their prints, toward the lone one.

He stopped, sniffed, and raised his head sharply to look down the trail. Walter walked to the dog. Pilot looked up at him and then toward the trail again.

"Hm. What's back there?"

The women paused, unsure whether Walter was asking the dog or them. After a few seconds he looked back at them, his eyebrows raised. "I don't know," answered Zoe, for this had been her house before it had been Maggie's. "I never wanted to follow it."

Knowing what she knew now, Maggie understood.

"I've only been here a few months, and it got cold out before I got the chance to walk it," added Maggie.

"Probably for the best." Walter smiled. "You'd need a machete to make it through." He peered deeper into the trees. "And maybe a chainsaw, too. Looks like a tree fell across the way."

The women were silent and shivering now in the slowly darkening cold. Maggie though of Jack. He'd be home within the hour. Then she remembered her conversation with him that morning. Hadn't he said he'd be home early today?

Walter interrupted her thoughts. "Well, it's getting dark, and I think we've seen all we need to see." They walked across the bridge and started across the lawn. Mrs. Ridgewood -"

"Maggie."

"Right, sorry. Maggie, if you see anything else, anything at all, you give us a call." He handed her a card. "That's my personal desk number."

Maggie took the card and nodded. "Thank you, Sergeant."

"Walter."

She laughed. "Right. Walter."

"I'll make a point to drive by here more often, alright? I need to get back up to the end of the road soon, anyway, to check on the property."

"Walter, what do you think is back there?"

"Not sure. Could be anything. Unless the trail bends hard to the right as you go, I can't think of anything back there."

"And what if it does go hard to the right?" asked Zoe.

"Well, like I said, that's land belonging to the farm back there, and then there's property still owned by the Maplestone family all the way to the dead-end. There's the farm, still occupied and working, as you know, and then the old abandoned homestead."

For some reason, the hairs on the back of Maggie's neck stood up. "What homestead?" she asked.

"Actually, the fella that owned the house originally owned the whole farm. The farmers used to rent from him, many years ago. Then it was the son in the house, but he sold the land to the family that owns it now, a generation ago."

"Oh! I remember that," Zoe piped up. "Mr. Brown came around every summer to see if we kids wanted to pick corn for some summer spending money. I remember his talking about the land and how his father had finally bought it from someone. I never put it together, but I did know about that house! There were some wild stories about how it was haunted and how the old couple that had lived there were recluses and *not* fond of visitors."

Maggie was astonished.

Zoe looked at her and explained, "You can't see the place from the road." She looked at Walter. "Is it even standing anymore?"

"You're thinking of the right place, and it's standing, yes. But barely. The place is near one hundred years old."

"What happened to the son?"

"Moved out West, I heard, but after that, who knows. For a while I heard about the town trying to get in touch with him - property taxes, bylaws and such – the house has been in disrepair for decades! But that faded over time. The Chief gets me to go out and check it out once a month to make sure it's not posing a hazard."

"Is it?" asked Maggie.

"In my opinion, it has been for years. It's falling apart, and judging by the graffiti, kids have been out there. But aside from putting up 'No Trespassing' signs and doing my checks, there's not much to do until the town decides to step in and tear it down."

Maggie was still trying to work out the chronology of events. "So, Zoe, when you were little, hearing the farmer talk about the land, how old were you?"

"I'd say around ten."

"So how old must the son have been to have sold the land, then?"

Walter interjected, "He was in his thirties when he moved back into the place, as far as I know. Sold the farmland to the Brown family soon after that. His parents had been dead, oh, at least ten years by then."

"So, he'd be in his seventies now, and his parents had been dead ten years when you were about ten, Zoe."

"Two years before Martin was born."

Maggie twitched at the easy leaving out of Sebastian, despite her new knowledge of the truth.

"Yes."

Walter looked confused. "If either of you are thinking about tracking him down, I'll save you some time. Nobody's heard from him in years. Those rumours you mentioned were true, Mrs. Armiston. And I'll add to them. Did you ever hear anything about the son?"

Zoe's brow darkened as she struggled to remember. "I don't know. We kids always dared each other to go into the woods and up to the place – I think Jack did go a couple times - but we never talked about a son. It was always the old couple. That said, we knew it was occupied after some time of being empty. I don't think we knew it was their son, though."

"That would make sense. Nobody knew much about him. The Maplestones homeschooled him, and he was rarely seen in public, nearly as mysteriously absent as his father was. His mother was the who did the errands and took the boy to rare appointments, etcetera. Neither parent worked. He was from money, or so it was said. People talked. And then, nobody saw her much anymore, either. Then there was more talk. There was rumour that -"

Zoe and Maggie looked on expectantly.

"Well, then the rumours were mostly about her. I believe she stayed for a while at the asylum in Waterville."

"Why?" Zoe and Maggie asked together.

"Something happened. I'd have to go back into old case files to remember the details. But for now," he motioned toward the house where Pilot sat at the base of the back porch, waiting, "let's get you ladies in out of the cold."

Zoe and Maggie tried to swallow their disappointment. There was more to learn here. Who knew if it had anything to do with what had been happening lately, or what had plagued Alice, for that matter? Regardless, as they had very few other leads to follow, both were determined to follow this one.

As they reached the house, Walter declined to come in for another coffee and again told Maggie to call with any worry or complaint. He shook their hands again, and the women thanked him, giving Pilot a final pat. They watched him back down the driveway to the road, and before they turned to go inside, Walter's patrol car was pausing on the road, letting Jack's truck in.

"Oh! Jack's home! And he's seen the police car," Maggie turned to Zoe, eyes wide. "What do I tell him?"

Zoe hugged her. "Everything? Nothing? I don't know, Mags, but I've got to go. I've been out longer than I expected when I left this morning, and no doubt Sam's home and starting dinner."

Maggie looked at Zoe desperately.

"Don't worry. I'll call tomorrow!" She half-ran to Jack's truck, hugging her brother and sloughing off his question about the police car. Maggie heard her mutter something about "Just checking something out." Then she was in her SUV, backing deftly around the truck and waving at Maggie.

Maggie suddenly felt very alone, but she smiled at her husband as he approached her.

"What's going on? Everything OK?" he asked.

Maggie hugged him and said, "It was an interesting day! I'll tell you everything, but let's go inside; I'm a popsicle."

"A beautiful popsicle, then." He smiled and walked with her to the stairs, squeezing her shoulder.

"Hey, I thought you were coming home early?" she asked as they took their boots and coats off.

"I did get off early, but knew you were in Wolfville so I stopped for a drink – just one! - with Adam."

She couldn't help it; the annoyance showed on her face.

"What? He was on a different project and was already done." He raised his palms and shrugged. "What, babe?"

"I just miss you, Jack." Surprising herself, she started to cry. "It would have been good to have you here today."

He walked toward her.

"Some stuff has been happening - I didn't tell you - but then today we saw a woman. That's why Walter was here. And I was scared!" She was really crying now. Jack took her in his arms, smelling of beer and sawdust. Not unpleasant. She let herself sink into his embrace.

"Baby," he led her to the couch in the living room, "what's been going on?"

She told him everything, not choosing her words, just letting them tumble out. He was quiet the whole time, his brow furrowed. Tears sprang to his eyes when she talked about her visit with Alice. She cried as she spoke.

She ended with Walter's departure and Jack's concurrent arrival. Jack stared at her for a few seconds, then wiped the tears from her cheeks. Then he wiped a tear from his own eye.

He hugged her, shaking, crying with her now. "God, Maggie, I'm so sorry. I wanted to tell you everything, but I don't think I let myself even think about it. I've been trying so hard to put it all behind me, but being back here has been so hard."

"Is that why you built the bridge to the woods?"

He pulled away a bit and looked toward the kitchen where the window still glowed in the twilight of the day. "Partly. Mostly in tribute to my mom. She's not herself anymore with this dementia. I guess I just don't know how to deal with that, babe. She used to walk those woods with Grandma for hours. They'd easily hop over the water, but - I always thought, even as a kid, that she should have a bridge." He stopped and bowed his head.

"Oh, Jack."

"Maggie, I hate myself for pretending Sebastian never existed and never telling you about him!"

It was her turn to hug him. They sat quietly like that for a while. Finally, Maggie broke the silence. "I'm exhausted."

He looked at her with concern, then sneezed. "Me, too."

"Let's warm up that soup and talk more over dinner?"

He looked thankful. "Good idea."

They talked during dinner and then for a long time afterward. By the time they were getting ready for bed, she was feeling the familiar closeness with her husband that she had missed so much. He'd promised to be around more and to help her with whatever was happening however he could. But he had a theory that it was going to stop now that she knew everything about Sebastian and his mother's breakdown.

She'd mentioned the woman again, and he had nodded and promised to try and find out whatever he could while he was on the job.

They lay in bed, utterly exhausted, and Jack took her hand. "What a day."

She turned and lay her head on his chest, feeling oddly alert. "Jack..?"

"Hm?"

"There's something else."

He turned his head on his pillow and looked at her darkened features, willing himself to stay awake. Loving her. Being grateful for her.

"What is it, babe?"

"I might be pregnant."

Chapter 12 – Quiet Time

Jack stayed true to his promise; he came home right after work every day, much to Adam's disappointment. But Maggie was kind and suggested Adam visit on game nights to watch hockey.

Maggie and Jack chose and decorated a Christmas tree together, lighting it in the big window of the living room that faced the street. Maggie relaxed into the comfortable companionship they'd found again and regained her efficiency and zest for work.

She'd taken three pregnancy tests at Jack's insistence, which all came out positive, to their shock and great joy. They'd celebrated with Zoe and Sam, finally making it to their place in Kingston for dinner. Maggie made an appointment to see a local obstetrician, whose secretary vowed to request Maggie's records from her last OB and then congratulated Maggie. Maggie made a comment about how she'd given up, so this was completely unexpected, and the secretary gushed over Maggie's surprise. "It's so often when you least expect it. I can't tell you how many women I've seen give up, after trying for years, and then returning to the office, pregnant!"

When she was alone, Maggie walked around in a trance, marvelling over the solved mystery of her nausea, sore breasts and the urge to pee waking her in the night. It was surreal. The appointment wasn't until after the new year, however, so she'd have to walk around in near disbelief for a few weeks more.

In the meantime, she had her staff meeting to look forward to. The invitation had been expanded to include the Christmas party, since the remote workers would all be there.

She didn't tell Max – or anyone else - about the pregnancy. She wanted to hear it officially from the new OB first. Still, she felt odd holding anything back from Max, and Kaia too, for that matter.

Max had called a couple of days after Maggie and Zoe had seen the woman. After Maggie had updated him, Max vowed again to take that walk with her, professing, too, that his inspiration to do some research was renewed. He was fascinated by the story about the abandoned house, convinced there must be a connection.

Maggie, though, was reluctant to delve deeper into it until after Christmas. She was enjoying her time with Jack, doing well with her work, and feeling generally better in the house. She wanted to make the most of it and was glad to let Max run with the research in the meantime.

She was looking forward to her trip to Halifax and the holidays. It would be only three days from Christmas when she returned; she was staying an extra night to spend some time with friends and get shopping done.

The day before she left, she called Zoe to touch base.

Zoe jumped right in. "How've you been? How's the morning sickness?"

Maggie groaned, but there was humour behind it. "Bad."

Zoe laughed knowingly. "What about the other things? Any more dreams? Anything else?"

"No. I feel good. Jack's around a lot. You know, he thinks life will just return to normal now that I know everything. And Zo, he's so much more positive. It's cool."

"That's great, Mags. I hope he's right! Still, I've been thinking about your dream and wondering about the boy you saw, too. I wonder if it was Sebastian. And why he'd come to you."

Maggie felt a twinge of anxiety, a stubborn reluctance rising in her. "I don't know, Zoe. I haven't been thinking much about it, honestly."

"That's good. You don't mind if I do, do you?"

Maggie laughed, her tension dissolving slightly. "Not at all."

"And can I still make that phone call to Ottawa?"

"Um…"

"It can't hurt, Mags. And you might not even get to talk to her at all. It's sort of a shot in the dark."

Maggie squeezed her eyes shut, considering. *You involved everyone; you can't expect them to just drop it when things change for you.* She hated it when her own internal dialogue was against her. Sighing, she gave in. "OK. Go ahead."

"Really? Awesome!"

Zoe paused, but Maggie was too caught up in her uncertainty to fill in the empty silence.

"Um, OK, if I don't talk to you before you go to the city, have a great time, and enjoy the break from everything!"

"Thanks, Zoe - for everything. I'm so glad you've been around!"

They hung up, Maggie heading for the kitchen and letting the conversation fade.

She was on vacation.

Chapter 13 – Zoe

Zoe sat in the dining room, gazing out the window at the traffic. She'd hung up the phone after talking to Maggie and immediately sunk deep into thought. Flynn, her tortoiseshell Persian, lay snoring on one of the sun-warmed dining chairs.

Sam often had to touch her to rouse her from her ponderings these days, and though she was willing to share what she was thinking, she could see how hard it was for Sam to appear interested. Her husband believed in keeping things simple. After surviving a difficult childhood, he had made being easy-going an art, determined to be content as long as everyone was healthy and enough money was coming in to pay the bills and get them on vacation twice a year.

Sam was at work now, though, and in the presence of only the cat, Zoe didn't need to be concerned about the length of her trance-like state.

She understood Maggie's desire to take a break from all that had been going on, and she was happy for her and Jack. Secrets were finally told, closeness had been regained, and the baby they had so desperately wanted was on the way.

But.

But Zoe was haunted by the vision of the woman at the edge of the woods. The talk with her mother that day, the cop's story of the abandoned old house, the rediscovered guilt and sadness over Sebastian's death and Martin's early neglect – all of this consumed her. So, while Maggie was enjoying happy changes, Zoe was facing anxieties both new and renewed. And while she was content to let Maggie enjoy a reprieve, she herself couldn't just let things go.

She had let so much lie dormant for so long, and the resulting sadness and shame weren't worth the modicum of peace she'd found as a result.

She reached for the phone, her sudden movement making the cat raise his head, eyes heavy with sleep.

She had tried to call Martin the night after everything had happened, but unsurprisingly, he hadn't answered. She'd been quite relieved, truth be told. It had been a long day, and her desire to just fall into bed had been overwhelming.

One ring.

Two.

Zoe sighed. She knew Martin didn't leave his small bungalow often. He worked on IT security from home and had his groceries delivered. Despite that, it was nearly impossible to reach him unless you showed up at his door. He hated the phone, he said. She resolved to leave him a voicemail; it was better than nothing.

You've reached Martin Ridgewood. The best way to reach me is via email, at mridgewood243 (no spaces) at ITSafe dot com. If you prefer I contact you via telephone, please leave your details and I'll get back to you ASAP. Thanks.

Beeeep

Zoe was always surprised by the coldness of the message. It was her younger brother's voice, yes, but none of the warmth she knew existed. He made his desire to be left to himself apparent, but as always, Zoe assumed he meant that for the rest of civilization. Not for family.

"Hi, Martin. It's your oldest and coolest – and only! - sister. I miss you. I want to stop in on the way back from visiting Mom this Sunday, if that's OK with you. Just text or call to let me know. I'll bring Tim's."

She paused, holding her breath.

She had so much more to say, but none of it seemed to want to come out just now. "Well, I guess that's all. I hope everything's good with you. Bye."

Zoe hung up feeling empty. She needed to make a connection with her brother, but if he didn't share that desire, there wasn't a lot she could do. Feeling defeated, she gazed out the window again. *I'm trying, though. I can't just give up.*

It was a comforting affirmation, somehow.

She had one more phone call to make but needed to check her cell phone for the number before dialling it on her home phone, which had the long-distance plan. She patted her pockets and looked on the windowsill. No phone. She checked her purse and the kitchen chairs, finally finding it under the cat, warm and blinking red with a message.

She scratched his head, eliciting grateful purrs as he rolled to his side, offering his tummy with shameless abandon. He loved her phone. "Funny Flynn," she murmured as she checked her messages with one hand and stroked his belly with the other. Just an email from Sam with ideas for the vacation they'd been talking about taking in late January. She found Libby's number and dialed it quickly on the home phone before she changed her mind.

Another voicemail greeting, to Zoe's disappointment, but this one much cheerier than Martin's had been. *Doesn't take much*, she thought with a snicker.

Hi there; you've reached Libby Ardani...

(The surname reminded Zoe that Libby had been married since she'd last seen her, to a client she'd fallen head over heels for when he'd come to the consulting clinic.)

Zoe waited for the beep.

"Libby! It's Zo! It's been a while since we talked. Email's great, but I've been thinking of you lately and thought a call would be better." She hesitated, then rushed ahead. "Actually, I thought you might be able to help with something, too. I'm not sure if you still keep in contact with that -" Zoe mentally kicked herself for not making an effort to remember the psychic's name before she picked up the phone, "- um, your psychic friend? If you do, well - just give me a call. Some stuff has been happening at the old house where my brother now lives with my sister in-law. Crazy stuff. I'm talking disappearing-blood-in-the-snow type stuff." She laughed, knowing she would sound crazy to most but not to Libby. "Anyway. Give me a call. Oh! I hope everything's well with you and the family!"

She hung up, rolling her eyes at her rambling.

She tried to work out how old Libby and Harish's baby girl would be now. *Almost a year?* The emailed pictures were adorable. The baby had big, almond-shaped eyes, like Libby, coffee-colored skin, like Harish, and shiny black curls – a gorgeous combination of them both. God. She couldn't remember the little girl's name, either.

She stood. "I'm so bad with names!" she remarked to the still-purring Flynn as she placed the phone back in the charger. It rang just as she released it, making her jump. "Sheesh, Zoe!" she muttered as she picked it up. "Hello?"

"Zoe? It's Libby!"

"Wow! That was quick!"

"I just heard your message! Tell me everything."

Chapter 14 – Charis

She knew it was Jacob as soon as the phone rang. Always at this time, mostly when she was walking between work and the parking lot, and always welcome.

"Hi, sweetheart!"

"Hi, Mommy."

There was a smile in his voice, and she smiled in return.

"How was school?"

"Mom, the kitty's climbing all over me! Huh? Oh, school was good. Boring. I did my presentation."

The familiar combination of recognition and annoyance at this jumble of thoughts came to her. Familiar because it was so like herself, annoying for the same reason.

"How'd it go?"

"Pretty good, I think. Can I feed the cats? They don't have any food."

"Sure, babe. And you might as well get your homework done. I'll get your brothers and be home soon."

"'K. I love you, Mom."

"I love you too, honey. Bye!"

"Byeeeeeee."

He sang it, like always, moving from lower to upper register in a crazy no-tune tune, and she hung up both giggling and exasperated.

This kid! My first, and so like me. Such a sweet, painful love.

She walked quickly to her car, hugging herself against the cold, thinking of a million things. Her thoughts resembled Jacob's words, tripping over themselves, inconsistent but pervasive.

She thought of the tasks ahead of her: the drive to the school, then getting the boys from the daycare program there, dressing six-year-old Michael while nine-year-old Sasha got ready at his locker down the hall, yelling updates and questions to her the whole time, then driving home. The routine was simultaneously comforting and tedious. She looked forward, always, to seeing her boys, but the constant chaos of everything soon became exhausting, especially as she was dealing with it on her own.

Once home, her night would be full of homework, dinner preparation and consumption, notes from school to read and sign, showers and bedtime routines, and if she was lucky (and if she still had the energy for it), some tea while she watched a movie before bed.

It was crazy, but it was her life, and she had chosen it. And sometimes, on good nights, there was time for a laugh and a catch-up during dinner, and a snuggle on the couch while watching tv. There were so many of these little rewards that the chaos was more than worth it. She wouldn't change it for the world.

At work and with her friends, she was regularly complimented on her ability to handle so much, but what many didn't know about was the constant anxiety she lived with. How it drove her to always do the right thing. To be in control. To be a perfect mom, employee, sister, daughter, friend, medium. All the while neglecting her own needs. What she wouldn't give to not be fuelled by anxiety every day.

As she approached the school, her phone rang. Not recognizing the number, she easily ignored it. Her routine was hectic enough without interruptions of any sort. But as she entered the busy hallway, meeting the eyes of one of the daycare workers so the boys would be rounded up, curiosity got the better of her when she noticed she had a voicemail. She dialled it without hesitation.

"Charis! It's Libby, from the Center. Hi!" A short laugh. "I wanted to talk to you about a friend of mine. I know you don't do this very much anymore, but she's having trouble. Big trouble; you wouldn't believe it -"

Pause

"Anyway, I thought of you. If you think you're up to helping her out, give me a call, or email me. I hope everything's good with you and the kids."

Charis sighed and felt the familiar internal conflict: the pull to do this strange work competing with the louder, more immediate priorities. She always felt as if she was juggling too much with too little time. Adding anything new was challenging.

She held her phone, deep in thought, but was interrupted by a full body-slam of a hug from her six-year-old. Her face broke into joy as she lifted him up, reflexively smelling his hair before kissing his sweet, soft cheek.

"Hey! How's my boy?"

Michael sunk into her, sighing.

She marvelled at the ease of his abandon into love. She prayed she would always recognize it and never take it for granted.

Then Sasha was there, too, throwing his arms around both of them and looking up at her with a smile.

"Hello darling. How was your day?"

"Good."

His eyes smiling into hers. It never mattered what they said during these greetings. The words didn't matter at all.

But once past the greeting, the words were non-stop. The boys had built up questions for her all day and were now excited to get them out, eager for her answers and opinions. And they had so much to tell! She sank into this frenzied familiarity as she helped Michael with his shoes, nodding where necessary, answering when prompted, all the while trying to speed the process along.

The drive home held much the same, and she was thankful that most days she was able to go with the flow of their attention and excitement, even teaching them something as they talked.

She didn't think about the voicemail from Libby again until they were all seated at the table, eating tuna casserole. The boys had turned their attention to each other for the moment, and her mind wandered to the message.

She couldn't help but feel a bit conflicted whenever anyone called or emailed about this kind of work. Charis remembered that once upon a time, she'd lapped up the opportunity and was grateful for the clients.

But that had been years ago. Since then, she'd had Sasha and Michael, been divorced, been promoted, and realised that she truly had no idea what the right thing to do with her "gift" (curse?) was. She decided on the thing that felt right - to focus on the tangible and give the energy work a break, much to the disappointment of those waiting in line to meet or be taught by her.

Life had been less complicated since then. She hadn't regretted her decision. She hadn't had time to.

Of course, people who knew her gift showed up now and then, bringing it all back, and Charis found herself helping out whoever was in need, using her skill instead of merely tolerating it or ignoring it completely. She was tired, though, and today, she felt that this new request was just too much.

Unconsciously, she put the message from Libby aside. She didn't wonder what friend needed help or what it was she "wouldn't believe."

Instead, she scooped up a forkful of tuna casserole and scolded Sasha for burping loudly.

She knew it would keep coming to her – Libby's anticipation of her reply. She knew she'd eventually call her back.

But not tonight.

Chapter 15 – Max's Research

The town library's lights had been dimmed for the evening, and Max was among the few remaining patrons of the day. It was four days before Christmas, and Kathy was working late. He had bought small gifts for everyone on his list and, determined to keep things simple for once, had declared himself finished with his shopping. This night was free, and his latest talk with Maggie had him itching to try to dig up some information.

He was at a long table in the centre of the first floor, surrounded by books. Maggie had already filled him in on everything she'd learned, so it was his turn to try and find even more. He'd looked up Twin-to-Twin Transfusion Syndrome and the psychological effects of losing one twin for both the mother and the surviving twin. He had been disturbed and saddened by what he'd read. The fact that Martin had survived, physically and mentally intact (as long as you didn't count being antisocial a mental disorder – *hm* – Max mad a mental note to look up premature birth cross-referenced with antisocial behaviour) was a small miracle. TTTS was a scary thing. Most often, one or both babies died. He couldn't imagine what Jack's family had gone through.

His current task was to learn more about Greenwood Square. He asked at the reception area how long the microfilm machines would remain open for use tonight. As the receptionist answered, "Ten o'clock," he thought enviably of Kaia, who had access to the twenty-four-hour libraries on the campuses in Ottawa. Seeing his look, the receptionist (her name tag said "Georgia") said, "You can get most of the old newspapers online now too, of course."

Yes, but there was something so *focused* about researching in a library. Always one to be easily distracted, Max preferred, in this area of life, too, to keep it simple.

He smiled at Georgia and headed downstairs to the musty newspaper room, the microfilm machines on the right wall. Sitting in front of one, he was momentarily at a loss for where to start. The pieces of the story he'd learned crowded his mind. Leaving the microfilm machine, he relocated to the table in the middle of the room, grabbing a scrap piece of paper and one of the pencils provided. He began to write:

- Martin and Sebastian were born in/around 1970
- The Maplestone son (assumed in his thirties at the time) had sold to the Brown family a couple of years before
- Maplestone would have been born in the late thirties or early forties.
- Maplestone's parents had been dead ten years when he sold the farm portion of the property
- Length of time the Maplestone couple had lived in the home: unknown. Assume thirty years, to place them there at the birth of their son.

Max sat back, running his fingers through his hair.

He didn't know much.

But three things occurred to him as he reviewed what he'd written, and beneath his first list he wrote:

1) The Browns most likely have more information.
2) The Maplestones most likely announced the birth of their son, no matter how reclusive they were.
3) Definite chance Maplestone Junior still alive.

Following the tradition to pass property down through generations, and much like the Maplestones and Ridgewoods, the Brown family had been there for many years and were still actively running the farm.

He resolved to talk to the Browns, whom he'd met once at a barbecue at the Ridgewood's before it was Maggie and Jack's. If nothing else, maybe he could get the first names of the son and his parents. Another thought occurred to him: he could follow up with Sergeant Stack if nothing came of his conversation with the Browns. He hoped it wouldn't come to that, though.

Simple. Keep it simple.

So. He thought some more. The easiest of tasks – something quick to accomplish - would be to look for the Maplestone birth announcement in his assumed time frame. Next, he would talk to the Browns.

Now that he'd determined some rough next steps for himself and knew what he was looking for, he was less likely to get distracted. He briefly wished he'd learned how to use the tablet Kathy had given him for his birthday the year before. It mostly sat on the shelf with his DVDs in the living room, though he had used it to beat Angry Birds. He shook his head and resolved to get familiar with the thing. Maybe even start carrying it in his backpack.

He was tired and wanted to be home for Kathy, so he gathered his notes and the books he'd be checking out and pondered his third and most difficult step: to track down the Maplestone son.

Chapter 16 – Acceptance

Maggie left the house with Jack early on Monday morning, kissing him extra-long in the driveway, until he gave a low moan and a delicious warmth spread through her belly, down to her thighs. They collapsed into a hug.

"Hm, I'll miss you," Jack said into her neck.

"That tickles!"

"It figures you have to leave just as I realize that the place I most want to be," he pulled back to look into her eyes, "is right here with you."

Maggie knew the giant smile on her face must be fantastically goofy, but she didn't care. Her cheeks turned hot under his heavy gaze and she felt, in that moment, like nothing on earth was wrong. Everything, everything, was right.

She pulled him to her again, standing on her toes to nestle her face into his neck. "It's only three days."

"Take good care of yourself." He slid his hand between them, his palm finding her abdomen. "Really good care."

She kissed him again, and it was hard to breathe. "I love you."

"We're disgustingly happy, aren't we?"

She laughed, surprised and charmed. "Yes."

They kissed again, then reluctantly parted, he to his truck and she to her little hatchback. Maggie did another mental run-through of her list as she put her seatbelt on. When she was convinced she'd packed everything she needed – laptop, memory sticks, camera, hotel and spa information (she smiled at the thought of going to the spa with friends) – she started the car and was off.

The staff meeting was at 2:00, followed by the Christmas party right after, so she had plenty of time to drive, check into her hotel and enjoy lunch with some colleagues. She decided to take the more scenic route through Berwick, Coldbrook, Kentville, New Minas and Wolfville and finally on to the highway. It was cold, but she was warm in her car, and the sky was bright and cerulean blue, not a cloud in sight.

Maggie wondered at the drastic changes that had taken place since that day with Zoe. She had felt she was on a slippery slope to being neurotic, but then she'd opened up to her husband, talked to loved ones, discovered she was pregnant. So much had happened. So much had changed.

At night, though, she couldn't lie to herself. When the sun went down and the house was quiet, when Jack lay asleep beside her or she had occasion to glance out the window, she still felt that seed of apprehension germinating within her. She knew it was limited, this ability to live with blinders on. Eventually she would have to face it all, maybe solve it. At least solve it for herself. But just now, this newfound bliss wouldn't be denied. She needed to let herself get carried away by it for a while.

Today was for work, but tomorrow was for her. She would go shopping with an old university friend in the morning, then they'd meet up with another friend for lunch and treatment packages at the spa. The three had kept in touch since graduation, getting together now and again to catch up. Maggie vowed as she drove that she wouldn't share her recent troubles, or even the news of her pregnancy, with them. She'd let herself enjoy their company. Period. She needed this break, and they were the perfect distraction from the thoughts threatening to burst the bubble of happiness she was floating in.

Maggie knew the staff meetings at the magazine were far less structured than those of an office or the types of places most of her friends and family worked; a room full of writers, photographers and a variety of creative artist-types did not accommodate sticking to an agenda, or the intended timeframe, for that matter. But this one took the cake. It was more of a pre-party gathering than a meeting, with the editor in chief taking care of business up front and then a group breakout session. The owners then announced that the magazine's financial gurus had reported that they anticipated a better profit than the previous year, and the senior editor alluded to some upcoming promotions. Maggie thought he made eye contact with her for a brief moment but put the thought aside. She had no idea whether they had something in mind for her.

After the meeting, everyone was full of good cheer and moved slowly downstairs to the open office floor, which had been transformed into a festive party area. Music filled the air, twinkling lights and decorations adorned every window, corner and light fixture, and there was a table with hors d'oeuvres lining the far wall, the hulking photocopier/printer an awkward presence beside it. Maggie was impressed at the stage set up near the chief's office where a live band was already entertaining.

She mingled and caught up with her colleagues, sipping ginger ale and indulging in the food.

"Maggie, can I see you in my office for a moment, please?" Toby Simon, her boss and the senior editor had taken her elbow to lead her away from the group she was talking to.

"Sure, Toby." Maggie followed, her mind racing. Nobody else was being taken aside; was something wrong? Was her work not up to par? Everything came rushing back to her: the events of the last couple of months, her distraction and stress. Still, she'd been confident she was meeting expectations with her work.

Toby closed the door behind them and closed the blinds. The office was already occupied by the editor in chief, and Maggie felt her breath catch in her throat. This couldn't be good. "Hi, Maggie," he said, standing to reach for her hand and pat her on the arm.

"Hi, Mr. Peterson."

They motioned for her to sit.

"How has the move been treating you?" Toby asked as he settled behind the desk. Peterson sat beside Maggie. Both regarded her soberly.

"It's – well, I have to be honest. It's been a bit more of a change in daily life than I'd anticipated. It's so quiet in the Valley!"

Both men chuckled. "I imagine so. Actually, I know so! My aunt is in Middleton; I visit now and again as she's all alone." Toby smiled.

There was a pause, and with their eyes on her, Maggie flushed.

Toby folded his hands on the desk, his face turning serious. "Sorry to take you away from the party, but we know you're most likely returning home tomorrow, and we wanted to speak to you in person."

Maggie swallowed. "Gentlemen, I hope you don't mind my asking, but am I in trouble?"

The men laughed, and Peterson was quick to lean toward her. "No, Maggie! Wow, we've been awful not getting to the point. Of course you're not in trouble. Quite the opposite."

123

Maggie exhaled the breath she hadn't even realized she was holding and sank back in the chair. "Oh good. I love my job! But nobody else is getting pulled into the office, so I got a little worried!"

They laughed again, and Toby handed an envelope across the desk. "That's because we handed out most of these yesterday."

Maggie looked at the red envelope, her name in calligraphy on the front. The fabled Christmas bonus. It didn't happen every year - it was, of course, dependent on how the magazine did - and it was rumoured to be a modest amount when it did happen. Still, it was a much-coveted reward at the magazine. She looked up at her bosses, confused. Only full-time contributors got bonuses. She certainly never had.

"Maggie, you've done more this year – way more – than we asked of you. Your articles are consistently interesting, beautifully written and on time! That's more than we can say for a lot of the nine-to-fivers we have hanging out here every weekday!"

Maggie smiled, then frowned, making the men laugh again. "But -"

Peterson leaned toward her again. "Right. I know what you're thinking: only the big contributors get the bonuses. Now I want you to know that yours is not as substantial as some of the others, but we felt we had to offer you something in appreciation for your work this past year. We're very pleased with your contribution to the magazine."

Maggie opened her mouth to speak, but Peterson raised his hand. "And, we want to promote you, Maggie."

Maggie gasped. She'd always been eager to ascend the long ladder of career advancement at the magazine, but promotions were rare, especially for those who worked mostly out of the office.

"It comes with greater responsibility, of course, and probably many more hours of work. We want you to have a regular section every month, which would mean a lot more coordination with the contributors and the production team. Weekly attendance at team meetings would be a must, and we might need you in more often than that."

Maggie nodded, her brow furrowed as she contemplated these terms.

"It would be a trial period," Toby added. "We'll try it for a few months and see how the readers respond."

"Oh wow. This is incredible! Thank you both for the opportunity. I'm blown away!"

Both men leaned back in their chairs, plainly gratified by her enthusiasm.

Peterson stood, and Maggie followed suit, accepting his outstretched hand to shake, again. "We know you'll need to think about it. You'll find your new contract, should you accept, along with your bonus in the envelope."

Maggie could do nothing but nod again, and turn to shake Toby's hand, too, as he had also risen from his chair.

"Thanks again, to both of you."

Less nervous now, but still shaken up, she turned to go. As she opened the door, she was stopped by Toby. "Oh, sorry Maggie. Could we have your answer by the New Year?"

Maggie thought for only a second before answering, "Of course. Thank you for the time to talk to Jack and think about it."

She walked straight to the ladies' room, aware but uncaring that eyes were on her and that if either Peterson or Toby saw her making that particular beeline, they'd know she was going to open her envelope in private. But this was so unexpected; if she didn't open that envelope now, she'd go nuts with the distraction of it all through the party.

Her bonus was not what her eyes sought as she opened the envelope, but she was pleasantly surprised when she spied the amount. Three hundred dollars would help pay the bills. She took a breath and pulled out the second sheet of paper - which was actually a formal job offer. Skimming it, satisfied that the terms were as described by Peterson and Toby, she blinked when she saw the salary amount. It was six thousand dollars more than her current salary, with a raise review at the end of each year.

Just then, there was a knock at the door, and she cursed the single-toilet bathroom as she often had before. *Ridiculous, with sixteen staff on this floor alone, and seven of them women!* "Be right out!" she called and quickly skimmed the final paragraph of the offer, which explained the month-to-month trial period for the first three months and the potential opportunity to sign a six-month contract if her section was successful. This was common at the magazine, and the best she could have hoped for.

Exiting the bathroom after actually using the toilet, she made eye contact with Toby across the room and smiled.

That night, she slept deep and dreamless until her alarm woke her and she was hit with the trifecta of first-trimester pregnancy symptoms: nausea, the strong urge to urinate and the ache in her breasts as she changed position.

She padded to the bathroom, enjoying the luxury of the hotel and already wondering whether their breakfast buffet matched the high standards of the room.

Sitting in the large dining area, she felt elated. She had called Jack the moment she'd returned to her room the night before, and he had been excited at her news. He instantly advised her to accept the offer but recanted as she described her concerns to him: the increased office hours would mean much more travel and time away, and if everything worked out with the baby -

Maggie, don't think like that. We're finally realizing our dream of being parents, here.

I'm sorry, Jack. I'm just being realistic.

Silence.

Look, if I fall in love with even the idea of this baby right now, before we know anything for certain, and so early in the game, I don't know how I'd handle it if - if we were disappointed.

As they ended the conversation, Jack had insisted she use her bonus on her shopping trip that morning. She tried to convince him they'd use it for bills, but he stopped her protests in their tracks saying, "Maggie, *have fun.*"

Finishing the last bite of her toast, she gazed out the window and anticipated the day with her friends. Her nausea gone now and an excellent night of sleep under her belt, she was ready to hit the shops.

The day flew by, the three friends falling easily back into their groove. Maggie hadn't anticipated how often she'd have to tell white lies or avoid certain topics, all to keep the secret of her pregnancy. But when one of her friends announced that she and her husband were trying for a baby, Maggie's resolve disintegrated. It was during their

127

pedicure that she finally confessed her secret to both her ecstatic friends and their cosmeticians, alike.

Afterward, Maggie felt elated. *Now I can tell everyone,* she thought, with a twinge of guilt. She'd gone back on her and Jack's agreement to keep things quiet for now.

She called Jack as soon as she arrived back at the hotel and was happily surprised when he confessed his relief at being able to talk to someone besides Zoe and Sam about the pregnancy. As their conversation drew to a close, Maggie found herself wanting to say it out loud again, to her husband.

"Jack..."

"Yes, gorgeous?"

Maggie laughed. "We're having a *baby*."

He laughed, too. "I know. Crazy, eh?"

"Yeah. Like, *wow!*"

"Hurry home to me tomorrow. I've missed you. The house is so -"

"What?" Her heart sped up. "Has something happened?"

"No, not really. I just - well, Martin keeps popping into my mind. It's weird. Nothing specific. He's just there. I dreamt about him, too."

"Tell me about the dream."

"I can't; I don't remember it. Just that he was there."

"Jack, maybe it wasn't Martin."

Jack paused for a moment on the other end. "You think it may have been Sebastian?"

"Yeah."

"Huh. Well. Don't think about it now, babe. Enjoy your sleep in that fancy hotel and then get your sweet ass home to me."

"OK, babe. Love you."

"Love you, too. So much."

As Maggie got ready for bed, she was disappointed that some of her euphoria had faded. She flipped the tv on, but nothing caught her interest, so she settled into bed to sleep.

Except her mind didn't have the same idea. Thoughts rushed around in her head, insisting on being heard after being neglected for so long.

"Back to reality," she said out loud.

What if the boy I'm seeing is Sebastian? Why is he appearing now? Is he linked, somehow, with the path? The woman? But that can't be; the timing is off.

What if it's not Sebastian?

Her stomach clenched as an idea solidified in her mind.

What if it's my baby I'm seeing?

She sat up in bed, the darkness feeling heavy.

It would make sense that my child look like a relative of Jack's, but that wouldn't explain the dual umbilical cords I saw in the washing machine. Oh, God. What if it's twins? We can't say it doesn't run in the family now!

She shook her head. It was too much.

No. Why would my child appear to me as a grown man? Why would he want me to follow the trail in the woods? It has to be Sebastian.

Still, she felt unnerved by her thoughts. She wondered if Zoe had contacted that psychic in Ottawa. Some cosmic insight would be appreciated, especially now.

Chapter 17 – Followed

She was in her back yard. Birds were singing in the trees, and she was aware of the distant sound of a lawnmower. She knelt in the soil, planting seeds of zucchini, carrots and tomatoes. It was long, dirty work, but she loved it. There was something fulfilling about planting a vegetable garden. Something reassuring about the promise of growing your own food.

She heard the phone in the kitchen ring. Wiping her hands on her jeans (she never used gloves), she ran to get it, wondering absently, *when did I plant a garden?*

She spoke to Zoe briefly; she'd asked for Jack, who was at work, to plan a joint gift for Martin, and Maggie was little help.

As she hung up, a movement from the window caught her eye. Her hand froze on the wall-mounted handset as she looked at the woman standing on the other side of the bridge.

Some memory from a different time tried to surface, but she was unable to grasp it. What was it? This woman. Where had she seen her before? She finally let go of the phone and walked to the window. The woman was looking at her, too.

There was something dripping from her left arm. And she held something in her right hand. What was that?

Maggie stepped outside onto a thin blanket of snow. Hadn't it just been warm? *When did it snow?*

The woman waved at her then. Waved with the hand that held something. Maggie moved closer, smiling and waving back.

"Hello! Did you come from the trail?" She stopped.

The woman was holding a severed hand.

Maggie's hands flew to her face, and she covered her mouth before she could scream.

The woman smiled and lowered her waving hand – the hand that was holding what must be her other hand because, at this closer proximity, Maggie could see her left hand was indeed missing from its arm, and severed roughly, at that, hence the steady stream of blood flowing into the snow.

"*Oh my God*!" she yelled and ran toward the woman, who quickly held out the severed hand, as if to say, *stop*.

Maggie skidded in her tracks, her eyes riveted on the woman. She watched as she brought the forefinger of the hand to her lips and said, *"Shhhhh. He'll hear you."* She looked in the direction of the farm.

Dark rivulets of blood flowed from the stump of the hand down her arm, and the blood on the finger smeared over her lips.

Maggie sank to her knees, screaming, and in some trick of perspective, the woman appeared on Maggie's side of the bridge, again bringing the forefinger of the severed hand to her lips as she shushed her. Her eyes were wide in – what? – fear?

Maggie flew backward at the shock of the woman's sudden closeness, and just as suddenly she was standing above her, smiling down at her, her mouth impossibly wide, stretching her face grotesquely. "There was so much blood," the woman said, her mouth widening into a gaping, black hole in her face as her jaw stretched to her chest and the word "blood" seemed to go on forever. Maggie felt certain she'd be engulfed by it and live in this terror forever.

She awoke with a shrill scream.

She lay still in her bed, sweating and breathing hard. Fighting off the urge to bolt to the toilet and vomit up the remains of her amazing, not to mention rather expensive, hotel dinner.

Breathing, breathing, she slowly acclimated to her surroundings. It was still very dark in the room, so she couldn't have been asleep long. She checked the clock: two-thirty.

She sat up in bed and turned the side-table lamp on, flooding the room with dim light.

What the hell was that?

She surveyed the room and voiced her concern out loud, "Seriously, what the hell?"

She studied her hands on the duvet cover. Of course, it had been the woman she and Zoe had seen, but why hadn't she recognized her? Why did she approach her rather than instantly feel afraid? Did the woman *want* her to approach?

She grimaced in the confusion of it all, but already the shock of the blood, the eerie advances of the woman and the gaping maw of a mouth were beginning to fade.

"Damn. *Fuck*, that was fucking *terrifying*!" She thought the exclamation, although to an empty room, would help. And it did, a little.

She got up and paced now, adrenaline still coursing through her. She shook her tingling fingers and stretched her arms above her head. She contemplated calling her husband, but only briefly. What she really wanted was to sleep. "Peacefully!" she said aloud.

Nothing could be resolved tonight. In fact, it was too much for her to absorb right now. She was pregnant and tired and felt as if she'd stayed out partying all night.

"Crazy, messed up, horror movie costume party," she mumbled.

She returned to bed, lamenting her lost sense of contentedness and angry at the intrusion on her little vacation.

"It was nice while it lasted," she muttered as she sank beneath the covers.

Then, *She was using her own severed hand to wave at me.*

Ugh. What did that mean?

She shuddered in the bed and felt the smooth, luxurious sheets, the duvet heavy and warm on top of her.

Her conflicting sensations of revulsion and sleepy comfort were confusing, but she was too tired to analyze them. Shutting off the lamp, she chose comfort.

Willing the images in her mind to fade, she closed her eyes. *I'll make sense of it later.*

Somehow, she began to drift, interrupted only by a final thought before sleep: *I didn't even know it was a dream. I didn't even think to wake myself up...*

Chapter 18 – Martin

You've reached Martin Ridgewood. The best way to reach me is via email, at mridgewood243 (no spaces) at ITSafe dot com. If you prefer I contact you via telephone, please leave your details and I'll get back to you ASAP. Thanks.

beeeep

"Martin, hi! It's Zoe. I just wanted to say Merry Christmas! I'm sorry we didn't get to connect last week. I tried calling you while I was in Wolfville. I miss you, brother.

"Anyway, listen: we're having Christmas dinner at my place tonight, and it'd be so great if you could join us. Mom is here. The kids are all home, too. Maggie, Jack and Maggie's brother Max and his wife Kathy will be here. Lots of good food. Anyway, show up anytime.

"If not, I love you, Martin. Merry Christmas."

click

Martin stared across the room at the now-silent answering machine.

Then turned back to his computer.

Chapter 19 – Christmas

Christmas. The old excitement burst within Maggie as she woke up and realized that this was that much-anticipated day of celebration, family and gratitude. She had always loved Christmas. Knowing that her brother was sleeping just down the hall in the guest room added to that nostalgic feeling, bred from years of following the same routine they'd gone through every Christmas as children: Max joining Maggie and Kaia in their bedroom in the wee hours of the morning to play board games and whisper in excited, giggle-filled tones until they were allowed to wake up their parents at six o'clock.

They were often so excited that one or more of them felt sick, and all of them had always been exhausted after opening presents. It had been a small price to pay for the joy of the morning.

She was glad Max and Kathy had decided to spend the night and have Christmas morning with her and Jack. Max was concerned about her, especially after hearing about her last crazy dream, but even more, he wanted to spend Christmas with family. She so admired that about her brother. The ritual of the holidays was sacred to him.

Maggie placed her hands on her abdomen, breathing in and sending her growing baby love and happy holiday thoughts. She wondered if it could feel her working to connect. She turned her head to the side and admired her sleeping husband, his features softly lit by the early morning light. It wasn't yet dawn, but she knew she'd get no more sleep.

She rose quietly, not wishing to wake Jack (and laughing a bit at herself for even thinking that was possible – Jack's family traditions on Christmas day had never started before the sun was up), and put on her slippers and cardigan. She went to the hall washroom and relieved her screaming bladder, then brushed her teeth and looked at Jack's watch, which lay on the lower shelf of the wall cabinet. Five-fifty. Ah, she'd slept in this Christmas!

Knowing her brother would be lying awake, she contemplated going to the room to get him as she opened the door to the hallway. She instantly jumped back in surprise, as Max stood at the door, smiling hugely.

"Maggie! Merry Christmas!" He hugged her, and she laughed.

"You scared me, you weirdo!"

"I've been awake for hours, I think! Kathy won't be up for a while, so I was so happy to hear you up," he whispered, his eyes twinkling.

"Tradition, eh? It's hard to give up."

Max looked offended. "Are you kidding? I don't ever want to give up our Christmas tradition!"

Maggie put her finger to her lips to shush her brother, but the memory of the severed hand the pale woman had held to her lips didn't allow her to complete the action. She lowered her hand, and Max's face fell.

"Come on; let's go downstairs," she said, smiling and tugging on his sleeve.

Max's first act when they got to the main floor was to plug in the lights of the Christmas tree. Maggie had put some coffee on out of habit, but realizing neither she nor her brother would drink it, poured two big glasses of orange juice.

She joined him in the living room. Max stacked and re-stacked the gifts beneath the tree, working to make everything perfect. Finally satisfied, he stood back and raised his palms at his sides. His smile radiated innocence, and Maggie recalled him as a little boy, so troubled and yet so sweet. She put her arm through his. "I'm so glad you and Kathy stayed last night. It means so much to have you here!"

Max patted her hand and continued to admire the tree. "You know, we didn't have the best childhood. I mean, we were poor, Dad was going through everything, and then there was all the anxiety, you know? Our family seemed plagued with it."

Maggie nodded, remembering.

"But, Christmas! Christmas was always wonderful, wasn't it?"

She nodded again, grasping his arm and feeling overcome with emotion.

"Christmas was like -"

"- a break from all the crazy," Maggie finished.

He looked at her. "Yeah."

"Mom and Dad came together to make sure it would be special for us every year. Mom with her crazy decorations and piles of cookies and squares and -"

"- turkey!"

"Yeah. And Dad, always figuring out what we three kids wanted the most and finding a way to get it. Remember the Atari?"

She laughed. "And the ghetto blaster?"

"And then the Nintendo!"

"Ah, and thus, the seed of your addiction was planted." Maggie smiled at her brother, whom childhood friends had dubbed a "vidiot" with awed affection. "You spent all day inside playing video games while we rode our bikes and played in the brook and climbed trees."

"Yep. My brain was just on a different level, I guess, my genius unimpressed with your outdoor attractions."

Maggie poked Max's ribs.

"Anyway. This time of year always kind of saved us, you know? And kept us going into the next." He looked at her sideways. "Don't talk about getting rid of tradition."

"Ah Max, I was just kidding. Look at us, in front of the tree *way* too early and happy as can be. I'll never stop doing this! And I vow to help it carry on through future generations." Maggie smiled. She'd known she'd tell Max and Kathy the news today but was surprised it had come out now. It seemed perfect, though, and Max's widened eyes and intake of breath was a satisfying reaction.

He grabbed both her elbows. "What? You mean? Maggie, what do you mean?"

"I'm going to have a baby! I think!"

Max was at a loss for words.

"It's very early, probably only about three months, and I haven't seen the OB yet -"

"Why? You're nearly through your first trimester! Why haven't you – wait, does this mean you and Jack haven't even been trying?"

"First of all, how do you know about 'trimesters'?"

Max released her arms and guided her to the table, then retrieved her orange juice from the counter to put in front of her.

"Kaia -"

"Oh yeah. The midwife course. It's too bad she didn't finish that."

"Well, there was the divorce."

"Right. I want to call her right now. Still seems weird not to have her here!"

"Wait, wait. Please explain this to me!"

Maggie sighed and sipped her juice. "I don't know how to, Max! I'm as shocked as you are! You know what Jack and I went through all those years, and it's been years since then. Even through all the trying, I never even had a failed pregnancy. I simply never got pregnant. When we decided to give up, I did, completely. I've truly believed all these years that I simply would never get pregnant."

"Yeah, weren't you guys even talking about adoption?"

"Yeah! We still were, even when we moved here. Just now and again, though. It's pretty expensive to adopt." Maggie sipped her juice again, then stood abruptly. "I need to get something besides this acidic juice in my belly or I'm gonna hurl."

"Nice."

"Anyway, you know how I'd been feeling so sick."

"Wow. We just attributed it to the stress."

"Exactly. Well, that day with Zoe when I was sick again, she clued me in that my symptoms could be something else." She popped a slice of bread down in the toaster, and then, as a second thought, popped it up. "Oh, sorry. Want one?"

"No way; I'm saving myself for Christmas breakfast!"

"Mmm, bacon and eggs and fried potatoes and toast with jam…" Her stomach gurgled unpleasantly. "Ugh, don't worry, you'll get your carbs."

The toast popped, and Maggie buttered it quickly, then took a big bite. She sat back down beside Max and looked at him, his blue eyes impatient for the rest of the story.

"So anyway, three positive tests later, here I am. I even did one of the tests at the drug store where they make you pee in a cup, and they – well, I don't know what they do, but they take your pee away and a few minutes later bring you your result!"

"But why haven't you seen a doctor yet, Mags? I mean, with all your troubles in the past, I'm surprised."

"Max, I only realized I was pregnant two weeks ago! Remember, I thought all the symptoms were because of the dreams and the visions." She shuddered. "It was just a timing thing, I guess. But I have an appointment with my new OB in a couple of weeks, don't worry."

Max finally looked satisfied and then happy. "Oh, my God, Maggie! This is incredible!" He grabbed her hand.

She laughed. "Thanks. It is incredible. I'm still having a hard time believing it and probably wouldn't if it weren't for all these symptoms."

Max got up and grabbed the phone off its charger, bringing it back to the table.

"What the – who are you calling at five-thirty in the morning?"

"Kaia. Hey, you said you wanted to call her! And now you have no choice. There's no way you're not telling her this!"

"But Max, it's four-thirty a.m. in Ottawa!"

He paused. "Oh, right. Crap."

He reluctantly placed the phone back in its charger. "Well, I gotta tell *somebody*!"

"Don't worry, we're seeing lots of family today. And you can tell Kathy as soon as she wakes up."

He gazed anxiously at the dusky back yard. "That'll be hours from now." His eyes remained fixed on the window.

"What do you see?" She turned to follow his gaze. Nothing. Just dark.

"Nothing. I think, though, that we should take that walk today."

"Are you crazy? That tree trunk is still there, and it's snowy! And cold!"

"No, it's going to be pretty warm today. The snow's probably going to melt."

Yes, she had heard that on the radio the night before as she and Jack had driven back from Zoe's. Their Christmas Eve visit with Zoe, her husband and kids, and Alice had been quiet and mostly spent in front of the tv in the family room, the twins and John playing cribbage on the floor and Alice sipping tea and thoroughly enjoying the presence of family. This was evident only in the smile on her face; she was having a hard time piecing words together that night. Jack and Maggie had left early to meet Max and Kathy at home.

"Right. Well, I guess there'll be a lot of free time this afternoon before we head to Zoe's. We could check it out then, see how far we get. But why the change of heart?"

"I don't know. I just feel like it's time, you know?"

"Yeah. Yeah, I know. No matter how hard I try *not* to know, I know."

They sipped their juice, and finding themselves with plenty of time before their spouses would awaken, they made cinnamon rolls to complement their Christmas breakfast. Feeling rather proud of their accomplishment, they played some video games on the PlayStation. Maggie was thoroughly enjoying their being children again when she remembered her job offer. She discussed it with Max, and he looked concerned.

"If it weren't for the baby, I'd say snap it up! It's really not that far a drive, but at least once a week could get tiring as you progress. And once the baby's born, you'd have to take some leave."

Maggie nodded. "I know. Again, timing." She turned back to the video game. "I don't have to decide until the New Year, so I think I'll take advantage of that time. I know I'll probably have to turn it down; I guess I just want to hold onto it for a while first."

"Congratulations, eh? That's pretty amazing."

Maggie smiled. "Lots is, these days!"

At 7:00 a.m. they figured they could call their sister and decided to use the laptop to Skype her instead.

"*Merry Christmas*, Kaia!"

"You crazy bastards."

They all laughed.

"We miss you, sis," said Maggie.

"I miss you guys, too. It's not fair you're both there and I'm here." It was common for Kaia to state the obvious or somehow twist circumstances that were in place due to her decisions into something "unfair". Her victim complex, though, was hard-earned, and Max and Maggie forgave it without a thought.

"Yeah. But at least with modern technology, we can see each other! You look good!"

Kaia rubbed her eyes. "I look like shit."

Again, they laughed.

"Maggie looks something, too!" Max exclaimed.

"What?" Kaia made a face. "She looks *something?* From here she looks gorgeous."

"No, she looks -"

Maggie clapped her hand over her brother's mouth. "Kai, I have something to tell you."

"Oh my God. If you say you're pregnant, I'm going to freak out, because I had a dream last night that you were!"

Both Max and Maggie shook their heads. "You're such a freak. But you're also right!"

"*No way!*"

"Yes!" Maggie repeated the same story Max had heard, and Kaia listened, mouth agape.

"Maggie! This is amazing!"

"What was your dream about?"

"Nothing; we were just shopping for maternity clothes for you. It'll probably happen."

"You'd have to come visit."

"I *will*!"

"So, you didn't actually see the baby?" Maggie's heart sped up. *Just confirmation it's one baby, not two. Please.*

"No, but you were really big. Like, ready to pop. So, don't worry Mags, I bet it'll all work out."

Kaia had misinterpreted the question, but Maggie took what she got. Kaia's dreams, over the years, always held elements of truth, as Max had recently pointed out.

Kaia shook her head. "I was beginning to think none of us would have kids."

They were all quiet, reflecting.

Max spoke first. "We had our reasons."

"Yeah, but God, Maggie, this is the best news I've heard in a long time. The best Christmas gift ever!"

Just then, Maggie heard the sound of footsteps upstairs. "Oh, someone's up!"

"OK, well, you guys enjoy your day. Thank you for calling so early; it actually brings memories back."

They all smiled. "Love you, sis," said Max, Maggie nodding in agreement.

"Love you guys, too. Maggie, call me after your appointment, OK?"

Max paused. "Wait - what are you up to today, Kai? Tell me you're celebrating."

"Yeah, Dad invited me over to have dinner with him, Pat and Karen. Do you want me to keep quiet about the gestation situation?"

Maggie giggled. "Yeah, maybe for a bit; until after the appointment. I don't want to - well, you know."

Max stood and walked to the stairs, looking up to see who was moving around up there. Maggie assumed it was Kathy as he smiled and climbed out of view quickly.

"Yeah."

"Tell them all I love them, though. And I love you too, sister."

They said goodbye, and Maggie closed the laptop. She walked toward the living room as Max, Kathy and Jack came down the stairs, Jack yelling, "*Christmaaaaas!*"

Maggie hugged him and laughed. "It's been Christmas for *us* for hours now!"

Kathy rolled her eyes. "You played video games, didn't you?" She eyed Max.

"Maggie played, too!"

"Who cares? Let's open *presents*!" Jack yelled, rushing at the tree and pulling Maggie behind him.

It was a happy morning as the four opened and exclaimed over gifts. (Max had tricked Maggie and had given her the sleeved blanket, while giving Kathy a sparkling pair of diamond earrings, to the delight of both.)

Jack gave Maggie books and clothes he'd kept track of when she had expressed her desire for them, but she was especially touched by Jack's gift of *What to Expect When You're Expecting*. And even more impressed when he admitted to having read the Introduction and first several weeks.

"To get caught up," he said, kissing her.

Maggie was pleased with the reactions to her gifts, many of which she'd bought on her Halifax trip with her bonus. For Kathy, scrapbooking materials was a no-brainer, but she'd also scored tickets to an upcoming concert she knew Kathy would love. Max was thrilled with the vintage Ewok Village she'd found on eBay (*"I had one of these when I was a kid!"*), and Jack was ecstatic with his collection of specialty coffees.

Breakfast was a satisfying affair of gluttony and conversation. Max excitedly revealed the news of the baby to Kathy, who was overjoyed and had the same questions the siblings had already asked. Maggie relished answering them again, with Jack adding his own perspective. Maggie was shocked to realize, as she somehow was every year, that it wasn't even ten o'clock when they finished eating. Kathy settled herself on the couch to do some scrapbooking, and Maggie excused herself to take a nap.

She had a dreamless sleep and stretched luxuriously when she woke at eleven-thirty.

She was curious at the sound of Jack's chainsaw coming from the back yard and rose to walk to the window. Max was walking out of the woods, carrying an armload of what looked like small logs, then piling them in the wheelbarrow.

"The trunk," she said and was startled when Kathy spoke from the doorway.

"I can't believe it took you this long to wake up with all the racket they've been making! Sorry, I didn't mean to scare you. I heard you get up."

"They've been busy."

"They got to talking about the path. Max wants to get back there, and Jack wants you to, as well."

"Why?"

"Mags, we all know what you've been going through. If something as easy as a walk on Christmas day could help figure it out, then we're all for it."

Maggie wondered about Zoe. She'd probably want to come, but Maggie knew how busy she was with family today.

"OK. Maybe it'll be a nice walk."

"Oh, I'm not going." Kathy shook her head. "I was going to make the rolls for tonight's dinner, and Jack doesn't plan on going either, I don't think. He was talking about clearing the path for you and Max."

Maggie furrowed her brow, wondering at Jack's reluctance. Of course, he must still have some negative feelings attached to that path. Maybe he wasn't ready to face them, and maybe, on this Christmas day, he didn't need to.

But apparently, she did.

Chapter 20 – The Long Walk

Max gulped some water, standing by the kitchen table and clutching his gloves in his hand. Jack came in, rubbing his own gloved hands together with an air of accomplishment.

"Firewood for a couple of weeks, I figure, babe!"

Maggie smiled. "Great."

Max looked at her. "And a clear path."

"Great again." She turned to head to the bathroom. Who knew how long this walk would be?

"Your gratitude is overwhelming!" Jack joked as she retreated.

A twinge of annoyance. *She* was the one about to walk into who knew what, after seeing and dreaming of some pretty unpleasant stuff on that trail. Or coming from it. To her, this was not a casual, pleasant Christmas day meander through the woods.

What was it? A confrontation? And if yes, with what?

Jack was waiting for her when she came out of the bathroom.

"I'm sorry, Magpie. I guess I'm just trying to inject some humour into the situation. I - truth is, I really don't know how to handle all of this." He shrugged apologetically, his rough, callused palms facing up.

She looked at the floor. "It's OK. I understand you have a lot of memories attached to that place."

"Not of the path; I never went back there. But Mom did, and yeah, the memories of that time aren't exactly warm and fuzzy." He moved closer to her and spoke quietly. "You don't have to go back there, Mags. It's Christmas. You don't have to do anything you don't want to."

"He's right, Maggie, you don't have to go!" Max had stepped into the hallway. "I'll go alone."

"Don't be silly, Max! I need to go." She looked at Jack. "Maybe it'll be nice."

He smiled. "Would it be nicer if I came?"

She couldn't help but smile in return. "You're sweet, babe, but Max and I will be OK. You stay. Make us some lunch for when we return."

"None for me!" Max called as he walked back toward the kitchen.

"Saving yourself for turkey dinner?" asked Maggie.

"Of course!"

She turned back to Jack, who was still standing close to her, concern etched on his face.

"Bring your cell."

"Yep."

She kissed his cheek, and she and Max started getting ready.

"It's pretty mild, but you should put some gloves on, and a hat, too," Max said.

"OK, Mom."

"Hey, you're growing my niece or nephew! I need to watch out for you even more now!"

At the start of the path, Maggie could see that the tree trunk that had been about seventy-five feet in had indeed been decimated. But Max and Jack had done more; the pathway to the point where the trunk had been was clear.

"Wow! You guys really worked hard while I slept!"

Max playfully wiped his forehead with the back of his glove. "Clearing the path wasn't that bad. But past the trunk - or what's left of it – remains untouched, so keep your expectations realistic, sis."

She nodded. "Thanks for doing this with me, Max."

He smiled. "Shall we?"

They started down the path, and Maggie fought her apprehension. She thought of that first dream, following the morphing baby/boy/man (Sebastian?) down the trail. But today was nothing like that dream. The air was crisp and refreshing. The sky was full of thin, wispy brushstrokes of cloud, but the sun shone brightly behind them. The landscape was grey and white, save the pine trees, hunter green and standing tall against the washed-out sky.

It took them only a few minutes to get to the remains of the trunk, and they stopped, gazing for a long time down the overgrown path.

"Well, this has been fun!" Maggie pretended to turn and start walking back to the house, but Max laughed and grabbed her, propelling her further into the woods. Quickly, though, he maneuvered so he was in front of her, grasping and breaking branches with both hands when they blocked the trail.

Progress was slow.

Occasional small sections of the trail had melted into slush, and despite her insulated rubber boots, Maggie's feet began to feel damp and slightly chilly. Her consequential little dance would have been comical to a casual observer; whenever Max stopped to clear particularly stubborn or thick branches, Maggie hopped up and down from one foot to the other, then stomped on the soft ground, willing her blood to travel to her extremities.

Maggie sang, as she often did when she was bored or nervous. Or happy, or sad. Max joined in sometimes, and together they sang bits and pieces of Blue Rodeo and Tragically Hip songs, then Radiohead and Cranberries, and Maggie spiced it up with some Great Big Sea. She mixed the songs together and sang the lead guitar parts to her favourites.

"You're nuts," Max commented, grunting as he cleared the newest jumble of branches.

Maggie smiled, enjoying how good singing felt and marvelling at how long it had been since she'd felt like indulging in it. She glanced at the time on her phone. They'd been at it more than half an hour, and she could still see the area where the trunk had been, though it was far behind them. She froze, then groaned.

"Max."

"Huh?"

"We're idiots."

"Some have said, yes."

"I have some seriously awesome pruning shears -"

Max stopped struggling with the thin branches. "These *are* pretty thin. I can snap most of them; others just need a twist - but shears would be great. Where are they?"

"Um, you'll have to ask Jack, but probably with all the tools in the back porch. Didn't you guys use anything to clear the first part of the path?"

He shook his head. "It wasn't so bad, and we were focused on the stump, more than anything." He looked back toward the house. "You going to be OK here or do you want to come back with me?"

She looked around. The woods were bright, and she could see quite far back on the trail. "I'll be fine."

"Keep singing," he called back as he ran.

She looked around again. All was calm and peaceful. She felt none of the fear she'd felt in her dreams. She thought of continuing to snap through the tangle of branches Max had been working on but realized what a wasted effort it would be as Max would return soon and snip through it in seconds. She tried to see further down the path, but some distance after this tangle, it did a lazy arc to the right. Maggie thought of the conversation with Walter about the farm property and that of the Maplestone home. She tried to measure how far back they'd come and guessed a little over half an acre. Not far enough to have cleared her own property yet.

She paced the path a bit, listening to the sounds of the trees. A twig snapping, the air whispering in the branches. She tilted her head back to see past the tops of the trees to the white sky; she breathed in through her nose, closing her eyes. She felt content.

Spying a fallen tree to the left of the path, she went to sit on it, and it took a few seconds for her to adjust to the hard chill of the trunk.

Bored, she began to sing again.

"Hello?

Is there anybody in there?

Just nod if you can hear me..."

She stopped and chuckled. Bad song choice, but she had to finish now that the song was playing in her mind.

Is there anyone at home?

She let her voice rise and carry, enjoying the sound of it echoing off the trees. In a powerful crescendo, she sang, *"I-I-I, have become –"*

"Comfortably numb!" Max finished, running back up the path with the shears.

Maggie stood and came back to the path. "Dude, I *know* Mom taught you never to run with scissors, and that's a pretty bad-ass pair of scissors you've got there."

"Meh, I'm invincible! And besides, I was worried about you back here."

"Well, be impressed, because it was easy-peasy. I sat here and sang like a fool the whole time. It was actually very peaceful."

Max did look impressed. "Good."

He looked around, catching his breath, and then approached the tangle of branches again. Before he made the first snip though, he froze, his arms cocked in midair, the shears open-mouthed and ready to demolish the thin branches. "Maggie. Please tell me you did this."

"What?" She rushed to follow Max's gaze to just below the bramble of overgrowth. There, in the slushy snow, were several footprints leading off in the direction of the turn in the trail and then stopping abruptly. They were unclear around the edges, as the snow was so soft, but she would wager they were made with bare feet.

"Like that day," was all she could say.

Max studied her. "Are you OK?"

"Yeah. I just want to keep going." Maggie was surprised at her own calm. She felt as if this was alright and that they were just supposed to keep on.

"Why isn't this freaking you out?"

"I don't know. Who knows when those were made? And I just feel that whoever made them isn't going to hurt us, you know? As if she -" Maggie had to admit to herself that she knew who it was she was referring to. She was sure the woman had made them. The one in her dreams; the one she and Zoe had seen. Even though it made little sense. "- as if she just wants help."

Max cut through the brambles and looked at Maggie; they continued forward, avoiding the tracks.

"I felt so peaceful while you were getting the shears," Maggie remarked.

"Did you have a clear view of that area from that trunk you were sitting on?"

"Of course! Good enough to know I was alone, anyway! I would have known if someone was there."

"What if -"

"What?"

"What if she lives back here? What if that building you saw in your dream really exists? What if she's back here?"

Maggie slowed a bit, falling behind Max. She looked back but could see nothing beyond the bend they'd followed.

Max had stopped to cut through some more tangled branches. "Much better progress now."

"Oh, God. Max, you shouldn't have said -"

He turned to her. "What? About the woman being back here? Weren't you thinking it, too?"

"I don't know. I guess all this time I figured she was a ghost! Not real. Able to scare us but not to hurt us."

Max's face changed, and he looked up the path again in the direction they were headed.

"I guess I never thought of her as a real woman, living back here in a shack with her severed hand and - and her screaming and her bare feet!" Maggie's voice had risen to a shrillness that made a group of birds fly up from the trees on their right. They both jumped, then looked at each other, grinning sheepishly.

"Hey, assholes! You should be down south, not here scaring us!" Max shook his fist at the sky, and Maggie laughed again, her tension lessoning.

"We have no idea what any of this means, Mags. But I think we need to figure it out as best as we can." He gripped her shoulder. "And as God is my witness, I will not let any harm come to you."

Maggie laughed at his proclamation but felt tears well in her eyes. She reached up to grip his hand on her shoulder. "I feel trapped. As if I have to do this, but all I really want is to live my life and be happy!"

"Maybe if we do this, you'll get to do just that. Two birds, one stone, and all that?"

"Right. Well, let's get a move on, then. It must be close to one-thirty now?" She checked her phone and found she was right. "Wonder how long it'd take without all the work to clear it."

Fifteen minutes later, she convinced Max to let her have a turn with the shears. He was reluctant but finally handed them over, flexing his fingers and wrists with a grimace. "Just for a few minutes."

Maggie enjoyed the work of deftly cutting through the thin branches, the majority of which were dead. By the time her biceps were aching from holding the shears in front of her, Max was begging for them back. They stopped and looked back at their progress.

"Wow. I wonder how far we've come?" she asked.

"It's hard to know. But I'd venture to say we're far off Ridgewood property." He winked at her, and they turned back in the direction they'd been headed.

East, she thought.

Max worked for another ten minutes or so, as the path curved again. She updated her bearings: northeast now. About two hundred feet ahead of them, she saw the path open up into a clearing and yes, a dark shape that looked like a small cabin. Maggie inhaled sharply, and when Max looked back at her, she pointed, and said, "Look."

"Shit," he said, looking at the dark shape. "I was so hoping that wouldn't be here.

"Me too. But I knew it would be."

"Me too. What do you want to do?"

She laughed. "Don't tell me you want to give up now!"

He blew out a lungful of air loudly, letting his cheeks puff up.

"Are you tired? I can take the shears again."

"Yeah, I'm tired, but there's not a whole lot of overgrowth now." He gestured at the trail ahead.

"You're right."

They stood for another moment.

"Let's go, then," she said and started walking.

The state of the building gave away its age. The wood bent and buckled under the strain of dampness and neglect. The roof was tin and rusted badly, but intact. They peered through the windows. It was one room, about twelve feet by fifteen.

Before either approached the door, they did a couple of circuits around the building. The tall grass brushed their knees where it hadn't been weighed down by the snow.

"I think we can rest easy, sis. Nobody's been out here in a very long time."

She nodded. It was the first time either had spoken since entering the clearing, but it failed to break the spell. "It's quiet, eh?" she whispered, and they both stopped. No sounds of birds or woodland creatures, and the air seemed still, a striking contrast to how the woods had felt to Maggie earlier when she'd awaited Max's return.

It was Max's turn to check his phone. "Nearly two."

"Really? Wow, I really got caught up in what we were doing. We're supposed to leave in an hour and a half!"

"With the path cleared now, it'll take a fraction of the time to walk back. Don't worry."

"OK. Well, we'd better do whatever we're going to do."

Max approached the door.

"Wait!"

He looked back at her.

"You should have warned me that that was what we were going to do!"

Max laughed and waited for her to catch up. She huddled close to his back, clutching his coat, and allowed herself to let out a little whine.

"Dude. Chill."

Maggie laughed. "Oh, I've gotta pee."

Max sighed now. "Do you want to go now or after we look inside?"

"Now! Don't look!" After surveying her options, she ran around the building and used her gloved hands to dig into the snow, making a hole which she squatted over, her bare behind resting uncomfortably against the rough cold of the wood building. She relieved herself, pulling out the toilet paper she'd knowingly shoved into her pocket, and when she was done, covered the area with snow again. She smiled, another song popping into her head and making her feel giddy.

She was singing it as she rounded the corner of the building where Max stood waiting.

"Watch out where the huskies go, don't you eat that yellow snow!"

Max burst out laughing. "Are you seriously singing Zappa after peeing in the snow?"

"Try the door before I lose my nerve. My feet are freezing!"

"Did you pee on them?"

She gave him a little push, and they approached the door again, Maggie revelling in their giddy cheer. She never would have guessed she could be laughing here, on the site of her dream from which the shrill screams of a woman had come.

OK, you can't think about the dream, she told herself and shivered a bit.

Max tried the door, and it opened an inch. "Not locked," he remarked, amazed.

"Or the lock rusted away."

"Hm, good point."

He pushed a bit, but the door didn't budge. "Something's blocking it."

A vision of the woman standing on the other side of the door and resisting Max's pushes came to Maggie's mind.

"Oh God."

"You alright?"

"Yeah; just my superfun imagination. Let's give it a good shove."

They both braced their shoulders against the door, facing the woods in the direction they'd come, and counted to three.

"One, two, *three!*"

It was more effort than was necessary. The door scraped along the floor until whatever was behind it met the wall with a thud. There was enough room for them to enter, which they did, both of them instantly taking a glove off to plug their noses against the ripe smell of urine, mouse poop and mildew.

"This place has been the home of whatever forest creatures could find their way in for who knows how many years!" Max closed the door, and they saw a large, sealed bucket and some ancient gardening tools against the wall. "Well, that's what tried to block us," Max said, and Maggie resisted making fun of his nasal voice.

She released her nose and let a bit of the dank air enter her nostrils. "We'll get used to the smell. Let's take a quick look around and then GTFO."

"Get the funk out?"

Maggie laughed. "The funk is definitely already out. Replace that 'f' word with something more crass and you've got it."

They looked around, moving very little and speaking even less. At opposite ends of the room, they looked at each other questioningly.

Max spoke first. "OK - gardening tools, a couple of paintings so old they're barely recognizable as art, some candles and an ancient lawnmower. All this sort of makes sense to me. But then there's the broken table and chair – *one* chair, mind you – the cot, and the cookstove."

"I hear you. At first, I thought, garden shed. Big one. Or storage. But those things don't fit with that idea. And Max, as far as I can tell, we're well back into the woods, not really near *any* of the three properties on this side. Why have a building like this so far away from the road?"

"Especially if it was lived in, even part-time, and the cot and cookstove seem to indicate that."

They thought for a moment. Max mumbled, "If I'm thinking right, we're probably behind the Brown's farm. Quite a way back, though -"

"Oh!" Maggie perked up, a pointer finger raised. "A hunting cabin!"

"I thought of that, too, but you'd need running water, don't you think? And a place to store your weapon? Also, there's no sign outside of a spot to gut animals or to hang their skins -"

Maggie clutched her stomach. "Oh, stop," she moaned.

"Oops. Sorry, sis."

"You're right, though."

"Guess it's a mystery for now."

They looked around some more and found nothing else to indicate what use the cabin was put to.

"It's starting to get a bit darker," Maggie noted.

"Yep, certainly too dark to see very well in here. We'll need to come back with a flashlight."

The promise to return seemed to signal the end of their visit, and Maggie was glad; the smell was having an undesired effect on her sensitive stomach. Exiting the little building, her nausea worsened as the smell of skunk wafted into her nose.

"Huh. I guess the woods are more active than they seemed."

Max breathed deeply. "I love that smell!"

She gagged. "You are so weird." She plugged her nose again, but it was too late. She bolted toward the trees yelling, "Look away if you want to have an appetite for Christmas dinner!"

She reached the edge of the woods and vomited loudly, clutching her stomach through her coat.

She dug what was left of the toilet paper out of her pocket and wiped her mouth, then rummaged around for a mint. Finding one, she popped it in her mouth and was instantly painfully hungry.

"Good Lord, this is confusing," she remarked to herself, still out of breath and wiping her brow.

Max, who was emetophobic, had not followed her, but raised his voice. "Shit, Mags! Are you OK?"

"Uh-huh." She stood upright and froze, noticing what looked like a trail, far more overgrown than theirs had been, leading away from the clearing. Disoriented, she turned on the spot. *I've been doing a lot of this lately,* she thought to herself. The new trail, if that's what it was, was nearly perfectly opposite the trail by which they had entered the clearing.

Max yelled, "What?" as he watched her get her bearings.

"Max, come here!"

"No way!"

She grunted in derision, shaking her head. "Wimp."

"What?"

"Nothing!" she yelled, and then under her breath, "Yeesh," as she covered her little puddle of vomit with leaves and snow. The Zappa song popped into her head again, but she couldn't feel less like singing. "It's all covered; now get your ass over here!"

Max jogged over to her. "You OK?"

"Yeah. I'm hungry, actually. Let's head back, but first, look." She pointed to the overgrown trail.

"Oh, wow!" He walked over to it, peered in, and shook his head. "I can't see shit back there."

"I'll need to call that cop, Walter. He asked me what was back here, and I couldn't tell him. He also said he needed to go to the old abandoned house at the end of the street soon. My guess is that this trail leads to either the farm or that property."

"I'd guess the abandoned house if pressed to guess at all," Max said, peering again into the woods. "Seems pretty straight and true for as far as I can see. Which isn't far, mind you." Max gasped and quickly turned to her, making her take a step back.

"No! Sorry, I didn't mean to scare you, but – oh, I'm such an idiot!"

"Well, we knew that."

164

"Haha. But remember I told you I was going to do a bunch of research while you were in Halifax?"

Maggie's interest heightened. "Yeah."

"I didn't find much, but I did find out when the Maplestones' son was born!"

Maggie's eyes widened. "When?"

"Birthdate: August 2nd, 1938. Name: -"

"You found out his name, too?"

"Yes! Greyson Viktor Maplestone."

"*Wow!*"

"The birth announcement said 'Viktor' was in honour of his Russian ancestors and after his father."

Maggie looked puzzled. "Since when has 'Maplestone' been a Russian name?"

"Maybe the Russian heritage is on the mother's side?"

"He's named after his father!"

"Right. Hm. Changed name?"

Maggie nodded, then looked around them. "The woods will be darker now. Let's head back?"

"Yes. Oh, and sorry I was less than supportive while you were - you know."

"Puking?" She laughed and seeing his grimace, said "Sorry, Max. My current delicate constitution isn't really emetophobefriendly." She linked her arm through his, and they headed back to the cleared trail.

Max had been right; they travelled much more quickly on the way home. Maggie had forgotten to look at her phone before they started back, but estimated they'd been walking for half an hour when she caught sight of the first part of the trail, where the trunk had been, and then the house in the distance. They hurried their steps, both feeling an urgency as the darkening woods seemed to close in behind them. Both laughed as they took simultaneous deep breaths when they exited the trail.

Kathy and Jack sat on two out-of-place lawn chairs by the back porch, holding mugs in their hands and waving.

Maggie was suddenly exhausted. She gratefully sat beside her husband after crossing the yard.

Max looked at Kathy. "She barfed."

"Awww," Kathy sympathized as she pulled Max down beside her.

"Are you OK, babe?" Jack asked.

"Yeah! No worries; just a combination of bad smells upset my tummy. I'm actually starving now!"

"Good! We're leaving in twenty minutes. But how'd it go? Anything happen?"

"We found a cabin of sorts," said Max, and Jack perked up.

"Really? Was it like in your dream, Mags?"

"I guess so. It was darker in my dream, and I was much further away. We went inside this one. Smelled awful." She crinkled her nose.

"Why is there a cabin in the middle of nowhere?" Kathy interjected.

"That's what we were wondering."

The four headed inside, Max and Maggie filling their curious spouses in. Maggie gulped down some orange juice and a ham and cheese bun that her husband had dutifully made for her while she was gone.

She fell asleep in the car as Jack drove the four of them to Zoe's and woke up feeling refreshed.

Zoe saw their car from the window and greeted them on the porch, a dishtowel in hand and her apron dusted with flour. She hugged each of them, welcoming them and making a point of meeting Maggie's eyes. Maggie held her back as the others went in.

"What is it?" Zoe asked, her eyes dark with concern.

"We went back there today, Max and I."

"Oh, my God! You got through all that overgrowth?"

"Thanks to the heavy-duty clippers that came with the house!" She massaged her biceps.

Zoe continued to look concerned. "What happened?"

"I'll fill you in later, but it was mostly a peaceful visit. There is a building, but what I really wanted to tell you is that there's another trail, leading to who knows where."

"I want to know everything."

"Yes, but not today. Call me tomorrow." She remembered that Alice would still be visiting. "Or in a few days. I'll fill you in. But in the meantime, I'm going to call Walter and tell him what we found back there."

Zoe nodded, and they turned to go inside. "Wait. What about - you didn't see anything did you?"

"I assume by 'anything' you mean 'any*one*', and no, we didn't."

Chapter 21 – Christmas Dinner

Maggie was relieved that dinner was ready soon after they arrived and got settled. She had just enough time to catch up with the twins and John and to greet Alice and Sam before Zoe called everyone to the table.

Looking around as she sat, she felt blessed. What wonderful people she had in her life. She also noted Martin's absence without surprise but with a twinge of sadness.

The dinner was delicious, and Maggie devoured enough to make her feel heavy and bloated. As everyone finished eating, conversation turned to Maggie's appetite and subsequently to Jack's happy announcement of the baby, for those who were unaware. Zoe looked at Maggie as if to make sure the news was no longer a secret, and Maggie smiled and nodded.

The twins squealed and jumped up to hug Jack and Maggie, in turns, and John pumped Jack's hand up and down in hearty congratulations. Big smiles and loud conversation took over the table. Alice, sitting beside John and diagonal to Maggie, gripped John's sleeve. "What are they saying?"

Maggie took a breath and listened.

"They're saying Maggie's pregnant, Grandma! She's going to have a baby!"

Alice put her fingers to her mouth, and her eyes widened. She took a breath, and the table quieted a bit. She seemed to gather herself and looked across the table at Maggie. "This is wonderful, dear!" Her eyes filled with tears. "Are they boys?"

Maggie grabbed Jack's leg, unable to answer her mother-in-law. Unable to breathe.

"Mom, we don't know what sex the baby is yet," Jack said.

Alice looked confused. "Oh! Of course. Of course, you don't. Will you be finding out?"

The table slowly resumed its noise and chaos, but Maggie remained shaken.

After dinner, Zoe sat beside Maggie on the couch, and Sam came to sit on the coffee table in front of her.

"Attack!" said Maggie in mock fear.

"We are totally cornering you," Zoe confirmed. "We just spoke to your husband, and he says you can both come to Cuba with us at the end of the month if you say OK!"

Maggie looked at Jack, still in the kitchen, cleaning up. He met her eyes and gave her an enthusiastic thumbs-up, yelling, "We deserve a vacation!"

Maggie laughed. "I don't know. I have the appointment with the OB."

"That's a week before we leave."

Zoe had done her research.

"But Zo, what if -"

"Maggie, you can't live your life in fear. Come on; we have to book soon to get this deal. Jack wants to go!"

She glanced again at Jack, who was deep in conversation with Chelsea now.

She looked to Sam instead, who hadn't said a word but was smiling at her, his white teeth gleaming and his blue eyes twinkling. So handsome, and the twins were fair like him.

Charmed by them all, Maggie threw up her hands in defeat. "I give up. I'm too tired and heavy with food to argue with you two!"

Zoe pumped her fist in the air, yelling, "Yes!" and Sam patted her knees. Jack noticed the little celebration and sprinted over to the couch, hugging her.

"This is going to be great, Maggie!" He sprinted back to the kitchen, leaving Maggie dizzy in the chaos.

Max sat by her when Zoe and Sam gravitated to the kitchen to discuss the details with Jack.

"Will you be alright to travel?"

Maggie was touched. "Yeah, I'll only be around fourteen weeks then, probably, which means the nausea should be better, too."

"This is great, Mags."

She thought about it. "Yes, it is! But I feel weird leaving the house. I feel like we did something good today by exploring back there. I don't want to stop."

Max looked thoughtful now. "I know; don't worry, sis. It won't stop. I'm going to keep researching, and maybe I'll even drive over and talk to the Browns."

Jack joined them. "Hm? Talk to the Browns? Are you staying at our place while we're gone? It's a good idea, guys. Take advantage of a big empty place to stretch out!"

Maggie and Max looked at each other, questioningly.

"That's not what we were saying, but that's an interesting idea," said Max.

"And it would give you the opportunity to keep exploring, though don't do too much without me!" Maggie wondered at the sense of possessiveness she had on the happenings around the house.

Max looked toward his wife, who was immersed in a photo album with John. "Let me talk to Kathy, and I'll let you know well before you go, OK?"

Maggie nodded. Funny how things worked out sometimes. Contentedly, she lay her head on the back of the couch as Jack and Max switched places. Sinking into his shoulder, she finally felt the effects of her busy day.

"Come on, babe, let's go home." Jack was gently patting her leg and talking in her ear. She'd fallen asleep.

"Oh yeah. Home. Bed." Those in the living room laughed.

"Hey, I'm pregnant! I'm growing a human!"

"And we couldn't be happier," said Ophelia, taking her hands. Maggie allowed herself another moment of happiness as her family echoed her joy back to her. Another round of hugs, and Maggie was warm and dizzy with love by the time she was led toward the door by Jack.

They called their goodnights and returned home, Max and Kathy in the guest room and Jack and Maggie snuggled in theirs.

Just before sleep, Maggie remembered the footprints in the snow.

Chapter 22 – Zoe

Zoe's phone blinked red at her from her bedside table. She rolled over, rubbed her eyes, and found Sam had already gotten up.

What time is it?

She unplugged her phone and ascertained that it was seven-fifty. She punched the air with her fist in triumph. It was rare that her internal body clock allowed sleep to carry her past six a.m., but she'd been run-down since Christmas two weeks ago, in the grips of a cold or flu. Whatever it had been, it seemed to be fading now, and Zoe hoped this extra-long sleep had helped.

Sam's muffled singing reached her from the bathroom, and she smiled. *I love Sundays.* Sitting up, she checked her phone for messages and was surprised to see that Martin had called late last night and had left a message. She checked her ringer setting – whoops: vibrate. Dialling voicemail, she allowed herself a swift intake of breath. She'd been trying to get in touch with her brother since well before Christmas. Why call now? Was something wrong?

"Hey, Zoe.

(pause)

"Look, I'm sorry I haven't gotten back to you; work has been busy. Ah, I guess the truth is that I'm just feeling sort of down these days." He laughed a bit. *"I should say *more* down. Anyway. Winter always does this to me, you know.*

(pause)

"I hope you and everyone else had a good Christmas. Mine was pretty much the same as any day, but that's how I like it. I know

you're probably going to see Mom tomorrow. I'll be here if you want to stop by on your way back."

click

Zoe's jaw dropped. *An invitation?* The last line had been spoken quickly, as though it were an afterthought, but it was there nonetheless, and she was going to take it! She jumped out of bed and walked toward the sound of her husband's singing.

"Hey, baby."

"Whoa! Jeez! I thought you were still sleeping!" Sam peeked around the shower curtain.

"Martin called me!"

"Just now?"

"No; last night. And Sam, he said *I could stop by*!"

Sam's head had retreated back behind the milky transparency of the curtain, and she could make out his movements as he rinsed his hair.

"What? Wow! Today?"

"Yeah, after I visit Mom. Hey, do you want to come?"

"No, remember I have pool with the guys tonight?"

Oh, yes; she did remember and was glad about it. Sam's infrequent boys' nights were good for him. He had such a sunny disposition anyway, but for days after spending an evening shooting pool or throwing darts with his friends, he had a renewed confidence and energy, so Zoe always greeted these nights with pleasure.

"Right! Sorry, it slipped my mind. What are you doing until then?" She slipped out of her nightgown, letting it drop to the floor.

"Hmm, no plans, except to hang out with this really cool chick I know."

Zoe stepped into the shower, to Sam's surprise and delight. "I see. She's very lucky. Would you mind spending some time with me, first?"

He wrapped his arms around her and kissed her, the water running over and between their mouths as they moved. "How can I say no?"

Zoe loved Sundays.

The trip to Wolfville had been arranged for some days; Maggie had called and asked if Zoe would go Sunday, when she and Jack would usually go, as she and Jack would be in Kentville to see the OB on Wednesday and thought it would be easier to visit Alice during that trip rather than make the drive twice. Zoe appreciated the effort to coordinate their visits so her mother would never go more than four or five days without company. When Maggie and Jack had been in Sackville, Zoe had felt the burden of her responsibilities so much more profoundly. Martin couldn't be depended upon to visit their mother with any sort of regularity, and Jack and Maggie had been able to get to Wolfville only once every two or three weeks. It had been a significant transition to have their mother in a home, and just now, Zoe felt they were finally all falling into the groove.

The drive in was easy, but the radio warned of heavy snowfall late in the evening. Zoe leaned toward the steering wheel to better view the sky. She shook her head. It was clear and blue. She looked at the trees lining the highway, which stood still and calm. *Nova Scotia weather!* she thought and made a mental note to keep an eye outside through her day. She'd been caught in a few snowstorms on this highway and didn't want to do it again today.

Alice was in a fine mood, remembering things very well. Zoe enjoyed talking with her about when she and her brothers were small and was pleased with Alice's ability to recall names and details. Good days like this needed to be cherished. Alice's only slip-up was asking where her reading glasses were when they were sitting on her head, but Zoe thought that had less to do with dementia and more to do with being scatterbrained.

When they said goodbye, Alice hugged Zoe tight. "Thank you for coming to see me."

Zoe smiled. "Maggie and Jack will be here after they see the doctor on Wednesday. It's their first appointment with the new OB!"

"Oh, I hope everything goes smoothly for them. Remember the hard time they had?"

Zoe nodded. "Let's just be positive, no matter what, eh? Worrying won't help."

Alice laughed and gave Zoe's arm a light smack. "How our roles have reversed!"

Zoe realized her mother had said those very words to her hundreds of times in her life, and she smiled. "You've rubbed off on me, Mom."

Alice hugged her again. "Not too much, though. You're such a good person, Zoe."

"So are you, Mom!"

"But we're different. I'm so proud to be your mom."

Zoe pulled away. "Don't make me cry! 'Bye, Mom - oh! I'm going to see Martin!"

Alice took Zoe's arm, and Zoe noticed a tremble in her mother's chin. "Make sure he knows I'm proud to be his mom, too. And tell him to come see me. I miss him."

Zoe nodded, squeezed her mother's hand gently and left.

Blue skies, still and clear. It was after four, and Zoe was already hungry. On a whim, she stopped at Joe's in town and ordered two lasagnas and one scott skins, their signature dish made with thinly sliced, deep-fried potatoes smothered in a combination of spices. John had introduced her to them during an early visit to him in his first year, and she'd been a loyal fan since.

Thinking of her son, she slapped her forehead. She'd gotten so excited over her visit to Martin that she'd forgotten to call him. She sent him a text to say she was in town but was on her way to Martin's and asked if he wanted to join them.

She smiled at his reply: *It's cool, Mom! I'm doing a review with a group of students I'm TA'ing for anyway. Next time. <3*

Zoe smiled at the heart. She'd had some rough years with John as he went through what she supposed were "typical" teenage issues, but she was so proud of how he'd done for himself. He was a teacher's assistant for one of his professors and even ran auxiliary classes in addition to attending the main classes with the students. This and his Master's thesis took dedication above and beyond what Zoe had faced while she was in school, and yet John never complained.

The food was ready and placed unceremoniously in front of her, the bill on top of the brown paper bag. She paid and was on her way to Martin's in Waterville, texting him when she was close and remembering to pick up a Tim Horton's coffee for him on the way.

177

She was tired and hungry when she reached his door and hoped for an easy visit.

"Hey, Zoe." Martin smiled and ushered her in. Zoe hugged him awkwardly, holding the warm package against her side with one arm and embracing him with the other. He laughed and took the bag. "What's this?"

"I hope you haven't eaten, but if you have, I'm so hungry I'll eat yours too!"

"My what? And no, I haven't eaten." Martin still smiled, and Zoe felt any apprehension she'd had melt away. He looked like the perfect combination of her parents. She looked like her mother, while Jack got the looks of the handsome Ridgewood men. Martin, on the other hand, had her mother's eyes, her father's colouring, and a personality and temperament that reminded her of both. It was fascinating. Now she wondered at the fact that there had been two of them, once, alive and identical. In looks, at least.

She took off her coat and hung it on a hook in the hall, taking the time to regroup. "It's lasagne!"

"Oooh, from Joe's?"

"Yes, and…"

"No way! You didn't get Scott skins too, did you?" His face radiated pleasure and anticipation.

"How did you know that?"

He did a hop and hurried into the small kitchen with the package, making quick work of opening the containers and transferring the food onto plates, dividing the spiced potatoes between them. Zoe shook her head. Martin had such a sweet heart, and he was

178

so accommodating. The problem was getting him to consent to a visit in the first place. But she was here now, and she was determined to enjoy it.

They ate quietly, making small talk here and there. Martin updated Zoe on his latest work projects, and Zoe filled him in on Christmas dinner and told him about her visit to their mother that day. Usually, Zoe worked much harder to fill the silent pauses with chatter, but she was so hungry she forgot to speak.

Once they were finished, Martin sipped his coffee (after a quick blast in the microwave) as Zoe placed their dishes in the sink. "Thank you, Zoe. That was excellent."

"Yeah, it was good, wasn't it? You're welcome." She sat back down at the tiny kitchen table, sighing in contentment. "You know, I was so happy to hear from you this morning."

Martin looked uncomfortable. "I'm sorry, Zo -"

She placed her hand on his. "No, Marty; it's OK! I just meant I haven't seen you in months! I was glad you called."

He smiled.

"You know, there's something I'd like to talk to you about."

Martin looked uncomfortable again but didn't reply.

"It's OK if you don't want to talk about it. I'll just start telling you, and you can stop me if you want."

He looked at her, confused. "What's this about?"

"Well, I guess it's about Sebastian."

She had expected him to look shocked or angry, but Martin's face didn't change. "What about him?"

"This is going to sound pretty crazy, but I think Maggie's been seeing him."

"Ah."

"That's it? 'Ah'?"

"Well, what do you want me to say?"

"I don't know! I guess I just wanted to tell you. And - and I wanted to apologize, Marty. Maggie and I went to see Mom a while ago, to talk about that time after Sebastian died."

"Why? That would just upset her!"

"Because some things have been happening at the house. Maggie's been dreaming about a boy, and we both saw a woman, by the bridge."

Now Martin looked surprised. "What bridge?"

"Oh yeah, you haven't seen it. Jack built it. Actually, none of that is important. Just know that some things have been going on that have brought back a lot of memories, and mostly I just want to apologize to you."

"What for?"

She started to cry, and Martin placed his hand over hers. This comforting gesture somehow made her feel worse, and she covered her face with her hands.

"Zoe, what's going on? I know I've not seen very much of the family, so I've missed a lot, but - listen to me." He gently pulled her hands away from her face. "Listen to me."

She took a deep, shuddering breath.

"You have nothing to be sorry about."

"I just – I wasn't a very good sister to you after - everything was so hard with Mom so screwed up. We were alone so much, and I think I took it out on you!"

"What?"

"I mean – oh, that sounded bad! I didn't harm you physically or anything, but I didn't give you the love and attention you needed, Marty, and I'm so sorry!" She buried her face in her hands again, sobbing and miserable that her words weren't coming out as she'd intended.

Martin waited a minute, letting her cry. Then, he gently pulled her hands away from her face again, this time holding them in his own on the table. "Zoe, that wasn't your job."

Zoe shook her head, sniffing.

"I don't remember any of that, Zo. All I remember is you taking care of me. You teaching me. You were more of a parent to me than Mom and Dad were. I mean, I never felt close to Mom, anyway. I never felt that she loved me, but I've been old enough for a long time to know that that wasn't my fault. It was more like self-protection. She needed to protect herself from loving me."

"What? That makes no sense! How can a mother not love her child?"

"Of course she *loved* me, like any mother loves her child. But she couldn't get close to me, or build a relationship. She didn't make me feel loved."

Zoe, confused, looked at her brother, aware of her hands sweating in his and her cheeks cold with the tears that had covered them – but unable to say anything.

"Do you understand?"

"No! You deserved love as much as Jack and I did! More! You'd lost your soul-mate! Your twin!"

"You lost him, too."

More tears, now, and she wanted her hands back, but Martin held them fast.

"Zoe, Mom had to protect herself from loving me because then it wouldn't hurt so bad if she lost me, too."

"Oh, Martin…!"

"Hey, it's OK. And don't start thinking I'm all evolved or enlightened or anything. Just because I understand, it doesn't make it better." He let go of her hands and grabbed a tissue out of the box on the windowsill behind him. It was pitch dark outside, and Zoe could hear the wind against the building.

Zoe accepted the tissue and blew her nose loudly. "What do you mean? I mean, I know it's hard for you to be with family -"

"With people, Zo. People in general. And who knows? Maybe I'd still be this way if my upbringing had been more typical. But I spent so much of my life trying to figure out the 'why' and 'how' of things that I forgot to pay attention to what it was doing to me, my relationship with my family, my life in general."

Now Zoe grabbed his hands. "Maybe now that you recognize that, you can make some changes."

"Maybe." He seemed reluctant. "But it's not a simple decision. This is who I am, and I'm afraid I'm not a very good person."

He'd said it so matter-of-factly that Zoe knew he believed it. She laughed. "Martin, I was just thinking what a good person you are! You are! You're wonderful! One of the most genuine people I know!"

"You have to say that."

"No! I -"

He raised his hand to stop her. "I'm not. I've resented Mom all these years. Not you, not Dad or Grandma. Mom. I needed her. I always felt like I had this hole in me. Maybe it was missing Sebastian. I don't know," he shrugged, "but I blamed Mom for it. I blamed her for not making it better; for not filling it with her love.

"Oh. Shit, Martin. I don't blame you for that! I only wish I'd done more to help you."

Martin smiled again. "You know, you're right. Maybe it's time to make some changes. I've actually been seeing a psychologist."

"You have? That's - that's wonderful!"

He blushed. "It's been a few months. I've been working stuff out with him. It's been good, I think."

"I'm so happy that you're helping yourself. And please know that I'm here to talk to or help in any way I can, too."

"I know you are. You always have been, Zoe. Thank you for that."

They hugged over the little table, bending awkwardly but not caring.

The wind whipped at the window.

"Oh wow; I hope this isn't the storm they called for."

Martin walked to the patio door and flicked the switch for the outside light. Its pale glow revealed big, heavy snowflakes, the kind that would have floated lazily to the ground if it weren't for the harsh wind shoving them in one direction, and then the other, before they landed in relief. "It doesn't look too bad yet, but you should get on the road if you want to miss it."

Zoe nodded and headed back toward the front door.

She got bundled up, checked that she wasn't forgetting anything, and hugged her brother. "I'm so glad I came. Thank you."

"Me too. I'm going to try hard to make sure you hear from me more often. And Jack, too."

Zoe didn't comment on his omission of their mother. She'd take what she could get.

"Good. Love you, brother."

He smiled, then asked, "Oh, what you were saying before?"

She turned to look at him. "Hm?"

"About Maggie. Is she OK?"

"Yeah! More than OK, actually. She's just -" Zoe decided not to spill the news about the baby yet, though she couldn't quite put her finger on why. "She's just going through a transition period, maybe."

Martin looked like he wanted to say more but decided against it. Both of them recognized that the other was treading carefully on the new ground they were building. "OK. Be careful driving." He opened the door and looked at the snow. "It's getting heavier. Do you want to stay?"

"No; I'm OK. I'll take the back roads and stay away from the highway."

"Yeah. Alright. Goodnight."

There was no *"Let me know when you get home safely."*

That was OK. Baby steps.

The snow whipped against her cheeks painfully. No longer fluffy, it had quickly turned hard and icy. Zoe was eager to get home quickly, but her heart sank in the realization that this would take a while.

Not more than a kilometre away from Martin's house, her car slid on some black ice. Zoe yelped and whipped the wheel to the right, a voice in her mind saying, *No! You know you're not supposed to do that on ice!* The tires caught on pavement and, still turned hard to the right, took her front end straight into the shallow ditch.

"No!"

Zoe put the SUV into reverse and gunned it. The car rocked backward and stopped, and at the whining insistence of her engine, she released the gas. Remembering the "rocking" technique Sam had taught her, she alternated between drive and reverse, the car indeed rocking, but not moving anywhere useful.

"Shit."

Then, hitting her steering wheel, *"Shit!"*

185

She picked up her phone. Her first instinct was to call Sam, but he was a good twenty-five minutes away, and it would be ridiculous to try and get out here. John was her next option, but he was probably still busy with his students, and, well, Martin was just up the street. Still, something in her resisted calling her brother. They'd sort of had a breakthrough, hadn't they? She didn't want to push her luck. But looking out the windshield at the falling snow brightly illuminated by her headlights, she realized he was her best choice.

He answered on the first ring. "Hello?"

"Hi, Martin! Hey, remember how you said you wanted to start seeing me more?"

"Uh oh."

"Not even a kilometre away from your place, I'd bet. Bring sand if you have it."

"Doesn't everyone in Nova Scotia?"

She laughed wryly. She was pissed off and just wanted to be home with Sam.

"Be there in a few; sit tight."

"Thank you."

She dialled Sam as she waited.

"Hey, baby."

"Hey, I'm glad you called. Bad storm!"

"Yeah, it put me in a ditch."

"What? Oh my God, are you OK?"

"Yeah, no worries. Martin's on his way to get me out."

"Babe, you should stay at his place tonight. Don't try to drive home in this."

"We'll see. I'll call you after I'm out. Don't worry, OK?"

"Easier said than done. I'm sitting by the phone."

"Love you." Zoe spotted Martin approaching in the rear-view mirror, his body illuminated in the red glow of her brake lights.

"Love you too."

"Here's Martin. Talk to you soon."

"'K."

She watched her brother approach, his hands shoved deep into his pants pockets. Weird; she couldn't see his car. Had he walked? But he wasn't carrying a shovel, or sand.

She raised her hand and waved, still watching him in the mirror, and Martin stopped and raised his hand, too, smiling.

She got out of the car and moved to the back of it, levering herself out of the snowy ditch with a good grip on her still-open door. The snow whirled around in the angry wind, and she raised her hand to her forehead, shielding her eyes to look at her brother.

She couldn't see him. He was just gone.

"Martin?" She turned around. "Where'd you go?"

At the sound of an approaching car behind her, she turned, still shielding her eyes from the snow, which was good, as the headlights coming her way, slowly now, were blindingly bright.

It was Martin's car. He stepped out and went to the trunk, retrieving a shovel and sand. Regarding the SUV, he walked to Zoe's side. "Ah, that's not so bad. I'll dig the excess snow out from behind the rear wheels and dump a bunch of sand for traction. Good call, sis."

Zoe was dumbfounded.

Martin got to work and, in less than ten minutes, advised her to stand back by his car and out of the way so he could back the SUV out.

On the third try, it mounted the lip of the ditch and was up on the road.

Martin walked back to her, smiling. "Phew, that's my exercise for the night!"

Zoe stared at him.

"What's wrong?"

"Martin, you were here."

"What?" He laughed. "Is that some sort of weird way of saying I was the master of this situation? Yes! I totally kicked its ass." He bowed low. "You're welcome."

"No. You walked up to the car while I was still inside. I got out and looked up and you were gone. And then you drove up."

Martin's face turned serious. "Oh."

"Martin -"

"So, he really is showing himself to others now."

"*What*?" Zoe gripped his arm and shivered uncontrollably.

"It's OK, Zoe. Listen. Tell Maggie I see him, too. Tell her he just wants to help."

"Sebastian? It was *Sebastian* I saw?"

"Well, did he look like me?"

Zoe felt faint. "What the hell, Martin?"

"I've always seen him. Made me feel kinda crazy...*er*. To tell you the truth, it's sort of a relief to know I'm not the only one." He smiled, completely calm.

"But why? What does this mean?"

"I don't know, sis. I don't actually see him as though he's a tangible person, like you're describing. I dream of him, and I feel him around all the time. He's always been with me, I think. In my dreams, he's at the old house. When I was a kid, he would talk to me about Mom in the dreams. Said I needed to forgive her. Said - said she was trying to help someone who needed it. Then that stopped. And recently, it started again, but about Maggie."

"Tell me more!"

"That's all there is. It's never really made any sense to me, Zo. All I cared about was that I never felt that I'd completely lost him. I was just so happy to see him. I'm sorry. I wish I could help more."

Zoe nodded, dazed by these new revelations.

Martin gestured around them. "Look."

The snow was floating around them, and the wind had died down.

"The eye of the storm, maybe, and it's still icy. You should maybe stay with me tonight, after all."

"No. Thanks, Martin, but I've got volunteer work with the co-op tomorrow." Really, she just wanted to get home and have a bath. Maybe not even have a bath, actually. She just wanted the comfort of her husband and her own bed.

"You're still cooking meals for seniors at home?"

"Yes, Mondays. Martin, would you be willing to talk to Maggie about this?"

He shuffled his feet in the snow, the lights from both cars casting shadows of his feet in four directions. Zoe noted the beauty of it, took the quiet moment to breathe the clear, cold air into her lungs.

"I don't know, Zoe. Maybe. Maybe soon. But this 'being more social' thing (he made quotation marks in the air with his fingers) - I think it's a long-term goal. Oh, don't look so disappointed, please. I'll talk to her. Just - I need a bit of time first. I thought I was the only one, you know? I just need a bit of time."

Zoe nodded, her heart aching for her brother. She hugged him, muttering into his shoulder, "Thank you for helping me. I'll talk to you soon?"

"Yes. I promise. Drive home carefully, OK?"

"I will."

"Call me when you get home, just so I know you're OK."

Chapter 23 – Confirmation

Maggie's breath caught in her throat. She gripped Jack's hand convulsively until he grunted at her side and she realized she was hurting him.

"Maggie?" Dr. Barker looked questioningly at her.

"You mean you're not even going to do a blood test?" Maggie heard the hysterical tone in her voice and took a deep breath.

The doctor smiled and leaned forward. "Maggie, I understand this is a scary situation for you, considering all you've been through." He looked at Jack. "Both of you. But like I said, home pregnancy tests are close to one hundred percent correct!"

Jack and Maggie were both silent.

"And you took three! All I'm saying is that I think we can safely skip the blood test. If you're as far along as we've calculated based on your last period, we should be able to hear the heartbeat, and that's a better confirmation than any, don't you think?"

"But you said with my tilted uterus, it might be more difficult."

Jack squeezed Maggie's hand now, and it was his turn to lean forward. "Doctor, I think what Maggie is saying is that she'd rather do whatever test is the most likely to tell us a quick, reliable answer. If she lies down on that table and you can't get a heartbeat, that'll be easier to accept with the tilted uterus and a positive pregnancy test, done by you, than it would be if you hadn't even tested her - see?"

The doctor looked embarrassed. "I'm sorry. I see, yes. I want you to know I would never have suggested it if I didn't think we'd be successful, but you're absolutely right. Maggie, if it makes you more comfortable, let's do a urine test first, and once we're done with our appointment, I'll have the nurse draw some blood so we can test your HCG levels, too. Sound good?"

Maggie could have hugged him. "Sounds awesome. Thank you."

He handed her a transparent plastic cup with a yellow lid. "You know the drill."

Maggie's hand shook as she took the cup. Three weeks ago, she had decided to be confident and share her news. Now she felt as disbelieving as she had when Zoe had first suggested she might be pregnant. Her symptoms had faded considerably, which could just mean the end of the first trimester, but it made her nervous nonetheless. She stood, but Jack stopped her before she could leave.

"Babe."

She met his grey-blue eyes.

"No matter what, we have us. That's enough. Right?"

"Right." It *had* been enough for so long, but now with the hope of having a child to share their love with, Maggie questioned if they could get through the disappointment if it didn't work out.

After the doctor had taken the little cup away, Maggie and Jack sat silently, holding each other's hands.

"What if..?"

"No Mags. Don't do that."

"Jack, there's something else. The job."

He looked at her. "What do you want to do?"

"If that doctor comes in here and shows us a positive test, I can't hold off anymore. I need to tell the boss. And I need to say no to the offer."

Jack looked sad. "Sucks, but you're right. With the baby, all those trips into Halifax would be hard. We could manage it though, babe. I know Zoe would help, too!"

"But I don't want that. We've wanted a baby for so long. Now that it looks like we're getting our wish, I want to cherish it. I want to take care of our baby. I'll still work from home, of course, but -"

Jack nodded. "OK. Yes. If it's the right decision for you, it's the right decision for us. I just don't want you to regret anything."

Silence again until Dr. Barker came back, holding a paper towel in his gloved hand, with what looked like a litmus strip on top. Smiling.

"Let's listen to that heartbeat."

"It's purple."

"If you weren't pregnant, it wouldn't have turned any colour at all."

Jack and Maggie looked at each other, and Jack whooped and hugged her. "Magpie! We're having a baby." He pulled back and met her eyes again. "Please, you have to believe it now."

Maggie grasped his hand. "OK, OK! It's real." She turned to the doctor. "How do we do the heartbeat thing?"

The doctor smiled and indicated that she should get up on the table. "Just lie on your back. Jack, you can come hold her hand if you like." He waited until they were comfortable, then, tucking Maggie's pants down into her underwear, he said, "I'm going to spread some of this gel on your tummy. It helps the Doppler move around and helps transmit the sound waves."

Maggie jumped at the touch of the cold gel.

The doctor looked at her. "Are you ready?"

She nodded.

He placed the Doppler low on her abdomen, pressing in gently. Strange sounds filled the room as he moved it around, his eyes fixed on some point beside the table, but nothing that sounded like a heartbeat. "Hm. Your uterus is positioned a bit differently. We have to remember that." He moved slightly higher on her abdomen and pointed toward the small of her back. "Don't worry; this takes time with everyone the first time. When the baby grows and we know its position, it'll be easier."

His speech was surreal. His focused gaze on the wall made her feel as though he was talking to someone else.

Suddenly, what sounded like the frantic hoofbeats of a racehorse filled the room, and the doctor's gaze left the wall and met her eyes in a smile. "There it is!"

"It's so fast," said Jack.

"Is that normal?" asked Maggie.

But the doctor's eyes were already fixed again, this time on his watch. Maggie counted ten seconds.

"Just over one hundred and fifty BPM. Perfect."

Catching Jack's confused look, Maggie said, "Beats per minute."

The doctor moved the wand slightly and furrowed his brow. More swishing sounds, but distant. "Hmmm."

"What does, 'hmmm' mean? I don't like 'hmmm!'" exclaimed Maggie, and the doctor laughed.

"Don't worry! Do you have any twins in your family?"

Jack and Maggie met each other's panicked eyes. "Why would you ask that, doc?" asked Jack.

"Well, I'm picking up what sounds like another heartbeat. Don't get too excited; it sounds less clear than the first. Could actually be Maggie's heart, or the one baby's but from a different angle. But it could also mean there's another baby hiding behind the first, or one whose heartbeat is more difficult to hear due to the position of the uterus."

Maggie and Jack didn't say anything.

"Chances are it's a singleton, folks. But let's schedule an early ultrasound. I would have anyway, due to the uterus, but now we can check both."

"OK," was all that Maggie could muster.

Already the doctor was wiping the gel off her belly.

"That's it?"

"Ah, now you can't get enough!" He smiled. "I'll call the nurse in to take your blood and schedule your ultrasound, and I'll see you again after that appointment. You'll most likely be classified 'high-risk' due to the tilted uterus, though we don't always call those high-risk pregnancies. It depends on the severity. But with your previous troubles getting pregnant, your chances of seeing a lot more of us are higher."

"Oh, my God," said Maggie.

"Maggie, this doesn't change anything. What it means is that we're going to watch you more closely. You get to have more ultrasounds and see the baby more! I know many women who would pay good money to be classified high-risk." He winked, and Maggie couldn't help but feel a bit lucky at this bit of news.

"We're special, babe," remarked Jack smugly, and the doctor laughed as he dialled a number.

"I'm going to go ahead and make your first ultrasound in the high-risk unit. Much more specialized care, and they'll get you in more quickly. We'll see what we see and go from there."

Walking out of the hospital with an appointment card for just over two weeks later, the couple were elated.

"We'll get to see the baby right after we get back from the trip!" said Maggie.

"I'm so glad he said you could go," answered Jack. "And holy cow, it might be bab*ies*. I don't know how I feel about that."

Maggie stopped, and Jack turned to face her. "Jack, I feel like it's one. I can't explain it, but I do. I'm nervous, too, of course, but I feel like it's one." She walked up to him and held his arms. "But if it's not, let's think of Zoe's twins, OK? About how perfect and beautiful and healthy they are."

Jack dropped his head. "How alive they are."

"Yes. Not every twin pregnancy suffers TTTS, you know. In fact, it's only one in a thousand."

"You've been Googling."

Maggie grinned. "It's a skill. Now let's go. I'm starving."

"Should we stop for a bite before seeing Mom?"

"Yes, and let's take her some cake or something. We have some celebrating to do. But first -" She picked up her phone and dialled Toby Simon. After the short conversation, she turned to Jack, looking elated. "He said, 'Congratulations'."

"Nice."

"And he said if I can't take the position they offered, they'd still like me to write more, and that once I'm ready to travel more, the other offer will be waiting!"

"Won't they fill it with someone else?"

"No! He said they had the specific section idea for me and my writing. He also said he'd talk to Mr. Peterson and see what we could do in the meantime!"

Jack shook his head. "You've got a good spot, there."

"I know it. What a day," she shook her head.

"Now let's go get some cake!" Jack gave her hand a squeeze, put the truck in drive, and they were on their way.

Chapter 24 – Nola

Walter bolted up in bed for the third time that week. He sat panting in the dark until his heart slowed and the chilly air had cooled the sweat on his skin. He swung his legs over the side of the bed and stood, looking at the digital clock glowing red on his nightstand.

Three twenty-six.

"Shit."

He flicked the light switch in the bathroom and blinked in the bright light, acclimatizing. He didn't even know why he'd come to the bathroom. Out of frustration, he guessed. And refusal to lie awake for an hour or two, wishing he was asleep. He leaned over the sink and studied his face in the mirror. Blue eyes, faded with age now, like old jeans, and stubble on his cheeks and chin that he never seemed to be able to shave completely smooth anymore. He palmed his chin, rubbed his cheeks.

"You look unimpressed, Wally." It was something Nola would have said, but now there was only him to say it. A wave of loneliness clenched at his chest. Feeling chilled, Walter pulled his housecoat off the back of the door and put it on, then headed for the stairs, thinking of warm milk.

Why am I waking up?

It wasn't dreams. He didn't remember dreaming anything. He didn't wake up feeling particularly scared, either. Well, maybe that wasn't entirely true. Any of it. While he didn't remember the dreams, he felt the remnants of them clinging to him. And bits and pieces came to him as he worked at the station or made his rounds before he returned at night.

Walter poured some two percent into a saucepan and turned the burner on low. He took a mug out of the cupboard above his head and waited.

Thinking.

He let himself wonder whether it was Nola but quickly shook his head. All that talk about your loved ones coming to visit you after they'd passed on was just that: talk. He felt Nola's presence. Of course, he did! She was infused into this house and his routine and the car and the yard and the grocery store. Everything made him think of her. And sometimes it was as if she were right there beside him. He had loved her so completely - still did. But she hadn't appeared to him. He'd had no revelations or final messages from beyond.

He searched his mind for other possibilities. This was a skill Walter had worked hard to develop. His training in the force had encouraged analytical thinking from all angles.

But it taught a deep respect for instinct, too.

What do you feel in your gut, old boy?

He thought about Maggie Ridgewood and her phone call on Boxing Day. He'd thanked her for the information, but his interest wasn't piqued. He had gone out to the old Maplestone place very shortly after being called to the Ridgewood house and hearing Maggie's story of the woman at the bridge, dripping phantom blood into the snow. Nothing had changed. It had been so cold that day that Walter had only done a quick walkaround. No new graffiti; apparently it had been too cold even for the teenagers to visit the place. The property was quiet, save for the whistling wind in the trees. And just to satisfy his sense of due diligence, he had looked for footprints around the house and leading to and from the driveway.

Nothing.

But since then, he had been waking up during the night.

The milk was starting to foam, and Walter poured it into his mug. He brought it to the table and sat, reflexively opening the Maplestone file. He had found two in the archives and already gone through them twice. Two incidents had involved the police: one, the incident that resulted in Rose Maplestone's being committed to the psychiatric facility in Waterville, and the second the response to Greyson Maplestone's call to report his parents' death.

Some surprising information, yes, but somehow Walter felt reluctant to think about it too much. What significance could these events have to Maggie Ridgewood?

He took a large gulp of his milk.

Well, the blood would make sense. Walter shook his head, hard. *Only if they were seeing a ghost, you fool!* He stared at the report, not really seeing the words. *Or someone who knew the history and wanted to scare the daylights out of someone.*

Walter swallowed another mouthful of his drink and decided to return to bed.

I should go back out there. If that trail leads to the Maplestone property, I need to find it. And why is there a cabin-type building out in the middle of the woods?

He shivered. The more he learned, the more his refusal to believe in anything beyond the physical – the tangible – was challenged, and he didn't like that. He was a cop. He wasn't going to get scared. More importantly, he didn't want to find a problem he was unable to solve with his badge or his gun.

He laid his housecoat over the chair in the corner and got into bed, revelling in the warmth and falling asleep quickly.

In his dream - for he did dream again, and this one he would remember as clear as day when he awoke in the morning – he was standing at the edge of the Maplestone property, the house itself shrouded in mist. Nola was standing to the left of the building, midway between the house and the woods.

"Nola?"

"Wally, darling. I have something to show you." Her gentle smile, so familiar and so missed, was like a punch in the stomach. It sucked the air from his lungs and the tears from his eyes.

"Nola. Oh God, I've missed you." He ran toward her, his heart bursting in his chest. When he reached her, she took both his hands in her left hand and reached out to touch his face with the other.

"I've been trying to talk to you for so long."

"Nola, I'm so sorry! I have so many regrets; I love you so much."

His words came in a rush. He felt his time with her would be short, and he had so much to say.

"Wally, I love you with all of myself. Please, make me happy. Do not live with regrets. Live with joy until we meet again."

He fell to his knees, placing his hands on her slippered feet. It was spring. The grass was fragrant.

"Darling, come with me. Please."

Walter would do anything for her. He would gladly die so he could stay with her, even in this place far back from the road, with its strange stories and dark history.

She led him by the hand to the trees. Her skin was soft but cold.

She stopped and pointed.

Walter knew, before he saw the barely noticeable gap in the trees, that she was showing him the trail.

"Help her."

"Who?"

"She's stuck. She needs help. She keeps trying. We try, too. But it's hard for them to hear us. To understand."

She started to fade, her body dissolving into the mist before his eyes.

"No! No, Nola! Please!"

"I'm not gone. I'm never gone. You can help. You can help her. Help them help her. I love you."

He woke up, and his room was bright with morning sun.

Chapter 25 – Two Calls

Maggie moved around the bedroom, alternately packing an item or two and checking her list. Her brain felt full, too full, of things to remember as she packed for the trip.

Jack breezed into the room, carrying a large pile of folded laundry. "Two days!" He put the clothes on the bed and grabbed her arm, stopping her in her tracks, bewildering her. "Two days 'til paradise, my love." He pulled her close. "Do you think you'll be able to relax?"

She tried to smile. "Of course. I just - there's so much to think about, and I can't help but think of all the things we'll still have to do when we get back! Vacations are supposed to be relaxing!"

"Babe -"

"I know, I know. I just wish the ultrasound could have been scheduled before the trip."

"The doctor didn't seem concerned at all, and he said we'll see more if we wait."

"Oh, Jack. I know. Logically, I should be very happy right now. Instead, I can't seem to calm down. I can't sleep. My mind keeps going."

"Is it the dreams?"

"No! In fact, I don't remember any dreams, really, since I was in Halifax."

"Well, that one was enough to last a lifetime!"

Maggie walked to the window and studied the footbridge. "I still feel her."

"The woman?"

"Yes. And the boy, too. I know there's something there, Jack. Something that needs to be solved."

He walked to the window and gently turned her toward him. "I know it, too. Hell, my mom knew it. But do you think, just for a little while, you can put it aside? You'll come back to it. Just focus on yourself, and me, and the *beach!*"

She couldn't help but laugh. "You're right. I mean, how lucky are we? Zoe and Sam are amazing for pushing us to come."

He crossed to the laundry, picking up his pile and sorting it into his suitcase. "Magpie, it took very little pushing to convince me." He winked.

Maggie studied her list, but it looked shorter now, and easier to accomplish. *Deep breath. You're allowed to relax for a while.*

Jack startled her out of her thoughts. "You know, the fact that Max is staying here should comfort you. Isn't he planning on talking to the Browns? Maybe doing some more research?"

"Oh, thank you for mentioning that! I need to call Max and finalize plans! Shit. I might have forgotten until we were on the plane! I think I'm starting to understand that 'pregnant brain' thing." She walked out of the room, muttering, "We could have forgotten to give him the key!"

He called, "Hey, if you're going to call him now, tell him I wouldn't mind if he solved this whole thing while we were gone!"

Maggie answered, but all he heard was "- need to be part of that -"

Maggie dialled her brother, hoping, as she did every time she called him, that his ringer was on.

"Hello?"

"Max, I want to talk to you about your stay. I'm actually kind of worried because you don't know anything about the fireplace and how the heat works and where we keep the salt for the driveway -"

"Whoa, there! Hold your horses, sis!" Max laughed. "I'll come by a couple of hours before you leave, and we can go over everything you want, OK?"

"OK."

"Are you freaking out?"

She let out a short laugh. "Yes! Yes, I am! And Jack tried to help me with that, but it keeps coming back. I guess I feel conflicted with leaving, you know, with everything going on."

"Don't worry, Mags. This thing seems to have been going on for a long while. I think it'll still be going on when you come back. You're only going for what, ten days?"

"*Eight*! Oh my God, you don't even know how long you're staying!"

"Calm down, calm down! Jeez."

"Sorry. God, I'm awful, aren't I?"

"No. You're unexpectedly pregnant, transitioning to a new life in the country, having dreams that would fit perfectly into a horror film, and seeing things in the waking hours, too. And you're not the only one! So, it's definitely not all in your head. All that put together and you're doing pretty well in my books."

"Huh. When you put it that way, I guess I am."

"But Mags, do yourself and your poor husband a favour and let go of everything for a little while. Just have a fantastic vacation! Then when you come back, we'll figure out the ghosts!"

She laughed.

"Hopefully I'll have more information by then, too."

Again, she felt reassured. "Thanks, bro. Wow. I *need* a vacation!"

"Good thing for you is that in two days, you'll start one. You'll be warm, too, while the rest of us are here freezing our asses off."

"I'll bring you back some beach sand."

"Great. Thanks."

"Haha, don't be bitter, Max. Anyway, I'm going to go finish packing. Thanks for the calming lecture."

"That's what I'm here for. Oh – when do you leave on Friday?"

They finalized plans, and Maggie hung up the phone, only to notice the red indicator light blinking. She sat at the table and listened to a message from Zoe:

"Hi guys, it's Zoe. Just checking in to see if you're packing! Actually, I'm also calling because I got some information today from my friend in Ottawa. Maggie, call me!"

Maggie deleted the message, feeling her heart sink. She didn't want to deal with this now, but she knew if she didn't, she'd think about it the entire vacation. She dialled Zoe.

"Maggie?"

Maggie laughed. "Yep. Just got your message; you must have called while I was talking to Max."

"Mags, Libby called me today."

"Oh; that's the psychic's friend, right?"

"Yeah. She'd pretty much given up on her, but she called her back today! Her name is Charis, and she says she feels compelled to talk to you?"

"Oh? I don't feel very lucky about that, somehow!"

"That's probably because she only helps people who really need her. I guess she's pretty young – your age – and she's a single mother of three boys."

"Holy cow. Also, I don't really like confirmation that I need her."

"Not just you, Mags. You're not in this alone. I saw her, too. And there's a history there, remember?"

"I'm sorry, Zo. You're absolutely right. *We* need her. Thank you."

"We're in this together. Got a pen?" Zoe recited the psychic's number. "Are you going to call her today?"

"I don't want to, but I think I have to. I don't want to be thinking about it the entire vacation."

"OK. Will you call me back when you have?"

Maggie sighed. "Yes."

She hung up the phone and laid her head on her arms, breathing in the smell of the wood table, feeling the draft from the back door. Finding a modicum peace in the moment.

"I want a nap."

"So, take one." Maggie jumped, shot Jack a look, and put her head in her hands this time.

Jack couldn't help but laugh. "Conversation with Max that bad?"

"Nooooo, the conversation with the psychic is what has me stressed."

"What? She called? What'd she say?" Jack sat down at the table.

She peeked between her fingers. "Since when did you even believe in that stuff?"

"Hey, I didn't say I believed in it! I'm just curious!"

"She called Zoe. I've got her number, and I'm supposed to call her." Maggie noted Jack's effort to hold back his enthusiasm.

"Babe, you know you can wait until we're back from vacation."

She took his hand across the table. "Thanks, but I've got to call her before we leave. I want to get it over with."

"Cool!"

Maggie grinned. "How do you *really* feel, Jack?"

Jack smiled in return.

"Well, I'm afraid you'll have to wait a little while. I'm taking a nap."

"You OK?"

"Yeah, no worries. Just tired, and you know I've been stressed over the trip and - everything. I'll call tonight. Or tomorrow."

Jack's face was momentarily blank, then he nodded, apparently having registered that this is what his wife needed right now. "Good. You sleep; I'll cross more things off the 'To Do Before We Go' list."

"You're a good man. But why don't you take a break, too? Take the afternoon to see the guys, or hey, you could nap, too!"

"I can't nap right now! My mind would never stop. And if I go out with the guys, I'll just want to be here getting things done. Besides, I like being here with you."

Maggie walked around the table and sat on her husband's lap, kissing him long and slow. "I like you here too," she said quietly, breathing in his scent and closing her eyes.

After a moment, Jack took her hand, led her upstairs to the bedroom and tucked her in, her eyes closed and face relaxed already. Maggie, drifting down, down to sleep, sensed him there, felt their deep connection, felt happy.

Resurfacing, for him, she muttered, "Tonight. I'll call her tonight."

Chapter 26 – Make That Three

It was seven-thirty. Charis folded laundry and watched TV, thinking that if she had the kids, she'd be ushering Michael up to the bathroom to start getting ready for bed. The pang in her heart, so familiar, reminded her of their temporary, but poignant, absence. She wondered if she should take herself to a movie, but her fatigue convinced her to stay in, finish the laundry and get to bed early.

The phone rang, and she instantly knew it was Libby's friend. She considered not making the trip across the room to pick it up, but a sense of obligation or – urgency? – compelled her. She paused her TV show and grabbed the phone.

"Hello?"

"Uh, hi. This is Maggie Ridgewood. I'm hoping to talk to Charis?"

Charis instantly liked her. Her energy was sincere and honest. Good fundamentals. And again, that sense of what felt similar to urgency but was closer to commitment. Like the Universe eyeing her and saying, *You're in this now. No backing out.*

She took a deep breath. "Maggie. Libby's friend. Hi there." She tried to put a smile in her voice.

"I hope I'm not catching you at a bad time."

Charis saw her. Black curly hair. And on vacation. And pregnant.

And there were a woman and a boy around her.

"Nope! Not at all. I'm glad you called. It was the right thing to do."

"So, how does this work?"

"Well, we just talk. I connect to your energy and see what I see. Then I tell you and hope it helps." Charis gave a short laugh.

"OK."

"There's no guarantee I'll see anything of use to you, but you're a breeze to connect to, so I think this'll be easy."

"Uh, thanks?" Maggie laughed. "I don't know what you usually do for compensation, but -"

"Nothing right now, actually. I used to charge for whatever it is I do, but it never felt quite right, so I stopped."

"Oh. Then how do you continue to do it? I mean I know you have kids. Sorry; that's none of my business!"

"No, it's OK. It's a good question. I don't do it much anymore, I guess."

"That's too bad. I hear you're quite talented."

"Yeah, but I have a full-time job and three little boys."

"Wow. That's enough for anyone!"

"Still, it doesn't solve the question of what I'm supposed to be doing with this. I mean, it's sort of sad that practising was a casualty of not charging anyone. Wow. I've never thought of it like that before!"

"Sorry about that! I didn't mean to make you question your life choices!" Maggie laughed. "Oh, wow, you must be less than excited to work with me!"

"Not at all. In fact, I have some new perspective on my own choices, I guess. Pretty valuable. Thank you."

"Uh, no problem. Ha."

"Well! I guess I could sum all of that up by saying I won't charge you unless I come to see you. I ask for my flight and expenses to be paid then. I simply can't afford to pay them myself."

"Of course. Do you think you'll need to come?"

"Well, that's up to both of us to decide after we talk. I think we'd both benefit from my visiting that building in the woods with you, though."

Maggie gasped.

"Oh. Right. I've been getting images while we talked. That's how it works for me; I connect to someone and get things. Like pictures or words or smells. Sometimes it's like a movie in my head. Right now, I see you and a man working your way through a path in the woods, toward this building. The building smells awful inside. I see you being sick."

"Oh my God. You really *are* the real deal."

"Whatever that means. OK, I've also been seeing a pale woman, missing a hand. She's showing it to me rather - horribly. Have you seen her? I think you have."

"Yes -" Maggie didn't know what else to say.

"Is this OK? Am I going too fast?"

"Not too fast – go as fast you need to -"

"OK, I want you to know that sometimes when people die and something is left unsolved in their life, they hang around. Try to get help to solve it. Understand?"

Maggie laughed. "Yeah, I've seen movies."

Charis couldn't help but smile. She did like this woman. "I've seen it especially in cases where there was violence involved, or it's been a long time since the event occurred without resolution, and in this case, it feels as if both are true. Sometimes these souls, or ghosts, or spirits can't see the reality of their situation anymore. So, these events that were so important to them, and still are, become skewed to how they *feel* about the events. Do you understand?"

"You mean what I saw might not represent reality but *her* version of reality, based on how it affected her and still does?"

Charis saw a flash of the woman they spoke of, her gaping maw, her eyes eerily calm. "Oh!"

"What?"

"Nothing. Sorry. I just saw – well, yes, I can confirm now that what you've seen is skewed. I can also confirm that something happened to her that both terrified her and threatened to drive her mad. Nice summary of my rather messy explanation, by the way."

"Thanks!"

"You're a writer."

"Yes."

"Anyway. The boy is trying to help you. Maggie, listen to me: the boy is not your baby. I know you're afraid of that."

Maggie started to cry. "Oh. Oh, thank you!"

"A few more things, and then I'm afraid I'm done for now. I need to sleep on this for a while. Try to interpret everything I'm seeing."

"You've done so much already, trust me."

"Just telling you what I see. First: go on vacation. Have fun. You'll have a nice break. OK?"

A huge, shaky sigh. "OK."

"Next: your house needs a resident while you're gone. You've thought of that?"

"Yes, my brother is staying, but – "

"Don't tell me anything yet. I'll ask if I need to know. I need it to just come, OK?"

"Sorry."

Charis laughed. "No need to apologize. I just want clean information, with no influence from you or what you've told me. Once I have an emotional connection or start to learn yours, it's harder to interpret what I get and differentiate reality from desire or emotion. Understand?"

"Yes."

"Human will is so amazing. Each person's perceptions, or even their hopes or fears, are very hard to differentiate from reality."

"Wow, I've never thought of it that way."

"People often don't. But it makes this stuff a lot harder. After I know too much or get attached to someone, it's harder to trust what I see. There's a lot more interpretation."

"You aren't able to do this for loved ones, then."

"Not purposefully. I still see things for them all the time, but I have no control, and connecting to them to try and figure things out helps a lot less!"

"That's - thank you for explaining. It's mind-boggling, actually."

"It's refreshing that you're interested. OK. It's good your brother is staying. He's going to learn a lot while you're gone. But don't worry. Leave it to him, right?"

"Right."

"Lastly, give him my number. He'll need me. It's about a man with a colour in his name. Like 'Grey'."

"Can I tell you?"

"Yes, the name might help."

"Greyson -"

"Stop. No last name, Yes, Greyson. I can help find him. But not yet. Not you. I need to talk to your brother, OK?"

"Yes, of course, but we're going to find Greyson?"

"Yes."

"Do you know his connection to all of this?"

"He is connected to the property you visited, and the woman. You have more helpers, too."

"Oh."

"You're not alone in this."

"OK."

"Aaaand I'm done, but you have a question for me."

"You are *amazing*."

Her heart skipped a beat. "No, I'm *not*, Maggie. I'm not. I'm a normal person, just trying to live life, with normal problems and wishes and hurts and joys. Please know that."

"Sorry, I didn't mean -"

"No, it's OK. I just don't want you to think of me as being powerful, or better, or - whatever. Some people are born singers. Some, like you, are gifted with words."

"Not right now, it seems!"

"Ha! My talent is this. I connect, I see. It's a skill like any other. Can you think of it that way?"

"I'll try. But it's kind of a rare skill!"

"Yeah. Even more rare is that I'll never tell you something *just* to tell you something. Sometimes, I just don't know. I'll be honest with you. Can you accept that?"

"Yes."

"Good. Now ask your question."

"You don't know it?"

"Argh!"

"Oh. Right. *Sorry!*"

"I'm not a god, Maggie. I have little control over the information I get. But I'll admit this: if I was going to be able to answer your question, I'd probably already know it."

"Oh -"

"Ask anyway. I might get something."

"It's about the pregnancy. I want to know if I'm having twins."

"Ah, the boy you've been seeing. He's a twin. Related to - ah, I can't see him, but he's not blood-related to you. Your husband's family?"

"Yes."

"I understand your concern. And the concern of others. Others in the family want to know, too, right?"

"Yes." Maggie was crying again.

"I'm sorry, Maggie. I can't see your baby, or babies. Maybe when I visit."

"You'll visit?"

"Sorry, I'm getting tired. I should have let you decide that, but I've already seen it."

"OK. I'll need to talk to Jack."

"Of course. Anyway, to get back to your question, I can't see whether you're having twins, but I'll tell you this: I see happiness. I see health. I see a future with children. You will have another pregnancy, though, so I still don't know whether this one is twins."

Maggie was silent, so Charis continued, well aware that she had just revealed something to Maggie that was critical. "Maggie, you need to relax into the pregnancy. You're already a mother. You will hold your baby. Past troubles? I don't understand them, but I see that you had a horrible time trying to get pregnant. But these troubles, they are there, firmly, in the past. You can be happy in this pregnancy."

"I'll be pregnant again?"

"Yes. You are a wonderful mother."

"I am?" Maggie hiccoughed and giggled. "Sorry, I'm crying like a baby here."

"It's OK. This is important. But you're not supposed to know the details about this baby, or babies. You just aren't supposed to know yet. I don't know why, but it has to do with this woman. She wants you to help her, and you're not sure if you want to."

"God."

"One more thing: do you know a police sergeant?"

"Yes!"

"You will talk to him again. He needs a bit of a push, but he can help, too."

"I will, yes."

"After your trip."

"Thank you so much."

"I am seeing a bunch of other things but none that I can articulate right now. I simply can't interpret them."

"Do you want to try?"

"No, I don't need to. I mean, I'm not supposed to yet or I'd feel compelled to. Strange images, though. You've been going through a hard time with this."

"I'm so glad I've talked to you. Thank you for taking the time. You have no idea how much it's appreciated."

Charis closed her eyes, took a breath. "I don't like to do this because I don't know what I'm supposed to be doing. But sometimes it just feels as if I have to do it anyway. That's how it feels with you. Also, I like you."

Maggie laughed again. "I like you, too. I'll talk to you when I get back?"

"And not before. Have fun. I mean it!"

"I'm determined to, now. Thank you again."

"You're welcome. 'Bye, Maggie."

"Talk to you soon."

Charis stood, thinking, for a long time after hanging up the phone. She'd been getting some confusing images since Libby's call, and now they made more sense. She was disturbed at the new clarity, though. And now had more questions than ever.

"Too late to back out now," she said aloud, but there was no feeling to it. She knew she was in this until it was solved.

She pressed 'Play' and went back to her laundry.

Chapter 27 – Max Stays

Max grunted as he rolled paint to the top of the wall. He worked in large "W" shapes, getting lost in the monotony of it, enjoying the sound of the roller leaving colour on the wall. He thought of Kathy at work and Maggie and Jack on vacation and felt contentedly alone in the big, empty Ridgewood house. He and Jack had conspired for Max to paint the nursery while Maggie and Jack were away, and though the task had seemed a bit daunting at first, Max was thankful for it now. This was the second coat of the palest yellow, and it was turning out nicely.

Max stood back to survey his work. He usually didn't like yellow, but this was such a soft, sweet shade that he was pleased with it. *Nice.* Just a few finishing touches around the edges and windowsills and he'd be done.

His phone rang. He raced to gently place the roller in the tray and then absentmindedly wiped his hands on his old jeans before answering, "Yellow!"

It was Kathy. "Haha! How's it looking?"

"Really great, actually."

"Good. Will I be able to start the chair rail tomorrow?"

"Yeah, it'll be dry by noon, for sure. It's going to look really good, I think."

"Maggie's going to love it!"

"I hope so. A part of me is protesting as I work, saying she'd want to do this herself."

"I know; I thought of that, too. But we'll make it look so nice that she'll be happy it's done for her. Besides, she can still pick all the furniture and decoration; we're just giving her a nice palette."

Max shook his head. Kathy always had a way of putting things. "You're right."

"Did you eat lunch?"

Max glanced at his watch. 2:18 p.m. "Holy cow!"

Kathy laughed again. "I knew it!"

"It's OK. I'm nearly done! It was actually good getting lost in it. Really cleared my mind."

"What you been thinking of?"

"Nothing."

Another big laugh from his wife.

"It's true. It's been great."

"I don't doubt it. But that's a good thing. Give your brain a rest."

Max paused. "I guess I'm just taking advantage of the quiet. I have a long list of things I want to do while I'm here."

"I know, but you have a lot of time to do it."

They both breathed, comforted by each other on the other end of the line.

"Are you spending the night tonight?"

"Nope. In fact, that's why I'm calling. I've been asked to work late -"

221

Max started to protest.

"Sorry, sweetie. Michelle called in sick. Hey, it's extra money."

"I know. Sorry. It's just quiet here."

"You were just saying you were enjoying the quiet!"

They both laughed.

"I think it was easier to enjoy the quiet when I was looking forward to seeing you tonight. So, does this mean you won't even be here for dinner?"

"Yeah, sorry hon. It just doesn't make sense with how early I have to be in tomorrow."

"What's with the crazy schedule lately, anyway?"

"I don't know; it's like they're testing me, or something. They're giving me more responsibility, too."

"Maybe a promotion is in your future?"

Max could almost hear her shrug.

"Who knows. At least my paycheques are bigger."

"Yeah."

"OK, you; I have to get back. Go *eat*!"

Max chuckled. "Don't worry! I miss you."

"I'll come right after work tomorrow. Do the chair rail, we can have dinner together, and I'll spend the night."

Max perked up. "Excellent! Love you, sweetheart."

"You too." She made a kissing noise and hung up.

Max surveyed the room again. He estimated he'd need less than half an hour of work before he was finished, and worried he'd not want to come back to it if he stopped now, he picked up a smaller brush. He savoured the first dip of the shiny black bristles into the smooth paint. *This is like a type of meditation*, he thought.

By the time he was finished, his stomach was growling, and his watch told him it had actually taken him close to an hour. "Looks great!" he said aloud, and the sound of his voice in what had been a silent room, save for the sound of his brushstrokes, surprised him.

He suddenly felt very alone in the big, quiet house.

I should have had music on.

He busied himself by putting the lid on what little remained of the paint and cleaning his brushes. By the time he was finished, he was painfully hungry and the idea of cooking was abhorrent, so he quickly got dressed to go out.

A glance out the kitchen window showed a darkening forest beyond the lawn, and Max felt his stomach constrict. The thought of sleeping here alone tonight was less than appetizing, but he reminded himself he was doing this for Maggie, and his sense of duty strengthened his resolve. He'd been here two nights, both with Kathy's company, and even with her beside him, he'd lain awake for hours, listening to the house, with its creaks and groans, and hearing the sounds of the forest. But it wasn't just the sounds; it was that *feeling*. Since Maggie and Jack had left, hurried and excited, an unshakeable feeling that he was never alone here, even in his apparent solitude, had taken quick hold of him.

He had made himself busy with the nursery and had enjoyed the comforts of the fireplace and well-stocked pantry. He tried to think

223

of it as a little vacation, and in a sense, it was. Thursday he'd had no classes, and the next day was a parent-teacher day. With this little reprieve so soon after the Christmas holidays, he'd finished up his grading very quickly and had plenty of time to relax. But it was hard to relax here.

Still, he hadn't been over to talk to the Browns and had given little thought to how he'd proceed once he did. He thought of Walter Stack, whose number Maggie had left for him, and of the other number she'd left: the one for the psychic, who apparently wanted to speak with him.

He'd decided to call her only if he felt the need to, and he certainly hadn't, yet.

Max shuddered in the draft by the door and went out to the car, head down against the biting wind.

The sandwich shop in the mall was deserted except for two employees. In no hurry to go back to the solitude of the house, he sat with his cold-cut sub and chips, and took out of his backpack a folder containing his notes and the printed birth announcement of Greyson Maplestone. Reading them over as he devoured his sandwich, he came to the same conclusion as before: the next step was to talk to the Browns. He simply couldn't go further without new information, and he was loath to contact the police sergeant Maggie had talked about unless he had to.

He looked out the window, absently bringing the last of the chip crumbs to his mouth and watching the growing darkness.

He, Maggie and Kaia had dubbed themselves "friendly introverts," though he and Maggie made more efforts at socialization than Kaia did. Regardless, he still grew nervous when approaching others, especially if he didn't know them well. And he did not know the Browns well. He supposed he'd been avoiding the thought of going to see them on their expansive, cold farm, with the fields covered in snow and the animals in the barn.

But there was another reason. Something told him that this one step would mean the beginning of a torrent of other actions: what he had said to Kathy earlier about taking this time to quiet himself was true in a deeper way because, after he'd visited Maggie's neighbours, he wouldn't have quiet again for a while. It would be like knocking down the first domino. To some, that would be exciting, he knew, but to Max it was scary. It was the same reason he didn't teach at the university. He preferred less responsibility. He preferred lower expectations on himself.

His sisters understood.

He shook his head and gazed forlornly at his empty sandwich wrapper. He was still hungry.

He ordered another sandwich to go, then drove back to Greenwood Square in the dark. He'd forgotten to leave the outside light on, and the place was shrouded in the deepening night. He found the keyhole with difficulty and then let himself in. He worked quickly to make a fire and enjoyed his second sandwich. *Lunch and dinner: done!*

Feeling contentedly tired, he made a conscious decision to sleep well – to ignore that feeling of an anxious presence, to put aside thoughts of talking to the Browns, and to just rest. The fire was warm. Max texted his love and goodnights to Kathy and, pulling over the throw from the back of the couch, gave in to his exhaustion. He slept soundly until the morning sun streamed in through the windows.

He stretched.

It was weak sunlight, its brilliance compromised by the covering of pink-grey clouds. Max padded to the kitchen, shivering in the chilly air, noticing the creaking of the pipes. He went to the thermostat and turned the heat up. Maggie had told him to do so, but he'd held off. Today, he'd had enough.

Why did I sleep on the couch? He was cramped all over, as though he hadn't changed positions all night. Still, he'd slept, and that was all he'd wanted.

He puttered around the kitchen, brewing tea and toasting toast, boiling two eggs and enjoying the sound of the forced air heating streaming through the vents. By the time he'd eaten breakfast, the kinks had worked themselves out of his body, and he was full of energy. He looked forward to Kathy's presence later on, but until then, he was determined to be productive.

He would visit the neighbours.

First, though, a shower. But on his way, he found himself wandering into the nursery and opening the can of paint to do some touch-ups.

Procrastination. Gotta love it.

Max had lost himself in the painting when he heard the doorbell ring. Puzzled, he set his brush on the lid of the open paint can and ran downstairs to answer. He was greeted first by the muzzle of an ageing German Shepherd.

"Whoa! Hello there!"

A man in a police uniform regarded him, looking just as surprised to see him. "Oh. Hello. My name is Walter Stack." He reached out to shake Max's hand.

"Ah, yes. Maggie actually left me your number."

"You're a friend of hers?" Walter eyed him with some suspicion.

Max laughed. "Yes, I'm her brother, Max. I'm staying here while she and Jack are away."

Sergeant Stack scratched his chin, nodding. "Ah, I really am getting old. She did tell me that. When do you expect her to return?"

"Early next week. Is there something wrong?"

"No; sorry about that. Unannounced visit, old police dog at your door -"

Max thought the old man referred to himself, then let out a chuckle as he realized he was actually referring to his dog. "It's no problem, really. Is there something I can help you with?"

Walter paused, eyeing him again. "Well, I'm not sure if your sister told you anything about my last visit, but she did tell me that you and she had taken a walk on the old trail back there in the woods." He gestured toward the back of the house. The dog lay down and placed his muzzle between his front paws.

The outside air swirled a gust of snow into the foyer, and Max felt it hit his legs through his pyjama bottoms.

"Ugh, sorry! Please come in; it's cold! And your dog looks tired."

"Old Pilot looks like that even after hours of napping these days."

Walter pulled the dog by his collar, just the gentlest of tugs, and Pilot was up and instantly headed for the kitchen.

227

"He's been here before!"

"Yes, your sister was kind enough to let him in last time. That's why I brought him to the door. Hate to leave him in the cold."

"Of course. You're both welcome. I'm sorry, though; I'm afraid I got caught up in painting and lost track of time. I haven't even gotten into clothes for the day."

"No bother. I won't take much of your time. I've been meaning to go up to the old Maplestone place since your sister called me, and it's a clear day today, despite the clouds. I thought I'd take old Pilot up there and let him sniff around a bit."

"You're going today, then?" Max gestured to the coffee machine, and Walter nodded.

"Thanks, I'd love some. Warm me up a little. Yes, I'm heading up there today, and I thought I'd stop in and see if your sister was interested in accompanying me, as she seemed so interested in it last time."

"She'll be sad to hear she missed that, but if you don't mind, I'd like to come with you. I've been meaning to look into the history of the place – and the people – while I'm here, and honestly," he bowed his head and busied himself making coffee, "I've been avoiding it, I guess."

"Yes, well, that does happen, especially when there are other things to take care of. What are you painting, if you don't mind my asking?"

"I'm working on a surprise for Maggie. It was Jack's idea. For the nursery."

Walter looked surprised.

"Oh God, I've got a big mouth. But then, I don't see her minding that I shared that with you." Max smiled.

"Well, that's wonderful!"

"Yeah, it really is, considering all that time she and Jack tried so hard to get pregnant, with no results - crap. I'm doing it again. You must be a very successful interrogator!"

Walter laughed loudly, his eyes twinkling. "People do tend to trust me easily." He shrugged. "My wife and I were never lucky enough to have kids. Sounds like your sister and her husband went through some tough times in that area, too." He got a distant look in his eyes. "In any case, I'd be happy to bring you along to the old residence. Shouldn't take long; there's not a whole lot left of the building; much of the second floor has collapsed, now. It's the outer edges I want to take a look at – the woods."

Max poured coffee and got cream out of the fridge. "You looking for the trail?"

Walter paused, his eyes fixed on Max again. "You suspect that's where the trail you and your sister found comes out?"

"Or starts."

"Hm." He poured cream and spooned sugar into his drink.

"Sergeant Stack -"

"Walter, please."

"Walter – have you been able to find out anything about the family itself? I was able to find the birth announcement for the son, but that's it. I was heading over to the Brown farm today to try and dig up some more details."

"Why?"

"I'm interested in the history. And you know, people who've lived in this house – or even stay in it - see things and feel things." He felt stupid. Here he was, talking about ghosts with a cop.

"Now, I don't know about all that. But that is why your sister first called me out here. And yes, I've found out a thing or two about the family. Still digging, though, and not sure if I've found much of use, yet."

"Yes, but anything might help sort out some of the questions."

"Hm. You could be right there. But let's go out to the old place, see what we see, and then we'll talk." He looked thoughtful. "I've never really paid any heed to, you know, life after death." He waved his hand as though shooing away a fly. "Ghosts."

Max continued to look at the old man, waiting.

"But what your wife and her sister-in-law saw?"

Max nodded.

"What they said they saw that day, well it sort of makes sense with what I found."

Max sat at the table with Walter now.

"Please, what did you find out?"

"Well, the woman of the house, Rose Maplestone, was committed to the psych facility in Waterville for a time. The whole family was sort of reclusive, I guess you could say, but the event that got her locked up was a great shock to the town."

"Rose - was she Canadian?"

"Ah, you know about the Russian heritage, then?"

"Yes, and I'm confused about the name."

"Maplestone was apparently a legal name change by Viktor Kotova when he entered the country."

Max stood up and paced. "Why?"

"I don't know. There isn't a lot to find, at least on paper, about this family, and it doesn't look as if anyone ever researched Kotova's family history."

Max sat again. "The event?"

Walter appeared to become very interested in his coffee, not meeting Max's eyes. "It was officially recorded as self-mutilation. Not a pleasant bit of information here, I'm afraid."

"Self-mutilation?" Max felt a chill run up his spine, and the back of his neck tingled. He felt sick. "You can't mean - the hand?"

Walter merely nodded.

"You're telling me she did that to herself? She cut her own hand off?"

Walter shrugged and raised his drink to his mouth, only to lower it again, his brow furrowed. "To be honest, Max, I don't understand it, either. And I don't know how your sister saw that. I won't try to explain it. But the report says she nearly bled to death from the injury, and that they found her on the street here, in front of the house."

"What? How?"

"Apparently, she said she'd come from the woods. Someone spotted her and called it in. She was pretty much incoherent besides that. Seems as though nobody ever really understood what happened there."

"My God."

"That's what made me think of the building in the woods that the two of you found."

"You think she came from there?"

"I don't know, but it's a possibility, wouldn't you say? Anyway, she was locked up for less than a year. There are notes – I got her file from the psych facility's archives – that say she was mentally fit and eager to get back to her son. They called it 'latent post-partum psychosis', citing that she'd potentially been untreated since her son's birth and it had manifested itself, finally, in this one horrid act."

"How old was Greyson at the time?"

"The son? I figure, from the dates, that he was about four, nearing five. It was late '43."

Max leaned back in his chair, his hands in his hair.

"I didn't mean to share all of this with you, Mr. er, sorry, I don't know your last name!"

"East. Call me Max though, please."

"Mr. East. Max. I mean, there's nothing wrong with my telling you now, nearly seventy years later, and in the absence of any family members, but - I don't know. I hadn't planned on sharing this with anyone just yet."

"Why?"

Walter frowned. "I've seen a lot of things as a cop. A lot of things. Cases that were dreadful, I tell you." He shook his head and gently smacked his palm on the wood table, making Pilot cock his ears and open his eyes. "But this - this one feels strange. There's something wrong here. I feel it in my gut."

Max nodded. "I don't really understand it all, but I feel like you're right."

They sat in silence for a few moments.

Max stood. "I'd like to have a quick shower, if you don't mind, and then we can head out?"

"Sure, as long as 'quick' is a promise." Walter smiled and sipped his coffee.

Chapter 28 – The Maplestone House

Ten minutes later, a clean and freshly-dressed Max, along with Walter and Pilot, who seemed to have gained a bit of spring in his step, were heading out the front door.

"The dog seems more chipper."

"He always perks up when he's got a purpose. He likes going on ride-alongs; always has. He's been a valuable member of the force." Walter scratched his dog between the ears, and Pilot looked up at his master, his tongue lolling happily.

As they set off in the cruiser, Max marvelled at how things had worked out. Yesterday, he'd been wary of starting anything today. Walter had been his last resort, and he hadn't even considered going up to the old abandoned place at the end of the street.

They passed the Brown farm, where Steve Brown paused in his shovelling to wave at them. Max raised a hand, feeling happy. A connection with the Browns today, too. Unsolicited. Small as it was, the little acknowledgement was a gift.

He strained his eyes to see through the trees as they neared the end of the street. The dog sat up in the back, peering eagerly out the window, as though he knew they'd reached their destination.

Max swivelled his head to look around. He'd only been up this far once. He and Maggie had taken a walk to explore her new home, and the leaves hadn't yet left the trees then. Now, the dead-end was stark and desolate. The old and long-unused back gate to the air force base was rusted and overrun with vines, and the fields were white, their blankets of snow run through here and there by animal tracks. Beyond the vast fields on the right were train tracks, more forest and the river.

Max tried again to see through the trees on the left to the old house, but although the maples were bare, the pines were thick enough to obstruct the view. "I can't see it at all! Is there even a driveway?"

Walter pulled over and put the car in park. "Yes, but it's not worth trying to navigate in this snow with the car. I'm afraid we'll have a bit of a walk."

Pilot scratched at the door to be let out. "All right, all right, old boy." Walter took the time to wrap a knitted scarf around his neck, press his fur-lined hat lower on his head to cover the tips of his ears and put on his big mittens. He looked at Max, who was jealous of his companion's attire. "You going to be OK with this? Snow's not too deep, but it's cold."

"Yeah, of course." He looked back into the woods again, which were indeed separated to the right by a driveway-sized gap. "How far back is it?"

Walter laughed and got out of the car, leaning down to talk to Max. "Not far. Not even ten minutes, I'd guess. They built it just far back enough to be covered by the trees." He closed the door, and Max listened to his boots in the snow as he moved around the car to let Pilot out. He then walked back to the trunk and retrieved a roll of yellow tape and a "No Trespassing" sign.

Max finished tucking his jeans into the tops of his boots and got out. Walter gestured with the tape and sign. "Need to put new ones up every time. Part of the job, though it doesn't do much."

"That scarf looks warm."

Walter tightened it around his neck. "Nola made it. My wife."

"Nice."

Walter grunted, and they started through the field on what Max guessed to be the driveway. Pilot went ahead of them, limping a bit but sniffing excitedly and wagging his tail.

After a few moments, Walter broke the silence. "She died, my Nola. Near two years ago now."

"I'm sorry to hear that." Max breathed deeply, the cold air filling his lungs and the brightness making him blink. Why did being outside always make everything more real?

Pilot barked and stopped, looking back at them.

"We're coming!" called Walter, "Go on ahead, then, if you want!" The dog ran off.

"It was a shock," he said.

Max looked at the old man beside him, suddenly aware of his loneliness. His face was a map of frown lines. He wondered why he thought of them as frown lines when they could just as well have been made from smiling.

"It must have been very hard on you."

"Still is."

Max nodded.

"You know, I told you back there at the house that I don't believe in ghosts. Never have. But for so long after Nola died, I was desperate to believe, if only to be able to have her around me again."

As they neared the trees, Max did see a clearing ahead and a large, dark shape to the right.

"But she never came. I only felt emptiness."

Why was this man, this stranger, telling him about his dead wife? He thought about Steve Brown waving at him in the car after he'd worked so hard to put off a visit. He hadn't even seen the man since he'd first met him. He thought of Walter just showing up at the door. He felt as though he was being pushed down this path by forces beyond himself. He had very little control, here. He could either hide from it or go with the flow. He looked around. The stark, silent forest somehow gave him peace.

"Then I did dream of her."

Max stopped in his tracks, and after walking a few more steps, Walter did, too, and faced him.

"I dreamt of her at this place." Walter gestured beyond the trees. "I've been avoiding coming back here, even since your sister called. You know, I've been back here dozens of times just to check on the place. Part of the job. Nothing ever stood out as being unusual. Then all this business started." He shook his head. "I guess it was easy to believe it was just local kids fooling around when I hadn't seen Nola, or felt her presence." Walter took off a mitten to rub at his eyes.

"Walter, nobody knows what's going on." He stepped forward, unsure whether he should comfort the man or change the subject. "You're here today, right?"

"Right. But only because she told me to come. Told me to help. I don't understand it, boy. She died so suddenly, then stayed away. And then she came to tell me to come back here?"

Max looked off into the clearing again, the side of the building visible, now, through the trees. "I think something here's been waiting to be solved for a long time. I guess we're just part of making that happen. Your wife isn't the only one coming back to guide us." Max told Walter about the boy they believed to be Sebastian.

"But why? Why would that boy care? He couldn't even have been born when that family lived here."

"I don't know yet. But I think our being here today is supposed to happen."

"Well. Let's go then. You cold?" He turned and started walking again, shoving his hand deep into his mitten.

"I'm fine," Max lied. His fingers and toes ached.

They reached the clearing, and Max's jaw dropped as he looked up at the house in ruins. Even now, though it had been vandalized, the porch had become completely detached, and there wasn't an unbroken window in the place, Max could imagine how impressive it must have been before - before what?

"How can something so big hide so well?"

Walter looked at him thoughtfully. "Like a secret."

"Yeah."

Pilot had disappeared, and Walter headed off behind the house, calling for him, while Max headed for the front doorway, whose door hung diagonally by a single hinge. He manoeuvred over the tilted porch and grunted as he jumped the gap between it and the doorway. "Why wasn't this place ever torn down?"

Walter raised his voice from around the corner. "You be careful in there! Second floor's mostly caved into the first, and who knows what else is wrong with it since I was last here!"

Max stood in the doorway and let his eyes adjust to the darkness. It seemed like a family room. He saw a pile of yellow tape, black words of caution across it, in a heap on the floor. Walter's efforts, he assumed, thwarted by vandals. In the middle of the floor, a gaping hole, obviously burned away by an attempt at a fire. His feet felt heavy in the doorway, unwilling to carry him forward. The place smelled of wet and mildew. Nothing like the shack he and Maggie had found, but unpleasant nonetheless.

He heard Walter behind him.

"Probably safer not to go in."

Max turned around and had to shield his eyes from the brightness of the snow. "Well this is what we came for, no?"

"No. *That* is what I came for." Walter pointed at the line of forest at the left edge of the clearing.

Max squinted until he saw it: a nearly indiscernible gap in the trees.

A path.

"Wow. It's really here."

"Come on."

Max felt no regret leaving the dank building, and the men trudged through the snow.

"Where's the dog?"

"There." Walter pointed again to the small opening in the trees, and Max saw Pilot there, sitting purposefully.

"Did he find it?"

"Not really. Just helped me to. This is what she showed me in the dream."

"She showed you there was a path?"

"Yep, and there it is. So, it must be important." They stopped at the trees, both peering in, and Max was daunted by the overgrowth, which was much greater than that on the path at Maggie's. "When you mentioned it back at the house, I nearly shit myself, I have to admit."

Max laughed nervously. "Do you think the other end is what Maggie and I saw? By that shack in the woods?"

"'Twould make sense. Maybe they used it as storage, or to hunt, as your sister suggested. Though she seemed doubtful."

"Yes, we talked about it, but it didn't really seem like the purpose of the place."

Walter turned to face him. "What did?"

"I don't know. It seemed as if someone stayed there. There were a cot and a table."

"People often did that to hunt."

"Yeah..." he trailed off, looking doubtfully into the trees.

"I'm going to have to go back and see the place m'self."

"That'd be good."

"The report on Rose Maplestone -"

There was a sound behind them, like a muffled voice, and the dog stood and barked in the direction of the house. Walter started off toward the building, and Max was impressed at the speed the old man could carry. "What was that?"

"Sounded like someone's in the house."

Max saw the dog struggling up over the porch as they worked their way through the snow, but by the time they reached the house, Pilot was sitting on the ground, wagging his tail.

"What'd you find, boy?"

Pilot looked unimpressed.

The men gazed up at the house.

"Hello?" Walter yelled at the front entrance. "If there's anyone in there, make yourself known now!"

Silence.

Max started over the porch, and Walter did not protest.

"Hey."

Max turned back.

"Take this. Just shine it around. No way to get up to the second floor now, so if there's someone inside, they'll be on the first." He handed Max a flashlight.

Max flicked it on as he took a step into the house. The light revealed nothing unexpected: the charred hole in the floor, the walls covered in graffiti - Max took note of a lone heart amongst the swear words and colourful tags, 'Chris + Margot' sprayed inside it - the pile of tape, some old bottles, and what used to be a hallway further back, now filled with part of the collapsed second floor. He shone the light to the right, where there was a door leading to a brighter room. Judging by what was left of a countertop in view, Max thought it to be the kitchen. He turned back to Walter. "I'm heading into the kitchen."

"I'll come."

Before Max could say it wasn't necessary, Walter was up and over the porch. Max held his hand out and helped him leap across the small gap.

Walter looked around. "Not much changed here, 'cept *that*." He pointed at the pile of tape. "They usually take it with 'em. Not sure what the hell they're gonna do with it." He shrugged.

They headed toward the kitchen, Max following Walter, who seemed to know how to navigate the oft-broken floorboards. "Well. This is new."

Max stepped into the kitchen and looked in the direction of Walter's flashlight beam, though it was bright enough in here to turn it off, probably.

At the other end of the room, there was an antique bassinet. In stark contrast to the ruin of the building, it was clean and white, the corner of a plush blanket hanging over the side. Walter walked over to look, but Max hung back, the back of his neck tingling.

"Why would that be here?"

Pilot barked outside, and Max jumped, looking toward the entrance. Just then, Walter let out a yell and recoiled from the bassinet, nearly falling. He recovered and backed toward Max, whose every nerve was on edge.

"What is it?"

"My God." Walter stumbled to the wall and leaned against it. "Let's go back to the car, boy. I need to radio the station. *Damn*, why didn't I bring the radio?"

Max walked toward the bassinet.

"No!" Walter's voice held a note of desperation, which threatened to unnerve Max, but he continued forward.

The dog barked outside. *Why isn't he coming in?* Max asked himself.

He reached the white baby bed, holding his breath as he looked inside.

Nothing.

It was empty, save for a pile of dirty leaves. The blanket was dirty, too. He stepped back and regarded the vessel with new eyes. One wheel was severely bent, and the thing tilted a bit because of it. The light must have made it seem brighter – cleaner - after they'd walked through the dark living room; the bassinet was clearly dingy and old. He turned back to Walter, his palms facing out. "What?"

Walter pushed away from the wall. "You don't-?"

"There's nothing here, Walter. Just a pile of leaves."

Walter barrelled across the room and, placing his hands on the edge of the bassinet, looked closely inside. "What the hell?"

"What? Walter, it's just leaves."

"It wasn't, son. It wasn't just leaves."

"What was it?"

Walter breathed deeply. He straightened up, took a hand out of its mitten and rubbed his face, then scratched behind his ear, all the time looking into the bassinet, his brow furrowed.

Max put a hand on the old man's shoulder. "You OK? You know, the light is really off in this place."

"That really spooked me."

"It's definitely creepy in here."

"Let's go."

The men left the house, both taking their time, lest their fear be given away. Walter sat on the edge of the broken porch, rubbing his face again. Pilot sat at his master's feet, looking up at him.

"Walter, please tell me what you thought you saw."

"I know what I saw, boy. It's not there now, but it was. I know what I saw!"

Max took a breath and looked off toward the trail in the woods. "You heard a voice too, right? That's why we came back?"

Walter looked at him. "There's something wrong with this place."

Max felt the familiar presence around him. "I think we knew that before we came."

Walter put his elbows on his knees and hung his head.

"Are you OK?"

Walter didn't answer.

"Walter, why is this place still here? You'd think the town would have ripped it down by now."

His question had the desired effect. Walter perked up and placed his hands on his knees, pressing himself up straight and looking up at Max. "Sit down, boy. You're making me strain my neck."

Max felt relief at the old man's attitude. He sat uncomfortably on the tilted porch with the open door behind him. His back felt warm. He tried to focus on something else. The painful cold of his toes. The sun, still veiled in cloud, but obviously high in the sky now. Lunchtime. His stomach gurgled.

"The short story is that nobody wants to pay to have it levelled."

"What's the long story?"

"Well, the Maplestone boy still owns it."

Max chuckled. Greyson Maplestone had to be many years older than Walter, yet he was still called "boy."

"What's funny?"

"Nothing. Where is he?"

"I don't know. I did some digging, and though he still owns the property, nobody knows where he is. No death records, though, so I have to believe he's still out there somewhere. There's record of him taking Law at Dalhousie over in Halifax. Then it seems he went out West, to B.C. After that, we just don't know."

"I wonder if he found a law career?"

"I thought the same myself. Took a look and didn't find anything in any of the Western Provinces under the name Maplestone."

"What if B.C. was wrong? Have you checked the rest of Canada?"

"Not yet."

"Will you?"

"Yes, son. I do my job." He gave Max a hard look.

"Sorry. It's just - well, *is* this part of your job?"

"Well, I've opened a file on the incident at your sister's house. Gave me some room to move when I was doing research. It's got to be official police business, see, if I want to find out anything useful."

"OK. Good."

Walter smacked his palms on his knees and stood, and Pilot instantly headed for the driveway area. "Dog's got a sixth sense."

"Seems so," said Max, rising.

"Every five or ten years, the town has renewed its efforts to find Maplestone. Always coming up with nothing."

"How can that be?"

"I don't know, son."

Max raised his eyebrows, and with a last look at the house, the men started toward the driveway. Walter stopped and groaned.

"What is it?"

The old man gestured toward the tilted porch, where the "No Trespassing" sign and yellow tape still sat. "Come on. Give me a hand, and we'll make quick work of it. I'm starving and cold and just want to get out of here."

The men worked quickly, thinking to move the door back into place, crooked as it was, and then zigzagged the tape across it. Lastly, Walter posted the sign on the porch. "In case the damn door falls off," he said when Max looked at him questioningly.

As they walked away, Max looked back at the little gap between the trees. He thought of the voice he'd heard – they'd all heard – and shivered. He stamped his freezing feet in the snow. "What about the Browns? Didn't Maplestone own that property as well?"

"He sold it to them after his parents were long dead. He was in his thirties."

"Oh yeah, I think Maggie mentioned that."

"Well, I don't believe in dead ends, son. I'll keep looking. I'm mostly at the desk nowadays, anyway, and near retirement. Looking's my job."

They neared the car where Pilot sat waiting for them, his head hanging a bit.

"Dog's tired."

"Yep. He doesn't want to be, but he is. Me too."

Max smiled. He thought of getting a fire going and sitting on the ottoman right in front of it, his toes defrosting in the warmth. "I'm glad you're going to keep looking, and Maggie will appreciate it, too. I was thinking of going and talking to the Browns."

"Don't know what you'll find out, there, but go ahead, if you think it's worth it. Steve Brown might remember something about the family; he was a young man when his father finally brought the property, not married yet."

"That's what I'm hoping for – some memories of the Maplestones."

"Well, don't get your hopes up there; they kept to themselves, and that's an understatement."

They reached the car, and Walter rested his arms across the roof of it, taking his mittens off and folding his hands.

"You OK?"

"Yes, son. I'm just taking a breather. All that walking in the snow's got me roasting under these heavy clothes."

"Wish I could say the same. These boots weren't made for this kind of cold."

Walter laughed heartily. "Alright, then." He started to move, but Max stopped him. He rested his arms on the roof of the car, too, so he was eye-level with Walter.

"No, don't hurry. There's a fireplace back at Maggie's, and it'll sort out my ice cubes-for-toes quickly enough. I want to know what you saw, Walter."

Walter met his eyes but didn't speak.

"In the bassinet. What was it that had you so scared?"

Walter looked back into the woods, in the direction of the house, unfolding and refolding his hands. He looked back at Max. "It was real. The dream. She showed me that trail, Max."

Max nodded.

"It was real. I saw her again, in my dream. Doesn't matter why, either. That trail is real, and so was that dream." His eyes twinkled under his heavy-looking police-issue winter hat.

"Maybe you'd seen the trail before, didn't register it, and held it in your subconscious mind until you had that dream?"

Walter looked down, stretching, his arms still on the roof of the car. He took a deep breath. "You could be right there. In fact, after I read the report about the Maplestone woman being found out in front of your sister's house, and got that message from your sister, I thought a lot about the woods, and the trail, and what it could all mean. I could indeed have stirred some memory of that little opening in the woods. Then I had that dream." He stood straight now, shaking his hands at his sides, and then took his mittens from the roof. He looked back at Max. "But I've done walks around the perimeter of that clearing many times and never perceived that trail. Not one time. Not only that, but Pilot hasn't, either."

The dog lifted his head at the sound of his name.

"It had to have been there."

"Of course. But it's so overgrown. If a person's not looking for it, they won't see it. You didn't; not 'til I pointed it out to you."

"True. Anyway, I wasn't questioning the dream, Walter. Just analyzing. Sorry. I've always done that."

"It's OK, boy. You don't have to believe I saw my dead wife in a dream. That she came to me to give me a message. I know it. I know it now." Walter smiled.

Max smiled, too. "I do believe it. Hell, after everything that's happened -"

Walter opened his car door.

"And by the way -" he paused, regarding Max over the roof of the car, "- it was a hand. In the baby cradle, on the leaves. A severed hand."

Chapter 29 – To Nap the Unnappable Nap

Walter refused to come in for lunch by the fire but promised to get in touch soon. He wanted to get out to the shack in the woods.

Max got the fire going, then warmed up a can of chicken noodle soup and grilled a cheese sandwich. By the time he sat down by the fire, his toes were tingling uncomfortably as the blood returned to them. He was feeling pleasantly tired. He noted it was only twelve-thirty, but he felt as if he'd been out all day.

He called Kathy and told her what he'd been up to, and she promised to see him soon. Hanging up, he thought about returning to school on Monday, and anxiety grew within him. There simply wasn't enough time to do everything. He finished his sandwich, slurped the rest of his soup from the bowl, relishing the freedom to do so without being scoffed at by the more proper people in his life, and put his dishes in the sink.

He wanted a nap.

Just then the phone rang, making him jump. *No such luck.*

It was Jack, asking how things were going. Max gave him the Cole's Notes version of his morning with Walter (omitting the hand-baby for the sake of keeping things light) and asked how Maggie was feeling. Jack reported success in the relaxation category all around and proved it by noting Maggie's allowing Jack to make the call to Max rather than she herself. Max chuckled. "That is a bit of a surprise, but I'm glad she's taking some time to just chill."

"Well," Jack paused and then added with a laugh, "it *did* take some convincing!"

Both men laughed.

"So, what's next on your agenda?" Jack asked.

"The nursery's painted, and Kathy'll do the chair rail today. I think Maggie'll love it."

"Ah, thanks buddy; that's awesome!"

"It was cool, actually. I was really zenned out by the time I was done."

"Sounds the opposite of how I feel about painting, so I'll thank you again!"

"Ha! And I was quite honestly thinking about a nap before you called."

"Well don't let me stop you. Thanks again, eh?"

"The nap may have to wait; I haven't gotten over to talk to Steve Brown yet."

"There's time."

Relieved of his nagging sense of obligation, if only momentarily, Max said a cheerful goodbye to his brother-in-law and made a beeline for the stairs, the image of heavy, warm blankets and the blissful tide of sleep coming over him quickly becoming the singular thought in his mind.

His cell phone ringing in his pocket made him jump again, but this time with a groan. With great reluctance, he dragged it from his pocket and saw a long-distance number on the display. So much of him wanted to continue to the stairs and then to bed that he almost denied the call, but something had his thumb swiping the green answer icon instead.

"Hello?"

"Hi, Max? This is Charis. Your sister gave me your number; did she tell you about me?"

Max walked a couple of steps into the living room and sat on the couch, still surprised he'd answered the phone. "Yes, she did. Hi, Charis. Everything OK?"

"No worries; everything's fine. I just – well, I wanted to introduce myself to you. When I spoke to Maggie, I told her to go off and fully enjoy her trip, which I hope she's doing –"

"Actually, yeah, I just talked to Jack, and they're doing great." Max scratched his head and wondered if this was a get-to-the-point sort of psychic or a draw-things-out sort of psychic. Then he wondered what the hell that meant and thought again about wanting a nap. "Sorry Charis, I was just on my way up to take a nap. I had a tiring morning…" He trailed off, aware that if he started telling her about it, he'd have to tell her everything. He decided against it as he glanced longingly toward the stairs. "Is there something I can help you with?

"Yes. I mean, I'm sorry for interrupting your day. I'm usually not the pursuer in relationships with my clients -" She laughed a bit uncomfortably.

"No, no. It's OK; please go on." Max was touched by the sincerity in her voice. He sank further into the couch, resting his head on the back cushion.

"Well, I've been having visions – dreams and visions, really – ever since I talked to your sister. I feel as if I'll be needed before she's back. I don't want to freak you out here, but – as though someone's in danger."

Max sat up. "What? Who?"

"I don't know for sure. I can't see her clearly. A woman."

"Well – and pardon my bluntness, but – that's not incredibly helpful!"

"I know, and I apologize. But she feels older and has long, grey hair worn up in a bun."

"Umm, the only thing I can think is that your description doesn't match the woman the girls have been seeing."

"The ghost? No, it's not her. In any case, there's nothing we can do about it now, or I'd know more. But when and if anything happens, I want you to call me, OK?"

"What?"

"Please. You have my number on your phone now, and that's all I want you to remember. Just call me if anything happens."

Max sighed and rubbed his temple with his free hand.

"I know this must sound crazy, but I had to tell you. Just that. Just to please call me."

"OK…"

"Oh! And this: tell the cop to search for the 'K' last name, not the 'M' one!"

That made sense. Before he could reply or thank her, Charis spoke again.

"Again, I apologize. We'll talk soon, OK? And please don't worry. Just put this out of your mind for now."

Max managed a feeble, "OK. Thanks, I guess?"

"Talk soon, and thank you." Charis sounded relieved, though Max wasn't sure why.

She hung up.

Max held his phone out in front of him and stared at it, still puzzled at the bizarre conversation. Then, remembering the last part, he realized he'd have to call Walter about the "K instead of M" bit. The woman had sounded rushed, and Max wasn't sure how to feel about her, but something told him to call Walter right away. Of course they should search for the Kotova name when trying to find Greyson Maplestone. If the man had been so determined to leave his property behind, maybe he'd left his name behind as well.

Another sigh as he dialled the old cop (who reported, not a little annoyed, that he *had* searched for Kotova, but admitted it had been in the context of family history only) and was glad when Walter vowed to search again for law practices in B.C. with the name Kotova in them.

Completely spent, Max dragged himself up the stairs and into the bed in the guest room he and Kathy had taken over. He sighed contentedly, sinking deep into the bed as the covers began to warm against his body. He relaxed finally, willing that pleasant drifting feeling to come over him.

"Honey, I'm home!" called Kathy from downstairs, and Max groaned loudly into his pillow. He couldn't help but smile as he shouted hello to his wife. It was truly the only interruption that could have made him feel happy at that moment.

Chapter 30 – Alice

I'm so happy for Jack and Maggie, but scared too. I'm always scared when it comes to pregnancy and childbirth. Losing a child is terribly painful. I lost control. I was so lost that Rose was able to find me.

And for a while, I had someone, in a sense, who understood.

But she didn't, not really. She couldn't see straight anymore. When she died, things went sideways.

Marla helped me realize that it had to stop. My living children needed me. I hate to admit it, but I don't think my Martin ever got what he needed from me. I tried. I tried so hard, but my heart, still bearing an open wound, hid from him. It hurt just to look at him.

I'm so sorry.

And now, she's back.

The other night I dreamt of her. It started so softly, so comfortably. I sensed her, but none of the bad stuff. Just the familiarity.

I'm tired.

But then it turned. It went sideways, too, the dream. She showed me how she felt, how she always felt. She had lost the one chance she'd found to get everything back. Her own dream was taken from her.

But wait. I'm not sure that makes sense.

This happens a lot now. I lose track. It gets mixed up.

But she makes me feel so bad. It's hard to stop thinking about her.

So tired.

Chapter 31 – Missing

Max woke before the alarm again – he'd come to the conclusion that his body was protecting him from being jarred awake by Kathy's blaring alarm – and stretched, feeling his heels find the end of the bed. The sun was just peeking up over the trees, and a pale orange light filtered through the gauzy curtains.

He glanced at his wife, still wrapped in her cocoon of sleep, and fought the urge to wrap himself around her, too. She'd been working so much.

Max rose, threw on some khakis and a t-shirt, decided against the button-up shirt until just before he left the house, and went downstairs to get the coffee started. The clock in the kitchen displayed 5:55. Enjoying the bit of extra time, he boiled some eggs, made toast and made up two plates. Kathy was awake and moving about within minutes, so he set the oven to the lowest setting and left her plate inside to keep warm. Feeling rather accomplished, he sat at the table and enjoyed his breakfast, absently turning the pages of yesterday's paper.

He marvelled at the ease with which he and Kathy had slipped into their routine here. After the weekend, things had slowed to a crawl, especially when compared with his crazy Sunday! He and Kathy had gone over the details of Max's day, Kathy's eyes widening with each piece of news. Finally, they'd laughed a bit over the call from the Ottawa psychic, but each saw right through the other. They were both a bit uneasy about her prediction, too.

In agreement over the fact that worrying about what *might* happen wouldn't help, and comforted that Charis had basically said the same, they decided to put it aside. And though each of them had thought about it throughout the week, quietly watching for signs of trouble, they hadn't discussed it again.

Max wondered now if she'd been wrong; it was Friday already with no signs of trouble – quite the opposite! The nursery was finished – a bright and clean palette ready for Maggie and Jack to decorate. He and Kathy planned to walk over to the Brown farm on Saturday, just for a quick and casual (as forced as it might be) chat about the farm and the man who'd sold it to him.

He was shaken out of his reverie by the sounds of Kathy coming down the stairs. "Mmmm, what do I smell?" she called, appearing on the staircase with a smile on her face.

"Gosh, you're a beautiful woman!" Max exclaimed in earnest and kissed her as she reached the bottom. She smiled even more widely, and Max remembered her breakfast. "Oh! I've been productive this morning! Let me get your food!"

Max had barely put the plate in front of her when the landline rang loudly. He and Kathy looked at each other. "Do we answer it?" Max asked, feeling dumb. He'd forgotten his sister even *had* a landline, and his aversion to phones had not been cured by the deluge of calls on the previous Sunday.

"Of course, we do!" Kathy rolled her eyes and rose to grab the phone. She pressed the answer button and put the phone to Max's ear, grinning as he fumbled for it while she went back to her seat at the table.

"You sneaky –!"

"Max?"

"Hi, Maggie. Sorry, we were a bit shocked by the fact that you still have a landline!" He smiled as he teased her.

258

"Max! I've been trying to get you on your cell -" Max patted his pockets and inwardly cursed, remembering his phone on the charger upstairs.

Her answering tone had wiped the smile off his face in a hurry, and Kathy, his mirror in so many ways, sat taller, on alert, as she watched his face change. He met her eyes and nodded reassuringly. *I don't know what it is, but something's up. Don't worry.*

"Sorry, sis. I left it on the charger."

"No, it's OK." Maggie made a little sound and fumbled her words a bit.

"What's wrong?"

"It's Alice. Oh Max, Jack and Zoe are beside themselves – they almost left for the airport right away, but Sam and I convinced them to wait for us. I mean, after all, we can't stay here while they go back!" She spoke fast, her voice a higher pitch, revealing her anxiety.

Max, who was still confused, but whose heart had sped to a gallop at the sound of Maggie's voice, mindfully kept his voice calm. It was a skill well-honed over the years of teaching teenagers. "Maggie, what's happening with Alice?"

"Right! Sorry. Oh, my God, I'm all over the place. Just a second; I have to sit."

"Are you OK?"

"Yes! The trip has been wonderful! And I think I'm starting to show a little - it's so crazy, but – ugh, I'm getting off track again."

"It's alright. You're upset. Just tell me what happened with Alice."

Maggie laughed, and then made that sound again. She'd always done that when she was upset. A little, "Oh!" that was more of a groan than an exclamation. Max heard her inhale deeply. "OK. We got a call this morning from the seniors' home. Alice is just - well, she's not there. She's missing. Oh, God."

"What? How can that be? Don't they have security? Are the police involved?"

"Whoa, now *you* have to slow down!" They both managed a nervous laugh. "We don't know much. Yes, of course there's security, but it's not like a prison, you know? They do have footage of her leaving, though."

"What was she wearing?"

"They said she had a jacket and shoes on, but it looked like just a nightgown under the jacket."

"Ah. Well, that's something. If it were her slippers and housecoat, it'd be better, but maybe just the nightgown will raise someone's suspicions enough to call the police."

"I thought the same."

"And that's it? They can't see which way she went?" Kathy was beside him now, holding his hand. He mouthed "Alice" to her, and she nodded, squeezing his hand a bit tighter.

"No; she only appears on the door footage, not the parking lot. So really, she could be anywhere." Her voice broke. "Max, she must be freezing!"

Max glanced out into the back yard, now bright with sunlight, the crisp snow glittering and the sky a pale blue. He shivered. The clear days were always the coldest. "Maggie -"

"I know, I know. I can't think about that. I'm just at a loss, here. It feels awful to be so far away, you know? And Jack is trying to hold it together, but I can see his panic. Ugh. Anyway, we're flying home. Flight's already booked, and we'll be there late afternoon, just before four your time."

"Shit." Max glanced at the clock reflexively. 6:45. "OK; I'm calling in."

Maggie inhaled sharply and cried her "thank yous" to her brother, clearly relieved that he'd suggested it.

"It's OK, Mags. Someone has to be here, just in case. And we have a really good substitute system at the school -" Max turned as Kathy ran to the stairs, meeting his eyes. She pointed at herself, making a "phone" sign beside her face, and then pointed back to Max. "Kathy's going to call them now."

"OK. Yes. Oh, my God."

"Mags, I'm worried about you. Get back here safe, OK? You guys are coming as fast as you can, and you have good help here. Wait – I assume they've called the police?"

"Of course. And Jack asked them to call Walter in Kingston as well. Thank you, Max. I don't know what I'd do if you weren't there."

He could hear the relief in her voice. "Take care of yourself and that niece or nephew of mine on the way home. Promise."

"I promise." Then, "You're a good brother, you know that?"

"Damn right I am!"

A small laugh from Maggie before she replied, "See you tonight. Call if *anything* happens."

"I will."

They hung up, and Max tried to gather his thoughts. Where could she be? He didn't know Alice well, but he knew she had dementia with times of crystal clarity. "Where would she go?" he whispered.

Kathy appeared in the kitchen with his cell. "Called the school; you're being replaced as we speak, with best wishes from Beth and Anna."

Max smiled slightly; the office staff were always kind. "Thank you, love. Doesn't make sense for you to call in."

"I thought the same," she said, "but if you want me to, I will." She held his phone out to him.

"Oh, just put it on the counter," he said absently, his thoughts racing. "No, babe; it'll probably be a lot of sitting and waiting. Makes more sense for you to go to work, especially considering how much it sucks to fall behind there."

Kathy nodded but looked dubious.

"It's really fine, babe. I'm going to call Walter in a bit, don't worry, but right now I just want to gather my thoughts and see you out the door."

She crossed the small space between them and placed his phone in his hand, cradling it there. "Yes, call Walter. That'll tell you where you need to be today. I suspect it's right here. But first, you have another call to make."

It took him a second to remember, but then he looked at her in dismay.

"Yep. You did promise." She released his hands and started toward the front door. "I have to go. The sooner I get there, the sooner I finish and can come home to you. But call me, Maxwell East, if you hear anything at all!"

"I will!" he called after her weakly. He looked at his phone, and Kathy returned to swoop in and kiss him goodbye.

"I love you. Everything's going to be OK. I'll see you soon." She took his hand with the phone in it again and held it up a bit, her point clear.

"OK. I mean I love you too. Keep your phone on, eh?"

She nodded, kissed him again and flew out the front door.

He looked at his phone. He knew if he hesitated, he wouldn't do it. He found her number in his contacts, thanks to her call on Sunday, and dialled Charis.

Chapter 32 – Charis

The call came just as she got back to her car after dropping her two youngest at daycare. Her heart accelerated as she answered.

"Max."

"Yeah. I mean, hi, Charis."

"It's happening?"

"It's Alice, Maggie's mother-in-law. She's gone missing from her seniors' home."

"OK. This is it. I need to come. I'll be there tonight, barring any difficulties with finding a flight."

"Really? Wow -"

"Yep. I will need the cost of the flight recovered; don't worry, it'll work itself out. And my boys go to their father's tonight for the weekend, so that works perfectly." She ticked checkboxes off in her head, the urgency she'd been feeling creeping up on her now full bore.

"OK. They'll be back before dinner, they think."

"I don't think I'll make it by then, especially landing in Halifax and needing to rent a car -"

"Tell you what, I'll reserve it for you. Then at least it'll be waiting when you arrive. Does that help?"

"Yes! You don't mind?"

"Not at all. I think we could really use your help, and I appreciate your dropping everything and coming."

"I've just been waiting. Anyway, I'm in my car; I just have to stop at home and pick up a few things, then call in to work." She paused, clearly working details out in her head. "Then I'll head straight to the airport and get the next flight out."

Max gave a low whistle. "I thought *I* had a lot to take care of! Listen, thank you for this."

"You're welcome. And hey, text me the car details, OK?"

"Will do. See you soon."

"Tonight, I hope." She hung up, and just as he had after their conversation on Sunday, he held the phone out in front of him, marvelling at the strangeness of the call.

But this time, he felt absolutely sure it had been the right thing to do.

He walked to the living room and sat hard on the couch. He needed a second.

He took a deep breath.

OK. Next.

He needed to call Walter.

A knock at the front door had him rising to answer it rather than dialling the number. Somehow unsurprised by the timing, he opened the door to the concerned-looking old cop, his alert German Shepherd at his side.

"Max."

"Walter, glad to see you. Hi, Pilot."

"I take it you've heard?"

"Yeah. I took today off. I want to help any way I can. Looks like he does, too!" He gestured toward Pilot.

"Well, you can start by letting two old dogs in, son." Walter smiled.

"Of course!" He gladly moved aside, grateful for the presence of these two, knowing they'd know what to do.

"And yeah, Pilot always knows when something's up." Walter stamped his feet. "I'm glad you're around to help. Let's sit down for a minute, and I'll tell you the plan."

Chapter 33 – Greyson

The call from Sergeant Stack in Nova Scotia had come completely out of the blue. For years, he'd been both shocked and relieved that his name change had so effectively separated him from his old life. The one hitch had been his degree, but it had been an easy fix; he'd simply sent his legal name change documents to the university, and they'd sent him revised papers.

Easy.

He hadn't meant to abandon the house. Well, he hadn't meant to abandon it *forever* was perhaps more accurate. He'd meant to work something out with the town – have it demolished or at least kept up. Even when he'd left, it had been falling into disrepair; he just didn't have it in him to do a thing with it. The house had seemed to fall apart as his family did. The deaths of his parents hadn't been the only blows; every loss, every act of violence seemed to have impacted not just their bodies and their minds but the house itself.

It was as though each time he hit her, the impact reverberated and grew, weakening the very walls around them.

When she was at her worst, his father took her to the tiny cabin far back from the house and left her there. His anger had never been well controlled, but it was as though his wife's fall into depression (and eventually, psychosis) had unhinged him entirely. Just the *needing* of his father was unforgivable when she'd only served and pandered to him until then.

He shook his head. Remembering had never done him any good. Ultimately, it had been the remembering that had kept him away, prevented him from arranging care for the property. Eventually, he'd let go of the idea that he would someday take care of it, and he tried in earnest to just forget it. To stop imagining what state the house must be in now. Maybe the city had torn it down after so many years. Most of the time, he fervently hoped they had.

But sometimes, he hoped the opposite. He hoped they'd left it for him to take care of. To renew or ruin. To finish it.

On those rare nights when a case wasn't on his mind, he'd find his thoughts would wander there. It was always quiet at home; he'd never married, so he worked insane hours and devoted his whole self to his practice. It had served his career well, and served his efforts to forget even better.

He didn't have many friends. His partners were closest to him, but he never felt the need to deepen those relationships past work-related discussions and banter. He was respected, even if viewed as somewhat of an enigma. Nobody truly knew who he was as a person, and if he was honest, Greyson would have to admit that even now, in his early seventies, he didn't either. He knew the boy he had been and the man he'd crafted afterward, but they were untethered save the name he'd taken to honour whatever family he'd never known in his father's homeland. Family he'd imagined, as a boy, to be kind.

Despite his efforts at distancing himself from the darkness of his past, he never found the peace he sought. He'd been a successful lawyer, but he'd also been painfully lonely and sadly denied any pleasure or comfort. Denied by himself just as he had been denied by his father as a child. Unintentionally but steadfastly, just the same.

Retirement had been terrifying at first. What would he fill his mind with? To what purpose would he devote his energies, dwindled as they were? And then that had been easy, too. He advised and mentored young lawyers at the firm, consulted on cases, and served on the city council as law advisor. Somehow, too, he'd become involved in women's shelters. It had fallen into his lap through his work with the council, and though, at first, he denied the satisfaction he took from investing in women and children's homes and advocating for their safety and rights had anything to do with his past, he had eventually allowed himself that one truth.

That by helping someone else who'd been hurt, he somehow felt he was helping his mother, and maybe even the child he'd once been.

Age had softened his resolve to deny it all. It had happened, and though he'd left it behind long ago, its impact had made him who he was today.

So that phone call from Walter Stack in Nova Scotia had completely taken him by surprise but came at a fortunate time. If it had come before the years had done their work, he had no doubt he would have denied who he was, slammed the phone down and taken steps to ensure that the wall he'd built to hide his past behind was further fortified, for good.

But, as it had come at just this time, he'd opened up to that sergeant a little and had promised to figure out what to do with the house and property it stood upon.

When he hung up, he thought long and hard about the things the cop had said about the neighbours. The stuff about dreams - it seemed to Greyson that the cop had opened up more than he'd expected, too - and he realized he'd left much more than memories behind.

And that he had to do the thing he'd not even allowed himself to consider in all the time since he'd left. He had to go back home. Face it.

And finally, finally make peace.

Chapter 34 – Max and Walter

"So, the Wolfville police are checking with taxi companies?"

Walter nodded.

"What about bus stops and their routes? Shit, what if she's gone to Halifax?"

"Son -"

"She can't have very much money; I wonder if she'd just go sit and have a tea or something?"

"Son."

Walter sat at the kitchen table, his hands folded in front of him, his hat on the tabletop beside him. He was watching Max pace and waiting for his verbal stream to dry up.

Max stopped mid-pace and faced Walter. "She'd probably go to Zoe's! Or come *here*! Let's split up! Drive around to find her!"

"Max. Sit down."

Max, realizing his pacing and ranting weren't helping – not to mention the look on Walter's face that said the old man wasn't going to talk to him until he calmed down a bit - sat.

"That's better."

Max managed a nod and folded his hands as Walter had. Thought of it as a lock, keeping his anxious thoughts in.

"Yes. The Wolfville police are doing all the things we professionals do when something of this nature happens. And they're doing it fast because they've seen this before and they know how urgent the situation is."

Max studied his hands and mumbled, "Sorry."

"It's OK, son. I get what you're feeling right now, and I know it ain't fun."

Max nodded again and met the cop's eyes. "What do we do?"

"Well, you were on the right track. We need to think about all the places she'd be likely to go. Trouble is, she's got dementia. Even if she knows where she wants to go, she may not know why. Hell, she may not even know how to get there from where she is."

Max tried hard not to let his distress over Walter's words twist his features.

"So, we start with the most obvious, then move to more distant possibilities. And if none of those prove successful, we consider everything else."

Max raised his hands in exasperation. "Right. Because in reality, if she's having a bad day, she could think that hitchhiking to see her granddaughters in Middleton is the perfect thing to do on a day you've escaped the seniors' residence! Or go see a movie! Or, or!" Max, whose voice had crescendoed as he spoke despite his efforts to cage his anxiety, sat back in his chair and folded his hands in front of him again.

"Yes. Because of that, exactly." Walter glanced over at Pilot, who was just waiting for this cue and stood, if not a bit creakily, waiting for instructions from his master. "But first, the obvious, right?"

Max stood. "Right."

Walter picked up his hat and turned it in his hands as he talked. "The Wolfville guys have already sent someone to Martin Ridgewood's residence in Waterville, and I drove over to the sister's before coming here. No signs Alice Ridgewood has been at either, and we're lucky to have all this snow to confirm that." He gestured toward the window with his hat. "No new or unusual footprints. This was my next stop. I assume by now you'd have alerted me to any unusual goings-on around here in the early hours of the morning, so my next step is to walk around the house. I would already have done it if I hadn't remembered you were staying here while your sister and her husband are away." He rocked back on his heels as if to punctuate the end of his sentence, then pressed his hat down over his silver hair and the tips of his ears.

Max, moderately reassured by Walter's matter-of-fact demeanour and obvious experience, merely nodded. "Please, feel free to check outside, and in as well!"

Walter squinted at him sideways. "You lock the doors before bed last night?"

"Uh – I think so. I mean, Kathy would have done it. I'm not the best at remembering stuff like that."

"Common sense stuff?"

Max chuckled and spread his hands out in surrender. "Yeah, exactly."

"So, what I'm hearing is that you're not entirely sure the door was locked this morning."

"I can call Kathy?"

"Nope; let's do a thorough search, just in case."

"Good. OK." Max moved to get his boots, but Walter held a hand out. "I'm going to have you sit tight in here while I walk around outside."

Max sighed.

"Only because I don't want any extra footprints. We want to be able to see anything unusual."

"Right. I get it." Max watched from the living room window as Walter and Pilot started out in front of the house. He saw Walter get something from the car – a shirt? – and hold it out for the dog to examine. A piece of clothing from Alice? How would he have that already? *Maybe the Wolfville police sent someone with it this morning.*

Max turned and walked to the kitchen, going to the window so he could see Walter and Pilot as they progressed to the back yard. He observed his and Kathy's prints in the snow and shook his head. They'd walked to the bridge and even beyond it a bit that week, going over all that had happened.

Pilot sniffed at their prints. Walter held the fabric out to the dog again, who seemed to eagerly drink in the scent before returning to the prints. Both walked along the path to the bridge, and then over it, but Max couldn't tell whether the dog was leading by his nose or Walter was making sure they covered the area thoroughly.

Max looked at the clock for the millionth time that morning. 9:15. Alice had been missing and presumably out in the cold for hours. But maybe not. Max held his breath and listened. Considered the possibility that she'd come to the house sometime this morning. That she could be inside even now. The hairs on his arms stood up.

"Alice?" he said quietly, half hoping to hear her, half worried he'd need a new pair of underpants if he got an answer back.

Nothing. The house was silent. He exhaled.

Walter's knock at the front door made him jump.

He crossed the living room and let Walter and Pilot in.

"Anything?"

"You have someone staying here with you?"

"Yes, my wife. I should've said —"

"No, it's fine. I think someone had mentioned it. Just making sure those tracks in the back could all be accounted for."

"We've been in the back. Even crossed the bridge the other day as we talked about everything that's been going on."

"I saw. Looks like you have a habit of pacing outside, too. Not just kitchens?" Walter's eyes twinkled a bit as he teased Max.

"Oh. I'm afraid so. Hmmm… I bet that makes it harder to pick out prints."

"It does, son, but it's nothing to feel bad about. What it does mean, though, is that I can't confirm with a hundred percent certainty that you and your wife are the only people who've been out back. Pilot was keen on continuing down the path but not pulling like he does when he's hot on a scent. A lot can affect that, mind you." He leaned closer to Max and lowered his voice. "Including age."

Max smiled. "Maybe we should, though. Go through the woods."

"Yep, and we will. But the practical cop in me is putting it a little lower on the list. It's *cold* out there. The cruiser read minus eighteen on the way here, and that's without the wind chill. It's not likely she'd venture down that path in the clothes she was wearing. Bare legs under that nightgown, they figure."

"Speaking of clothes, is that what you had Pilot sniff?"

"Yeah, they brought a shirt of hers to the station first thing."

Max nodded, satisfied at his earlier reasoning. "So, if the woods are lower on the list, what's next?"

"A quick check inside here, top to bottom for me and bottom to top for you."

"We'll meet in the middle?"

"We'll *cross* in the middle, so that both of us see all the rooms in the house."

"Thorough."

"Yep. And then the Maplestone house."

"I'm coming."

"Nope."

Before Max could protest further, the cop held a hand up authoritatively. "We don't have time to argue, now do we? Let's just hope we find her in here, for now." He removed his boots and started up the stairs, calling "Me: attic, you: basement! See you in the middle."

Max, frustrated and determined to argue his case before the cop headed up to the Maplestone property, turned and walked resolutely toward the basement door in the kitchen. He recalled Maggie's story about the washer and the – ugh – unusual contents, about three-quarters of the way down the dimly-lit stairs. Stopping mid-step and pulling his descending foot back, he peered into the small space below him, allowing his eyes to adjust. "Alice?" He called out for her again, a little louder this time, and then held his breath.

Nothing. Not even his voice echoing back to him in the small space. He reached the bottom of the stairs and stood on the concrete riser which served as the divider between the room and the stairs, breathing again and eager to get this part of the search over with. He found a light switch beside the staircase and flicked it on, only to be disappointed at how poorly it lit the surroundings. It was as though the room swallowed the light and hid it somewhere behind the shadows. He gazed around the small space, noting the exposed insulation in the walls and consequently finding the answer for the lack of echo. What else? Washer and dryer. Folding table. A couple of wall-mounted shelves stocked with detergent and other laundry paraphernalia. Certainly, no nightgown-clad woman. He moved several steps to the right to look into an even smaller storage room and was met with stacks of boxes, presumably left from Maggie and Jack's move, but, judging from the musty smell, possibly from the family members who had lived here before as well. "No room for anyone to hide in here," he commented out loud.

There was a shuffling noise behind him as if in answer to the words he'd spoken.

He spun around, picturing an old woman crouched and ready to pounce (and simultaneously feeling ridiculous at the thought), and was met with the same room and contents he'd just observed. Washer. Dryer. Table. Shelves. Shadows.

Max muttered, "Yeesh!" and moved back to the stairs, shaking his head - partly embarrassed and partly to convince himself there'd been nothing to jump at in the first place. *Probably not even a sound from in here. Probably Walter or the dog upstairs.* He flicked the light off and had begun to climb the stairs when it came again: shuffling. Again, he spun, his every tendon on edge, and flicked the switch back on. Despite his earlier denial, he knew without a doubt that what he'd heard had indeed come from the basement rather than from upstairs. "Hello?"

He felt stupid. The room was too small to hold anything besides what he could clearly see. Even the shadows in the corners were small. Still, *something* was making a noise, and he wanted to be able to say conclusively it was just a mouse. *Or a particularly rambunctious spider*, he thought, noting the dusty cobwebs.

It didn't take him long to walk the length of the room, peering even under the table and behind the laundry machines. He moved the containers on the shelves around for good measure and found nothing but dust and more dust. He resolved to let Walter examine the room and see what he said, and made for the stairs, not a little relieved.

But stopped, beside the washer.

He remembered his sister's vision again and could see it in his head: a mass of blood-red cord and placenta, tangled around the agitator and itself. And writhing. "That's not what she saw!" he exclaimed to his imagination (which had always bent toward the extreme), his voice shaky. Determined to feel he'd been thorough (and maybe also to prove he wasn't an over-imaginative four-year-old), he reached for the lid of the washer.

A shuffle again, this time louder, and coming from the stairs behind him.

He gasped as he spun around, his nerves frayed. He saw a shadow. An animal!

Tired of his own imagination, he leapt to the stairs and looked up the length of them to find Pilot at the top, his front two paws on the first stair and his hind-quarters still planted firmly in the kitchen.

Max laughed and put his face in his hands, then looked up at the dog again. "Pilot!"

The dog wagged his tail and continued observing Max, his head cocked to the side at the sound of his name.

"You probably smell my man-fear." Max smiled as he climbed the rest of the way up. The dog backed out into the kitchen and sat, seeming to smile up at him. Max patted his head. "Hey, bud."

Walter came down the stairs then, looking at him questioningly as he reached the bottom. "Don't tell me you just came back up from the basement?"

Max laughed a bit, still patting the dog, and looked sheepish. "Just my ears playing tricks on me."

"What'd you hear?"

"I never found out, but I'm thinking a mouse."

Walter shuddered, and Max laughed again, surprised at the tough old cop's reaction. "Hopefully I'm not gonna have to confirm that," Walter mumbled and motioned Max toward the stairs leading to the second floor as he made his way to the basement.

"Wait – did you see anything?"

The cop gave him a look. "Am I currently accompanied by anyone but yourself and this dog?"

Max took a breath. "You know what I mean. Anything unusual or out of place?"

"Dunno. Nothing obvious. You tell me!" Walter smiled and turned toward the basement again.

Max turned back to the stairs and was delighted to discover that Pilot had decided to accompany him. "Thanks, pal," he said, and the dog moved past him, leading the way.

The second floor was the same as he'd seen it last. Freshly painted nursery, rumpled guest bed (he made a mental note to restore the room to the state he'd found it in when he and Kathy had first arrived), bright bathroom and quiet main bedroom, where the door to the attic was located. No dirty footprints, no eerie feeling of being watched, no stray senior citizens.

He pulled on the metal handle of the attic door and mounted the extended ladder. Cursing himself for not bringing a flashlight (and just as quickly realizing he hadn't the slightest clue where Maggie would keep a flashlight), he squinted into the damp darkness. Tiny, oval windows at both the front and back of the attic let in a bit of light, and his eyes adjusted quickly as he breathed in the musty air. He took a look from front to back and resolved that a walkthrough wasn't needed. There were boxes sparsely placed here and there, but he could see all four corners clearly. *Nobody hiding here*, he thought.

The loft was much the same: simply furnished for Maggie's office with a little sitting area at the end closest to the stairs. Max walked to the far end, noting the low, slanted ceilings and internally deciding that, while this would be a comfortable office for his sister, it wouldn't work at all for him. He pictured a perpetually bruised head and smiled at his own clumsiness.

Reaching the window, he looked down at the back yard from a new angle but saw nothing different. His and Kathy's footprints, now joined by those of Walter and the dog, the small bridge and the woods beyond. He heard Walter yell from below and spun around for the fourth time that morning, this time smashing his forehead on the slanted roof he had just moments ago recognized as a hazard to himself.

He yelled in pain and frustration and sprinted to the stairs, descending to the first floor as quickly as his legs would carry him. Pilot had already reached his master in the kitchen, who was leaning over the sink, a hand on his head and a grimace on his face. Max approached him and saw blood between the old man's fingers. "Walter! What happened?"

The old man looked at him, and his eyes widened. "I could ask you the same!" he exclaimed, pointing with his free hand to Max's forehead.

"Oh, I walked into a – roof," he replied, feeling stupid.

"The loft?" the old man questioned, smiling slightly. At Max's nod, he finished, "I very nearly did that myself."

"What *did* you do?" Max moved to the sink and motioned for the old man to remove his hand so he could assess the damage. Walter reluctantly pulled his hand away.

"I was saving myself for this." He pointed to his forehead. An ugly gash oozed above Walter's right eyebrow.

Max reflexively sucked in his breath. "Wow. I think you got the bad end of this deal, my friend."

Walter walked across the kitchen, stopped, and asked where the bathroom was. Max pointed and then followed the cop to the small room off the hallway.

"Shit. Sorry." The older man examined his injury in the mirror. "But *shit*!"

"That's going to need stitches." Max maneuvered himself behind Walter to get a look at his own forehead, which was badly scraped and already bruising on the right side above his eyebrow but clearly nothing serious.

"Matching booboos," Walter said.

"Not quite," Max replied. "Let's get you to Emergency in Middleton."

Walter turned and passed Max, dismissing the suggestion with a wave of his hand. "Just needs a Band-Aid or two," he said as he walked back to the kitchen. Pilot, now unimpressed by the whole scene, lay relaxed in the corner.

"What? Walter, I'm pretty sure I just saw your skull through that cut!"

"Pfft!" Walter started opening cabinets, searching for a first aid kit, Max supposed.

"OK, it might not have been your skull, but it might have! That's a deep cut -" Walter, pretending not to hear him, continued opening and closing cabinets. "What are you doing? There's gauze and some bandages in the bathroom." He walked back to the bathroom, hearing Walter mumble something about "Nola always kept..." and "...cabinet."

Max persuaded Walter to let him clean and bandage up his head, which only further convinced Max that Walter needed stitches.

"Later," Walter replied calmly when Max voiced his concern again. "I want to get to the Maplestone place first."

Max shook his head, but Walter again stopped his protests before they could start.

"I assume you didn't find your sister's mother-in-law upstairs?"

"Obviously not, but -"

"She's still out there then, son. And she's cold. That we know."

Max sat back in his chair, meeting Walter's eyes (and noting silently that Walter's right eyelid was now swollen so that eye was half shut). "I get that, but -"

"And the way I figure it is that the Maplestone property is the only place left in the 'obvious' category."

Max nodded in agreement but said nothing.

"I just want to drive up there and see if there are any new tracks, vehicle or human, that go off toward that house."

"And then you'll call someone else to replace you and take care of that?" Max gestured toward the cop's forehead, where the bandage was already showing a line of blood through the fabric.

"If needed," answered Walter, and Max shook his head.

"You're stubborn," Max commented, rising from his chair.

Walter rose too. "You're not the first to notice, trust me," Walter replied, passing Max as he made his way to the front door.

Max joined him and began getting his boots on.

"Where d'you think *you're* going?" Walter asked.

"I'll concede to your checking out the property up the street, Walter, but you won't be going alone," and before Walter could make the obvious reply, he added, "and Pilot doesn't count!"

283

Walter looked out the front door window toward the street, thinking.

"We'll leave the door unlocked," said Max. "If she comes here while we're gone, she can get in easily and get warm. Finding me here might scare her, anyway; I've only met her a couple of times."

Walter continued looking out toward the road. "Where's your car?" he asked.

"Kathy has it. I'll have to come in the cruiser with you."

Walter nodded and opened the door, letting Pilot out first, and Max quickly finished dressing for the cold, astonished that he'd won and now hurrying to keep up.

Walter was already belting himself into the driver's seat when Max reached the car. Despite his worries about the old cop driving with a fresh, still-bleeding cut on his head (resulting, he assumed, from a pretty hard blow), he kept his mouth shut and resolved to quit arguing while he was ahead.

The digital clock on the dash displayed 10:01 when Walter fired up the engine and backed out of the driveway, and Max wondered at how fast time seemed to have passed during the chaos of the morning. *Hold on tight, Max. It's not over yet,* he thought, his mind on Maggie and Jack flying home even now, and Charis on her way, as well.

Max did a facepalm, yelping as he inadvertently smacked his bruised forehead. In answer to Walter's shocked look, he exclaimed, "I was supposed to rent a car for the psychic!"

Walter furrowed his bandaged brow, grunted at the stab of pain that small action had brought him, and answered, "What are you saying? Son, I think it's *you* who needs a trip to Emergency!"

284

Max laughed at the realization that he must sound crazy. "No –
uh - Maggie contacted a psychic about everything that's been
happening. It was Zoe's idea. A friend of a friend, or something.
Anyway, she's coming. She's flying in from Ottawa."

"What? What for?"

"To help, I guess. She told me to call her when –" Max
groaned. "It doesn't really matter why, I guess. But I promised to have
a car booked for her at the airport, and I forgot. Shit."

Walter chuckled and then brought his hand to his bandage,
grimacing. "Huh. Throbs."

"You need -" Max began, feeling a bit of panic creeping in,
now.

"Not yet," Walter interrupted. "Soon." They drove in silence,
save for Pilot's panting in the back, for a minute or two. Then Walter
stopped the car, having arrived at the dead-end where the driveway to
the Maplestone place would have been evident had it not been buried
in snow. "Listen, let's take a quick look here. And then, you'll be
pleased to know, you'll be able to kill two birds with one stone."

It was Max's turn to look at Walter as though he was crazy.

"I think you might be right about this," Walter gestured toward
the now oozing bandage, "so you can drive the cruiser to the hospital
once we're done here and book that car for your psychic while we're
in the waiting room." He rested his head on the headrest of his seat,
closing his eyes.

"Oh, God. Walter!"

Walter opened his eyes. "Calm down, boy. I'm just resting my eyes. I'm a bit dizzy. Seems that knock to the head was harder than I thought. I'm not dealing with just a cut, here."

"A concussion," Max replied, the worry evident in his voice.

"Probably. And in these circumstances, it's my duty to get myself taken care of before doing much more."

"I agree. And it's alright for me to drive the cruiser rather than call an ambulance?"

Walter slid a look at him sideways. "It is today. I don't want to have to deal with this all day and maybe into tomorrow. Let's get me to the hospital quietly. I have a friend there who can take care of me quickly so I can get back to work."

Max nodded, though he knew even a friend at the hospital wouldn't let Walter go back to work with a concussion. Even a much younger cop wouldn't be released to work in that condition. "OK, I'll go take a look at the driveway for any signs that someone's been here. In the meantime, can you get yourself into the passenger seat?"

"I'm concussed, boy, not paralyzed."

Max exited the car, shaking his head. He watched Walter open his own door and, satisfied that he was moving OK, turned and ran to where he and Walter had entered the property not too long ago.

There was nothing. Just snow, clean and unmarked as far as he could see. For good measure, he ran to the gated dead-end to look for evidence that anyone had even been up this way. There were some tire tracks, obvious U-turns, but none, human or vehicle, leading off from either side of the road. He rationalized internally: *even if a taxi had brought her here, there's no way any sane driver would sit there and allow her to trudge off into the snow alone, especially dressed as she was.*

Satisfied, he jogged back to the car and got in the open door on the driver's side. Walter appeared to be sleeping, and, purposefully pushing his rising panic back down, he said his name in as calm a voice as he could manage. "Walter."

Walter jolted a bit.

Relieved, he continued, "Hey, you shouldn't sleep until after you've been checked out, OK? Help me out, here. Talk to me while we drive." Max glanced at Walter's seatbelt and, seeing it buckled, started back down the road, already mapping out the quickest route to the hospital in his head.

"I fell down," Walter said matter-of-factly.

"I figured." Max realized he hadn't even asked Walter how he'd gotten the cut. He'd been too preoccupied with taking care of it.

"You were right."

"About what?" Max struggled to carry on the conversation as he wondered whether he should just stop and call an ambulance despite Walter's wishes.

Walter sat up in his seat a bit then, rubbing his eyes, and Max was relieved enough to keep driving, now turning left on to Old Notch, having decided to go through Kingston.

"The noise you heard. The mouse."

"Oh! Is that what you yelled about?"

"Yeah. I don't like mice."

"Yeah, especially when they knock you over, eh?" Max made an effort to get Walter fired up, just a little.

Instead, Walter was quiet for a moment. Then, "It wasn't the mouse, really. It was *where* she was that made me jump and trip over my own feet."

Max's blood ran cold.

"See, I kept hearing a noise. Probably what you heard when you were down there."

"A shuffling," Max stated, rather than asked.

"Yeah, that's it. A shuffling. I finally realized it was coming from the washer."

Max nodded.

"You don't seem surprised."

"No, I -" He wasn't sure how to answer. "I was actually about to open the washer to take a look inside when the dog appeared on the stairs. I guess that surprise made me forget my intentions."

Yes, he'd omitted some detail but wasn't lying.

"Well, anyway. I don't know how she got in there, but I guess there are pipes and tubes and whatnot that could easily explain that."

Max breathed a bit more easily. "Weird," he said almost absently.

"You're telling me. I opened the lid and there she was, looking up at me. Spooked me. The fall wouldn't have been so bad if it hadn't been for that bit of cement at the bottom of the stairs."

Max remembered standing there as he had surveyed the dark room beyond. "Oooooh!" he cringed, "that explains the gash, and the concussion, too." They were in Kingston now, about ten minutes from the hospital in Middleton.

"Pretty straight...forward?" Walter asked, looking at Max questioningly.

"Yeah, that's right. You OK there?"

"Just - had to search for that word. The rest of the word. Anyway." He leaned back in his seat again, and Max put the gas on. He was in a police cruiser, after all. What could go wrong? The car sped up, and Max focused on the road, only glancing at the silent man in the passenger seat after a few minutes.

Walter had closed his eyes again.

"Walter!"

"Hm? Get tired so easily now. Sneaks up on you, time does."

"Walter, stay with me." Max searched his mind for something to keep the man awake. "Hey, why did you keep calling her, 'she'?" he asked.

"Who?" Walter asked, turning his head to look at Max but not lifting it from the headrest.

"The mouse! How did you know it was a female?"

"The babies."

Max nearly ran a red light, and Walter started. "Whoa, son! I thought you could drive!"

Max braked, hard, and Walter sat up.

"Sorry," Max said. "We're almost there, and, trust me, I'll be pleased to relinquish the driving back to you. When you're up for it, that is."

"Don't patronize me," Walter said, with none of his usual fire.

The light turned green, so Max continued toward Middleton, contemplating what Walter had said.

"What babies, Walter?"

"Eh?"

"You said you knew the mouse was female because of the babies."

"Yeah. She must have found her way in there to have her babies. Looked like she made a little nest. Lots of dryer lint, ha!"

"Oh." Max absorbed this.

"Guess it was hard to get food or something, though. None of them were moving. There was even one outside the nest, still as a stone. Its eyes were open."

"They were all - I mean, couldn't they have been sleeping? The mother was alive, right?"

"Yep, she was, but her babies weren't. I'm sure of that. I looked in there a minute. I was…hypnotized…no…mesmerized, that's it. And then she screamed at me. That's when I fell."

"Screamed? You mean squeaked?"

"No, dammit! She screamed. Guess any mother who'd lost her children would -"

Max thought of Alice. Alice in the cold. Alice lost, again. She'd been lost once before, when her own baby had died. He shuddered. He glanced at the clock and flicked the turn signal to pull into the hospital parking lot.

10:29 a.m.

Chapter 35 – Charis

The plane taxied smoothly onto the runway, and Charis marvelled again at how smoothly everything had gone since she'd spoken to Max. Once she'd gotten some essentials at home and talked to the boys' father to let him know she'd be away at least a day, everything had gone without a hitch.

When she arrived at the airport, she'd parked in a perfect spot and made her way to the ticket counters. She paused and considered her options, realizing at that moment that she hadn't the slightest clue when the next flight to Halifax was. She grabbed her phone out of her purse and opened her browser, intending to use one of those multi-airline sites to find the details she needed. The browser displayed the loading icon, and she made a frustrated noise. "There's no time!" she whispered. Following her gut, she picked an airline and approached the counter, making eye contact with the agent sitting behind the computer.

"Hi, there! Do you have your ticket?" asked the agent, with a smile that reached his eyes.

Charis inwardly breathed a sigh of relief. This guy was going to help her. "Hi. I don't, actually! This is sort of a last-minute emergency. I need to get to Halifax -"

The young man started typing before she'd even finished her sentence. "Good; you still have time, but not much!"

"You have a flight?"

"We have a flight that boards, um -" he glanced at his watch, "- in nine minutes, and takes off in thirty-nine." He looked at her. "That's ten forty-five boarding and eleven fifteen takeoff."

She was stunned.

"Sound good?"

Charis nodded. "Yes! It's absolutely perfect; thank you!" She handed her ID and a credit card to him.

The agent smiled and started typing wildly again. "Wish I could take credit and say I commissioned this flight just for you, honey, but the truth is, you got lucky." He leaned forward and cupped his hand around his mouth, whispering, "And not just with the flight." He used his other hand to point to his left.

Charis glanced casually to her right where another agent for the airline chewed her gum loudly while looking at her phone. She stifled a giggle with some difficulty. "You're not kidding!" she whispered back.

After that, it was as though she was carried along by a tide. She got through security and found her gate without a hiccup. (It helped that she had only a carry-on with a couple of changes of clothes and her toiletry bag. No laptop, no fluids over 100ml.) Passengers were already lined up and flashing their tickets and passports at the airline employees before walking through to the plane.

The flight itself had been much the same: Charis had sipped some water and watched the better part of a movie, and now they were landing slightly early at 1:40, local time. She'd never had a less stressful day of travel. *I need to fly at the last minute more often!* she thought but knew, on a deeper level, that there were forces at work to speed her along to where she was needed.

Exiting the plane and looking for the signs for car rental, she switched airplane mode off and waited to see what she'd missed. A text from Max was what she needed, and there it was, three messages down. She clicked it and noted he'd sent it only a short while ago:

293

Max: Sorry for the delay; you wouldn't believe my morning. In any case, here's the link for your booking confirmation. It's with Value; I hope everything is OK. All paid up, with my thanks. Let me know your ETA after you get the car. See you soon.

Charis clicked the link and, spotting the sign, sped up and found the elevator she needed to take. On the way down, she wondered what could possibly have made his morning more hectic than a missing extended family member.

Following the precedent of her day thus far, dealing with the car rental folks was quick and easy. She breezed through the paperwork (which required only proof of insurance and a photocopy of her licence, seeing Max had already taken care of payment) and was pleased with the little economy car she was presented with. *Thank God for built-in GPS,* she thought, making a note to call her cell phone's service provider once she had settled into the hotel that evening. Oh. And to book a hotel. She couldn't help but laugh a bit as she started the car and the GPS.

She immediately sat back in the driver's seat, letting the hand she'd extended to the GPS drop. She had no idea where she was going! The vague images in her head, left over from dreams and visions since talking with Maggie, simply weren't going to get her there. She dialled Max and was surprised when a woman answered.

"Hello?"

"Hi. I might have the wrong number here. I'm looking for Max?"

"Oh, hi. No worries. Is this Charis?

"Yes! I've just landed -"

Charis heard the woman relay this information, presumably to Max, and asked, "Is everything OK?"

"Yes. Sorry, this is Kathy, Max's wife. I've just picked him up at the hospital -"

"What? What happened?"

"Don't worry; he's OK. In fact, despite having a rather nasty bump on his head, he was actually there for someone else. Anyway, I took the rest of the day off and picked him up. We're headed back to Maggie and Jack's place now."

Charis's brow ached, furrowed with confusion as it was. "Nasty bump? Someone else?" she repeated, quite unable to voice her questions more clearly as the urgency of the situation pressed itself upon her again.

Kathy laughed a little. "We'll tell you everything once you've gotten here. Maggie and Jack won't even land for another hour or so, from what I understand."

"OK -"

"Hey, maybe it would make sense for you to wait at the airport for them? You could follow them here?"

Charis paused. She opened up and sent the question out. *Can I wait?* It certainly would make sense – but no. She was immediately hit with that powerful feeling of urgency again. A vision of blood in the snow, and a woman with dark hair crying. And beside her, Alice – she knew it was Alice – in a nightgown, lost in so many ways, and cold.

"No!" she exclaimed, partially in answer to Kathy's suggestion and partially as a result of her visions.

"Oh."

"I'm sorry, Kathy. I just - I need to come right away. Can you give me the street address for Maggie's house, please? I have a GPS ready to go here."

"OK. It's 121 - Max?" Charis could hear Max in the background. "121 Old Barn Road."

Charis typed madly. "Greenwood Square?"

"Yes, that's it."

"OK, thanks. Just a sec." She waited for the GPS to calculate the route. "It says I'm an hour and forty-nine minutes away."

"Good! We'll see you soon, then."

"Yes. And please tell Max I'm very grateful for the rental."

She listened to a muffled, "Thank you for the rental," and then Kathy was back on. "Is there anything at all we can do in the meantime?"

Charis paused. "I can't see where she is yet, but I know she's cold. You two can get some supplies ready while you wait. Blankets, socks. Have them ready to go. We're going into the woods."

Kathy gasped. "To the clearing? The cabin?"

"Yes? I don't know if it's what Maggie talked to me about; I don't see the building. I'll know more when I see the house."

"Max knew it! He wanted to go with Walter this morning -"

"Walter the police sergeant?"

"Yes. And then he hurt himself."

Charis saw a vision of a nest of mice. Dead. "Oh!"

"He's OK; just a concussion, but out of commission for at least today, and not too happy about it."

"I don't imagine he is."

"But they had planned to go back there!"

"I'm glad they didn't. She wouldn't have been there when they went, anyway, and it would have made them less likely to go back this afternoon, you know?"

"I guess."

"There's a reason I'm here, Kathy. Please wait for me before you go."

"But if she's there now, isn't it best if -"

"No. I don't know how to explain it, but it's worse if you go just the two of you. Besides, somebody needs to be at the house for the others."

"I don't understand -"

"For Maggie and Zoe and the others." Charis was itching to get moving and tired of the conversation. This was old to her: others needing explanation and convincing. They just didn't *see* as she did. She got that! But it still wasn't easy to feel that you were running ahead of everyone all the time, yet needing to keep them with you.

"Just a sec." Charis heard muffled conversation between Kathy and Max. She put the phone on speaker and threw the car in reverse. She had to get going.

Kathy was back. "You're asking us to do something really tough."

"I know. And I know you don't know me enough to trust me yet, but I'm telling you that if you care about Alice and her family – and I know that you do, in fact, you're part of it – you'll wait." She took the rental exit and left the airport in her rear-view mirror, already speeding up. "I'm well on my way, and if there was *any* chance I was wrong about this, I'd be telling you two to get out there now."

"You *know* that waiting is the best thing?"

"Yes. It's the only thing."

"OK. I'll make it happen."

"Thank you. And Kathy?"

"Yeah?"

"Don't worry. I drive fast."

Chapter 36 – Max and Kathy

Kathy faced her husband and inhaled, unsure where to begin.

He took a hand off the wheel and placed it over hers. "It's OK. I heard most of that last part."

"What are we going to do? I can't imagine not sprinting down that trail as soon as we get back to the house, but I feel like she's right, too!"

"Fuck. I know."

They sat silently, holding hands, as Max steered them onto Old Barn Road.

Finally, he said, "Let's just get back to the house and see what happens, OK? Seems like every time I make plans these days, events take over and change them, anyway."

Kathy nodded, her face blank.

"Let's just get back there and take this one step at a time." He squeezed her hand.

She shook her head.

"Hon? You OK?"

Kathy threw her hands up in exasperation, leaving Max's own going cold in her lap. "How did this day go from being served breakfast to leaving work early to get my husband from the hospital because he'd needed to get an injured cop there and then wait to see what was going to happen – which, incidentally, is crazy enough on its own! - to this? To knowing where Alice is and *sitting on our asses waiting for a psychic to show up?*"

Max couldn't help but let out an unexpected roar of laughter.

"Hey! It's not funny!"

"Well, the way you said it was." He tried to reel it back in and, having failed, covered his mouth as he laughed some more.

Kathy wasn't laughing. "Max! What would Maggie think of this?"

That stopped him. "I don't know! That's the problem. It's not *them* here dealing with this. It's us!" Max pulled into the driveway and turned the car off, pulling the keys from the ignition but making no move to get out. He looked at his wife, who was on the edge of tears, and took her hand again. "I want to help. I want to deal with this in Maggie and Jack – and Zoe and Sam's! – absence as they would want us to. But I don't know exactly what that means."

A tear rolled down Kathy's face, and then her face lit up, just a little. "Hey. Hey, maybe it's *good* that it's us here and them stuck on a plane. Maybe we can make better decisions because we're not as emotionally involved? We're not quite as close to it." She looked at him hopefully.

Max shook his head. "How do you always know what to say to make sense of even the weirdest situations?"

She shrugged and kissed him. "Survival instincts!" She smiled.

He laughed again now, pulling her across the seat into his arms.

"What?"

"It really *was* funny."

"What was?"

He pulled out of their embrace and raised his voice to a comical falsetto. *"We're just sitting on our asses waiting for a psychic to show up!"*

Now she laughed. "OK, quit it. Let's get inside. She was right about one thing: we can use this time to gather what we'll need when we find her."

They both nodded, Max's grin still plastered across his face, and got out of the car.

They held hands as they approached the front door.

"I really hope you're right about events taking over," she said, still uncertain about what to do next.

"Me too," Max said, a bit distractedly, as they climbed the front steps.

Kathy followed his gaze to the front door. The screen was closed, but even from here, she could see that the inner door was ajar. They looked at each other with wide eyes.

"Stay here," Max said, dropping her hand.

"No way," Kathy said, and she approached the door with him, ignoring his annoyed grunt beside her.

He opened the screen and pushed the heavier inner door until it was wide open. Kathy made to go in, but Max held her back, gently. He held a finger up and called out, "Hello? Anybody home?"

Kathy was confused at the greeting. He was acting as if they were showing up to a family barbeque. Then something clicked within her. "You're a frigging genius," she whispered. Alice was probably scared and very confused. If she was still in the house and they barged in, loud and questioning, the chaos would do her more harm than good.

She followed his lead: "Alice? It's Max and Kathy - Maggie's brother and sister-in-law?"

No reply. Not a sound.

"Alice?" Max stepped inside, and Kathy followed, surveying the interior. She immediately noticed a mess in the kitchen that hadn't been there when she left. She grabbed Max's arm and pointed with her other hand, questioning him with her eyes.

"Some of that's ours – the first aid stuff on the counter and table."

"But not the bread? The peanut butter?"

Max's face registered surprise before he replied, "No!"

"I feel like we're alone in here. In any case, if she's here, she knows we're inside. I think we need to search the rest of the house."

"You're right, but lemme tell you, I wasn't thinking I'd have to search this house again today."

"We'll do it together, and I'll do the rooms with dangerous ceilings." She winked up at him, and he stuck his tongue out at her.

"OK, Alice, we're coming in just to sit down for a while. Maggie, Jack, Zoe and Sam will be here soon!" Kathy figured it didn't hurt to narrate their actions, just in case Alice was in the house.

A closer examination of the kitchen didn't turn up much more than they'd already seen from the door: evidence of a sandwich being made and maybe tea as well. Kathy also discovered some drying blood in the sink, which wasn't a surprise, given Max's detailed recollection of the morning's events when she'd picked him up, but was nonetheless an unpleasant discovery. She grimaced and turned the water on without a thought. She turned it to "Hot" when the edges of the drops proved stubbornly dried onto the stainless steel of the sink. "Blech," she remarked unconsciously.

"Hey, maybe we shouldn't screw around with anything, eh hon?"

Max's voice made her jump. "Oh, shit! You're right." She hastily turned off the tap, noting with satisfaction that the stubborn bits remained. She looked at Max. "Do you think this is *evidence*? I mean, will there be an investigation?"

"I guess it depends on how this all ends," he said quietly, and she contemplated that, gazing into the sink.

"It's gonna be OK," Max said, moving toward her.

"Of course," she replied. "Let's look around some more. If nothing else, I think it's a really good sign that she was here. We know she made it alive, at least to the house! And hey – maybe she got herself some nice warm clothes, too."

"Yeah. You're right. It's good she was here." He didn't comment on Kathy's hopeful idea about the clothes. Yes, she'd been clear enough to come to her old house, but he found it odd that she'd make a sandwich and a tea only to leave again, apparently, without any evidence that she'd actually eaten it. There was no plate in the sink, no empty teacup. He looked around again and spotted one of the drawers under the counter not quite closed all the way. He opened it.

Kathy watched him and sharply inhaled when she saw the plastic wrap, which appeared to have been replaced hastily, jamming the drawer partially open. "Guess she took it to go?"

"Yep. At least that explains the lack of dishes," Max replied. "But, why?"

Kathy shook her head. "I don't know. Let's check the rest of the house and gather some supplies while we do: blankets and socks, as Charis suggested, and maybe a flashlight, too."

Max sent her a questioning look.

She looked at her phone and then showed him the display.

"It's *two-fifty*?"

"Yeah. And it's still winter; it'll be getting dark in a couple of hours."

Max looked out the window. "God*damn* it, I want to get out there!"

She took his hand. "I know. And you will. But let's do this first." She gestured in an arc, wanting to get started.

"OK. Yes. Just a sec." Max had the door to the basement open and was descending into darkness before she could protest.

"Hey!" she yelled, flicking the light on for the stairs. "What happened to doing this together?"

Max was already moving stuff around on the little shelves in the laundry room, keeping his eyes out for a flashlight. "Just let me get this part over with," he yelled. "It's dark and gross down here. Won't take me a minute." Not surprised that he didn't find a flashlight – or anything of use, actually - he took a quick look around the little storage room and made ready to climb the stairs back up to the kitchen. He looked around a final time, his eyes landing on the washer. "It's no mystery why they don't keep much down here," he mumbled and made a spontaneous decision.

He couldn't explain why later, but he reached out to lift the lid to the washer. Maybe he had something to prove to himself. Maybe he was remembering that day at the Maplestone house when Walter had seen something that he had not. Or maybe he reached out because he was simply compelled to – maybe the action wasn't completely of his own volition.

Whatever. All he *did* know when he told that part of the story later was that he was more shocked than he could have expected at what he saw.

Because he saw nothing at all.

The drum was empty. No screaming mother mouse, no dead baby mice, no nest to speak of. Nothing.

"What's happening?" Kathy yelled down the stairs.

That made him jump. The lid slipped out of his hand and slammed loudly as it shut. He jumped again. "Shit!"

"What?"

Max took a second to breathe.

"*What*?!"

"Nothing, babe." He climbed the stairs.

"Did you look at the mice?" she asked with a bit of a smile, her arms folded.

He raised his eyebrows. "I tried."

"Why?" She looked exasperated. "Wait a sec. What do you mean, you 'tried'?"

"There weren't any there."

"Wha – that's – I mean, they have to be there! They caused Walter's concussion!"

"It's not the first time he's seen something I haven't," Max commented. "Come to think of it, I haven't seen *anything* weird."

"You heard that voice at the old house up the street," Kathy reminded him.

"Yeah. But that's it."

"Are you complaining?" She looked amused.

"Nah. Just – well, I've been here a lot. Been involved in all this from the start. From when Maggie got involved, anyway. And I haven't even had a weird dream, besides the one at the very beginning of it all."

"Maybe that's not your role."

Max thought about that and, bereft of an answer, motioned toward the stairs leading up.

They explored the upper floors of the house without incident and ended up back in the living room on the main floor, sitting on the couch in front of the big picture window.

"We'll see her pull in from here, at least," Kathy said as she folded and refolded two blankets and then stacked a pair of pyjama pants (they had looked so warm and comfortable to her that she'd grabbed them without a thought), a thick pair of wool socks and a knitted hat they'd come across in the guest room closet before placing it all in a reusable shopping bag.

Max watched her. "I think we got everything we need," he said, feeling accomplished.

"Even this," Kathy said, holding up the flashlight they'd found in a kitchen drawer. "And now we need to make a call."

"The police?" Max had thought the same as they'd gone through the house.

"Yep. Now that Walter's out of commission, we'll need someone else out here to check things out."

"Especially now that we know she was here."

"We should have called them an hour ago."

"*It's been an hour?!*"

"More than," she replied, showing him the display on her phone again. 4:15 p.m.

"*Shit!*" Max marched to the front door, a determined look on his face. "I'm going."

Kathy stood and held the bag and flashlight out to him. She made no effort to stop him. She was feeling the need to move, too. But it would have to be vicariously through her husband; she knew she'd have to stay at the house. "Go," she said. "I'll call and update the police."

Max took the supplies and leaned in to kiss his wife. She grasped his arm.

"Be careful."

Chapter 37 – The Trail

As he left the house, a car turned into the driveway and pulled up beside Max and Kathy's car, presumably to leave room for later arrivals. It had to be Charis.

He knew he shouldn't be surprised at her timing, but he was, nonetheless. He left the supplies on the front step and went to meet her.

She got out of the car and said, "Max," holding out her hand. He shook it with both of his and said, "You *do* drive fast!" as she waved at Kathy through the window. He was overwhelmingly relieved at her presence.

She gestured toward the step and said, "You happen to bring a flashlight?"

Straight to business. *Good.* "Yes, actually, thanks to the logical thinking of my wife." He started back toward the steps. "Come on, I'll introduce you." But Charis was already disappearing around the side of the house.

"Later!" she called out. "No time! Kathy's staying here, right?"

Max, running to catch up, answered, "Yeah -" before nearly bumping into the petite woman as she stopped suddenly and pointed to the back porch.

"What's in here?"

"Huh?" He couldn't keep up! "Oh! That's the back door."

She laughed a bit and pulled her hat down over her ears, her curly hair straining against the restraint and springing outward around the folded brim. "I know. But she's been here. Can we go in?"

Max felt stupid. "Of course! And yeah, they keep some stuff in here. Mostly Jack's tools and stuff for work." He opened the porch door and let her in, and she looked back at him.

"What does he do again?"

Still confused at the quick stop to their equally dizzying start, he absently said, "Construction."

Charis stopped, looking at an empty spot on the wall. "Oh, no," she said, quietly.

Max squeezed into the tiny porch and followed her gaze. The entire wall was hung with tools. He was impressed with his brother-in-law's organization. "He's always talking about the cost of good tools," he said. Then he noticed the empty space where Charis's vision was locked. It was the only empty space, just the hook itself and the outline of the tool on display. "Huh," he muttered, reaching out to touch the space where a small axe should be.

Charis turned to him. "We have to go! Now!"

"What is it?" he called after her as she left the porch and stopped, looking around the back yard. He saw the desperate look on her face as he caught up to her.

"I'll tell you on the way. Where's the bridge?"

He pointed, and she was off again. He groaned, but not in annoyance at the effort required to keep up with this woman he'd met for the first time only minutes ago. Rather, he groaned at the urgency she brought with her – and the accompanying realization that they might already be too late.

She waited for him at the entrance to the woods, starting down the path as soon as he was across the bridge. He shoved his arm through the straps of the bag of supplies and pushed it so that it rested on his back while they made their way through the trees.

"Thank goodness the path is relatively clear," she said, finally.

"You should have seen it on Christmas day when Maggie and I came through," he replied. He had so many questions for her but rationalized that it would be better to let her talk when she was ready. After all, they had some time before they reached the clearing, even at the ridiculous pace she was keeping.

"Hmm, I can imagine. And the snow's not very deep. Lots of shelter from the trees," she gasped, showing some fatigue from the speed she was still keeping.

"Charis -"

"Seeing that empty space back there on the wall where that axe should have been," she said, "was like finding a missing puzzle piece. One that makes you realize you're part of an action story rather than a drama."

"Huh?" was all he could manage.

"I had a vision after I'd talked to your sister. One that had tried to make its way through while she spoke to me about what had been happening, but made no sense."

"OK."

"I saw a woman in a white nightgown. Long, dark hair. Her name was - a flower."

"Rose," said Max. They'd already veered to the right and the trail stretched far ahead of them.

Charis stopped and, hands on her thighs, took a second to breathe.

"Rose Maplestone," Max said as he stopped, too. He was relieved for the reprieve but didn't want Charis to stop talking.

She stood facing him, hands on her hips and still breathing quickly. "It's still not clear to me how she's linked to Alice, except that they have – or had – something in common. A loss."

"Alice lost a child. She went through a rough time afterward. But Rose was long dead by then." Charis said nothing, so Max continued. "Rose Maplestone used to live in the house at the end of the road. We're actually on their property now."

Charis's eyes cleared. "In my vision, there was an axe, too. She – Rose – was holding it; let's just say that she hurt herself, thinking in some twisted way that it would gain her something back. What else do you know about her?" Charis glanced at her watch, muttered, "Four oh-five," and looked at the trail in the direction they were headed. Max got the feeling their break was drawing to a close.

"Not a lot. I know she was institutionalized. Something happened – I'm not sure what – and she was found on the street in front of Maggie and Jack's house. What do you mean 'gain something back'?"

Charis looked puzzled. "What about – did she lose a child, too?"

"Not that I'm aware of. I know she had a son, and he was still living when she and her husband died. He was something of a recluse – they all were."

Charis started walking. "I still can't connect all the dots, but I know she wasn't herself," she said over her shoulder. "Sort of like

312

Alice isn't herself, which is probably why she started seeing Rose again. I'm worried. Let's just say that missing axe back there tells me we should hurry. Come on."

"Walter – our police sergeant friend – he knows more about what happened. He's in the hospital. He – uh, it's a long story." He slowed, hoping she'd be persuaded to finish their conversation. No such luck. He sped up as Charis skip-hopped into a jog.

"I think Alice knows more than we do, too," said Charis. "And that whatever happened to Rose happened back here."

Chapter 38 – Alice/Rose

Everything is cold, much colder than the first time. The first time, the cold was new. The ground was still soft. She had forgotten her shoes in the woods one day and hadn't gone back to find them.

Grass between her toes.

It was comforting.

She had needed comfort so badly. When it all happened, before – when she first showed herself, that is – it was because Alice was lost, as Rose had been. Her soul had been ripped apart and bared to the universe like an open wound. She was vulnerable, and she was angry. Almost challenging whatever was out there to try and hurt her more.

And Rose had felt that. It had felt familiar. She was drawn to Alice, and then once Alice knew her, she was drawn to Rose, too.

At first, Alice couldn't stay away. Marla walked through the woods with her because she saw that Alice had gained some comfort from the spirit who seemed to understand her pain.

The problem was, her pain had only deepened when she died. The state of her mind – it followed her – and she, refusing to leave everything behind, was consumed by it. As in life, her pain had twisted everything. She was overcome.

And back then, consumed by her own pain, Alice had been unable to help. Was at a loss as to how, and was finally reminded that she was needed, not just by this ghost, or the ghost of her missing baby, but by her family on the other side of the woods.

And then she'd dreamt about him – the one she'd lost. Sebastian. She saw him as a toddler, as a teenager, as a man, and he'd held her hands in his and smiled into her eyes. Her soul had healed a little then, and she was given the strength to move forward.

But Rose hadn't moved forward, not even in death. And she couldn't see a way out of the misery in which she dwelled.

And though it felt unfinished, Alice had let go.

Until now.

With the changes in her own mind came an opening for her old friend. She started coming to her in dreams, and then, as Alice lost more time, in her waking hours, too. On the bad days when everything seemed mixed up, there was Rose. She was the only thing that seemed familiar on those days, so Alice grabbed on to her and held tight.

It didn't occur to her that it was unfair. That she was being taken advantage of. What did matter was that she was given a second chance to help Rose.

All Rose had wanted was a second chance. It had been taken from her in life, but she could try again. If Alice would let her in, she could try.

Alice didn't decide to let her in or to keep her out. All she did was remember the feeling of wanting to help, on a particularly mixed up day, when she was vulnerable, and Rose took her chance.

So now Alice had brought her a meal, as Greyson once had when Rose was confined with her madness to the little cabin in the clearing.

She'd brought her a meal and the other thing she'd asked for, too.

She'd done everything she was supposed to do, except this next thing: the big thing.

Rose showed her why.

Made her feel the pain of being punched in her pregnant belly. Feeling it in her own body, and somehow in the body deep within her, as well. Knowing instantly that it had killed the smaller one inside her.

It had been just a moment. A mistake. A misspoken word to her drunken husband. She knew better. But she was so tired. Her belly so heavy. And she was worried, too. He wouldn't even acknowledge her growing belly. He drank more and more as she grew and grew with the life inside her.

Greyson was her solace and her joy. He marvelled at her growing belly and talked to his brother or sister within it. He had grown protective, too. He followed her around the house and through the fields and gardens and doted on her. It touched her heart during a time when her husband had worked to convince her that she did not deserve love.

And then there was that blow, deep and sure. That one blow that destroyed everything.

It happened quickly after that. She'd almost died on the cold tile of the second-floor bathroom, delivering her baby. Should have died, probably. Her blood had pooled around her as contractions wracked her body and ripped screams from her throat.

Viktor had sent Greyson outside and locked the door, but she heard her boy's pitiful cries from the ground below the bathroom window. He couldn't help her, poor little thing. It was a four-year-old against raging, drunken Viktor. So, she was on her own and birthing her dead baby in a river of blood. The child she already loved with every fibre of her being.

She knew it wouldn't matter if she died. No ambulance would be called, no funeral held. She wouldn't be missed in town or at church; he kept her too close for that. Easier to control that way.

She passed out at some point and awoke to the overwhelming urge to vomit. She rose to all fours, the world spinning sickeningly around her. The bathtub was closer than the toilet, so she hung over the edge, retching weakly as the vertigo threatened to overwhelm her.

She knew she could not pass out again.

Still hanging over the tub, her eyes closed, she listened. Greyson's screams had been silenced. She wondered where he was. She could hear crickets and tree frogs through the window and felt the chill of the evening air. Some time had passed, but the familiar sounds of night in the forest which had brought her such happiness before held no comfort now.

Her contractions had stopped. She gasped at the realization. At the same moment, she felt it all over her: the blood. Sticky on her knees and between her fingers. Slippery as she held onto the cool porcelain of the bath with all her strength.

She had lost her baby.

She cried out then and heard movement on the other side of the door. Viktor, by the sound of it. Heavy and slow; surely drunk. He'd probably thought she was dead.

The room spun again, and she slowly lowered herself to sit, her back against the tub.

She steeled herself for what she'd see when she opened her eyes. She'd been six months pregnant, if her calculations were correct. She'd never seen a doctor, but she knew her body and her cycle. Six months. She didn't know what a six-month-old stillborn baby would look like.

Again, she heard herself cry out. It was more of a yell, but desperate.

She let the tears come, her eyes still steadfastly shut against the truth of what had happened. She moaned and screamed, howling at the injustice of it. Not caring who heard her and knowing her husband was nothing to fear now; he'd already taken everything from her.

And then, from below the window, "Mommy?"

Greyson's tiny voice had shocked her. She gasped and, without thinking, opened her eyes to look at the window.

And saw.

Saw it all.

It was carnage.

She screamed again.

Was she really still alive? Could she be? She maniacally pressed her hands against herself, a kaleidoscope of bloody handprints appearing on her nightgown as she confirmed her own existence. Checked between her legs; she didn't seem to be bleeding anymore. She felt real. She reeled with vertigo again and retched before she could even think to get herself over the tub or the toilet.

Nothing came up now, anyway; she was empty.

She screamed again.

Greyson called out, "Mommy!"

"Oh, God!" she sent the plea out. "God help me!"

She heard Greyson crying quietly and tried desperately to ground herself.

"Greyson! Honey, it's OK! Mommy is going to be OK." She sucked in the putrid air, held it, then blew it out, surveying the room with wide-open eyes now.

There was just so much blood. She struggled again to conceive her continued existence when so much of her had spilled out.

But what lay in the middle of it all! She cried to God again and moved forward to place her hands on either side of her baby.

It was terrifying to behold, at first: a tiny, dark red doll of a creature. Limbs like twigs, fragile as a bird. Rose ever so gently maneuvered her hands beneath her ever-sleeping child and let out a yelp as the tiny body slipped a little in her hands. She grasped her baby then and brought its tiny, still body to her breast. For months she had envisioned a fat, smiling cherub of a newborn, a new life to bring life back to her family. A ray of light to shine on her always-dark husband.

And now she held this different child; this early, broken child she'd poured all of her hopes into. Such a tiny, tiny body to hold all those hopes, *she thought now. Guilt overwhelmed her, mingled with her disbelief that the last – how long? – five hours? six? – had even happened.*

But it had. For did she not sit now in a pool of her own blood? Wasn't she holding in her arms the dead babe that had, just half a day earlier, been growing in her womb? She doubled over involuntarily as her stomach clenched again. She wasn't sick this time; she was devastated. Her body constricted against it all, even as she held the tiny child between her breasts, against the beating of her heart. Life against death – life blindly pounding onward, despite the despair of its host, and death blindly still, despite the spark of life that mourned it. Rose inhaled, her thoughts whirling.

This child was not as she had pictured but was her child all the same. That's all it took; love surged through her, shot with adrenaline and punctuated by fire.

Her baby was dead.

"No, no, no," she whimpered and held the child to herself. Felt its weight and shape and dearly wished she could absorb it back into her womb. The thought did not seem strange to her. The loss of this life – that was strange.

She lowered her arms then, holding her baby in front of her. What had seemed terrifying at first revealed itself to be beautiful to her now. This tiny being, perfectly formed in every way, was more hers than any fat cherub of her earlier visions. She examined every part of her baby, marvelling at each discovery.

Not the least of which was her gender.

"Darling girl," she whispered through her tears, "I dreamt of you." She placed her own forehead gently, softly, on her daughter's. "I'm so sorry!" She cried quietly now, her tears falling on her daughter's deep red skin. She gently spread the tears over her child like a balm.

"I love you so much."

She caressed the peach fuzz hair on the tiny girl's head, ran her thumb over her little belly. Cradled her in her arms and brought her to her nose to take in her scent. Rummaged in the drawer for something to clamp her cord with and found a barrette that worked just fine. Then, finding her nail clippers, detached her from the placenta, which lay flat and dejected on the floor.

Free of her tether, her daughter was impossibly light.

"Let's warm you up," whispered Rose into her baby's tiny, perfect ear.

She swaddled her in a clean towel, lavender in colour, and soft. "This is your brother's favourite!" It was far too large, and Rose left the unused part of the towel hanging over her arm. Somehow, the weight it added to her child was comforting.

She didn't know how long she sat there, gazing at her baby's face, apologizing again and again, loving her, memorizing her every feature, but she knew she had passed out again when she awoke to a pounding on the door.

She recoiled at the shock of the noise and looked down at the bundle in her arms. Yes, it had been real. The child looked different now, her lips deep purple and her skin dry and papery.

Rose carefully reached for her lotion and, for the next several minutes, healed her baby in the only way she knew how. She was careful as she tried to soften her skin with the rose-scented cream. Taking care to look her last on each feature, every perfect detail, she made a terrible effort, too, to glance quickly over her bruises. Swaddling her again and kissing her forehead, Rose stood to open the door.

When she did, her husband was there. "It's about bloody time!" he shouted and stepped forward. He stopped suddenly and took in the scene behind Rose. "Holy Christ," he breathed, and then, "Da ty chto" as he noticed the little bundle in his wife's arms.

Rose stood still, saying nothing.

Her husband finally tore his gaze from his stillborn child and met the eyes of his wife. "It's dead."

321

And that was it. Those two words. They broke her. No onlooker would have seen it, but she felt it happen, like a thunderous crack inside her mind.

Viktor, for the only time in his life, seemed at a loss as to what to do. Finally, he reached out and took the baby. "Clean it up," he said as he motioned to the bathroom, "and then we'll bury it."

Rose couldn't move as she watched her daughter's murderer carrying her body away.

And then she cleaned the bathroom.

Alice saw it all; felt it as though it had happened to her. Rose showed her everything. She showed her in bits and pieces sometimes, and sometimes she showed her the whole thing. It was like a nightmare, but a nightmare that followed you everywhere. Alice asked Rose to stop, but Rose said there was only one way.

And today she had shown her how.

Alice didn't understand it all, but she was so desperate to appease the spirit that she followed the instructions. Truly, at this point, she couldn't tell whether she was dreaming or not. She just did what Rose told her to do, and when she couldn't, Rose used Alice's body to do it for her.

She tried to pretend it was just like before, but she couldn't pretend the cold away. And something else was different. Before, Rose had been quiet when Alice wasn't in the woods or at the clearing. When she arrived at the cabin today, though, Rose wasn't there waiting for her. Instead, she'd been with her the whole time. Not quiet, not ever anymore.

Rose was the one who reached out with Alice's right hand and took the axe off the wall. Alice watched it happening, fascinated by the experience. And then she'd felt it there, the wooden handle, the weight of the heavy head on one end, and knew her hand was hers again.

The next part was easy. She just needed to take a walk, as she used to. And bring Rose her meal because Greyson never brought them to her anymore.

Her legs were so cold as she followed the old trail that she fell a couple of times. Rose had helped her, then, by standing her up, just as she'd reached out her hand for the axe. She was grateful. The ground had been so hard and unforgiving. She didn't remember arriving at the clearing, but it had happened because now she was inside the little cabin. She wasn't shocked at not remembering; these days her memory was unreliable. It was normal for her. It's too bad it's not warmer in here, *she thought, and Rose showed her that it hadn't been warm back then, either.*

She didn't remember taking her jacket off, nor rolling up the left sleeve of her nightgown, but there she was, stooped over the counter at the end of the cabin, her left arm on the board like a piece of meat ready to be prepared for dinner. "Strange," she said.

And her other hand, still gripping the axe, but no longer hers, rose above her head.

Chapter 39 – Kathy

Kathy was biting her nails as she stared out the living room window to the quiet road beyond. Her foot bounced incessantly, her nerves shot.

"Ugh!" she exclaimed aloud, "I left work to be *helpful*, and here I sit, being *useless*!

She knew that wasn't fair. She was doing exactly what was required of her. It just felt - it was goddamn frustrating, that's what. She mentally reviewed everything that had happened since Max and Charis had gone into the woods.

She'd actually dialled the police as she watched the two of them disappear around the side of the house. Since it had occurred to her that they should have called them as soon as they saw that Alice had been in the house, Kathy had thought of little else. She wanted to get that accomplished first and foremost.

Her disappointment at the lacklustre reaction from the cop who answered her call had quickly resolved her guilt. She explained who she was and which case she was calling about and asked that someone come out to the house right away, as they were certain Alice had been there, but now she was nowhere to be found. At the lack of response from the cop, she went on to explain that her husband and a "friend of the family" had gone into the woods to find her.

"Good, good," was the cop's reply.

"Yeah, um, will someone be here soon?" Kathy had pushed.

"Well, here's the thing. As you probably know, Sergeant Stack was assigned this case, and seeing as he's out of commission for at least the rest of the day, we're pretty short-staffed, especially with the emergency at the shopping mall occupying the majority of the force."

Kathy shook her head. "Emergency?"

"Yes, ma'am. I'm afraid I can't go into detail -"

"No, no, that's alright. So, what you're saying is that you have nobody who can come out here to help us find our elderly grandma *who has dementia*?" Despite her efforts to remain calm, her voice had risen dramatically as she finished her question.

"No, wait now. I didn't say that. I just said we wouldn't be able to come right away. Once I'm able, I'll request a spare officer from the mall to go on out if things have at all calmed down."

The man's defensiveness had satisfied Kathy deeply. "Once you're able?" she repeated back to him.

"Yes, ma'am, after I'm done talking to you."

"Well, then, I won't keep you. I certainly wouldn't want the two of us to cause any further delay."

"Yes, ma'am. Thank you, ma'am. You should have an officer with you shortly."

"Thank you." Kathy very nearly hung up, but on second thought, decided to add some gas to the fire she'd just lit under this guy. "What's your name please, sir?"

"Oh, uh -" He cleared his throat. "This is Constable Spinny, Ma'am. I don't usually work the phones, but as I said, we're working with a bit of a skeleton crew today."

"Constable Spinny. Thank you for all your help. Just one more thing before we hang up."

"Yes, ma'am."

"Have you worked many cases like the one we have here? Missing elderly people in dangerously cold temperatures? I'm just wondering – I mean – do you know how they usually turn out? The family's pretty scared -"

"Oh, I understand. Of course. But I'm afraid I haven't worked a case like this before; I'm pretty new. And the cases we studied at the Academy -" he paused, "- well, let's just say I understand the seriousness of the situation you and your family are dealing with."

"I appreciate that, Constable Spinny."

He cleared his throat. "I'll radio the chief right away about the new developments you've reported."

"Thank you. Goodbye."

"Have a nice day, ma'am. I mean – I hope your day gets better. I mean – oh…"

"It's OK, Constable Spinny. Bye-bye, now." She hung up, feeling certain she'd sparked up that fire under Constable Spinny real good.

"Don't mess with Sydney Mines girls," she said, crediting her Cape Breton hometown for her fiery determination.

That taken care of, Kathy had found herself stalled, unsure of what to do next. Then she remembered Jack and Charis's visit to the back porch before they went off into the woods. (She'd thought they were coming in to talk to her before leaving and had been confused when they'd simply left again and sped off.) She wondered now what they'd found to spur them on, and she made her way out into the porch.

Hugging her sweater around herself in the sudden cold, she surveyed the tiny room quickly. "Wow, Jack's more organized than I'd imagined," she commented aloud, her breath a visible cloud as she spoke. Dancing a bit in her sock feet, she lamented her decision to forego her shoes as she took a look around. She thought of Alice in her nightgown and coat, her bare legs unprotected, and her stomach did a somersault.

Then she spotted it: a lone empty spot on the wall of tools. *An axe?* She wondered whether it had already been missing when Max and Charis had come in or whether they had decided to take it. Probably the former, she thought, her mind racing with possibilities.

She glanced around again before deciding her imagination wasn't helping her anxiety, then bounded through the door in long steps. Back in the kitchen, she flicked the electric teapot on as soon as she could reach it.

She made her tea in the silence of the house, again anxious to do something – anything – to take her mind off the waiting. Her mug in one hand, she went to the guest room she and Max had been sleeping in, intent on tidying up.

A text notification on her phone stopped her just as she was smoothing the quilt over the bed. She grabbed her phone, thinking *Max*, but thrilled to see Maggie's name on the display. Rather than open the text, she dialled her sister-in-law.

"Kath?" Maggie sounded tired and worried, which Kathy had expected.

"Maggie. You've landed already?"

"Yeah, actually about thirty minutes ago. We're just getting into the car now. The luggage took forever."

Kathy glanced at the clock on the bedside table. "Oh my God; it's past five o'clock! Oh no -" she turned to the window and observed the blazing pink and orange sunset in despair. "It's getting dark."

"Kathy, what's going on?"

Maggie's question brought Kathy's mind back from the woods. "She was here, Maggie. She was in the house."

"What? Wait – I'm putting you on speaker. Say that again."

"Hi everyone. Max and I came back to the house today to find -"

"Came *back?*" Zoe's voice. "I thought Max was there all day?"

"No; long story, but he had to take Walter to the hospital." This was met with a cacophony of exclamations and questions from the other end. She hurriedly continued, "He's OK, he's OK! Just a concussion, but he's admitted for the night. So, they were gone for the later part of the morning but left the door unlocked, just in case."

A jumbled mess of acknowledgement and understanding from them now, much calmer.

"Anyway, I left work to pick up Max from the hospital, and when we got back, we saw someone had been here. We've assumed it was Alice. The police know, and Max and Charis left for the clearing about twenty minutes ago." There were grumblings of confusion from the other end, and Kathy realized she'd just dropped a lot of new stuff on them. "Wow, that's a lot to take in, huh?" she offered weakly.

Jack's voice rang loud and clear. "Kathy, did you say 'Charis'?"

Then Maggie: "Charis, the psychic lady from Ottawa Charis?"

328

Kathy took a deep breath, "Yes. Again, long story but suffice it to say that she and Max talked last week and she made him promise to call her if anything happened involving an older woman –"

"What? She knew this was going to happen?" Zoe was clearly freaking out.

"No. In fact, she wasn't sure of anything except that she needed Max to call her. Guys, please don't be upset; Max was kind of knocked sideways by their conversation. He didn't know how to take it. But he did call her as he'd promised, and she dropped everything and got here." She paused, desperate to know whether she was worrying them more or being helpful.

"That's – guys, that's kind of amazing," she heard Maggie say, and Kathy exhaled the breath she didn't even know she was holding.

"Anyway, they're headed back there now, and I'm at the house. The Wolfville police have been doing all the checks there and keeping the Kingston police in the loop. Oh, and before taking Walter to the hospital, Max and he checked to see whether anyone had been to the Maplestone house up the street – there'd been no-one. And there should be someone from the police station here soon; I called to update the Kingston police, so they're up to speed on what's going on here, too."

Kathy heard Sam for the first time. "Sounds like everyone's doing everything they can, Kathy. Thank you."

Kathy smiled, utterly relieved, and said, "What about you guys? No problems with the flight?"

"No, it went almost unbelievably smoothly," Maggie offered, "and if Jack keeps driving like he is currently, we'll be at the house very soon."

"I can't blame you, Jack. Just be safe, guys."

Another jumble of their voices, in agreement this time.

"I love you guys," Kathy added, surprising herself, and welling up when they all echoed her love back to her.

Hanging up, she was suddenly overcome with exhaustion. She allowed herself to flop onto the couch and looked out the window for the millionth time that day. The colours of the sunset were fading quickly into hues of grey and deep blue. "*One* flashlight…" She shook her head. They could use their phones, too, of course, but that drained batteries fast. Rising quickly and mentally shoving her exhaustion aside, she went to rummage through the drawers in the kitchen again. "Just one more," she begged, her voice loud in the quiet room. She paused and looked around, deciding to flick on some more lights in the darkening house.

Twenty minutes later, she was harried and frustrated as she stood in the middle of the kitchen, taking in the chaos she'd created around her. "Shit!" she exclaimed. "And no freakin' flashlight to show for it!" Without pause (and with a fervour equal to that with which she had trashed the room), she got to work and cleaned it up.

At the sound of tires on the driveway, she bounded to the front door, expecting Constable Spinny's spare cop, but was elated to see Sam's sedan, Jack already emerging from the driver's seat.

She stepped into her boots and descended the porch steps. Jack walked right past her, his face a mask of desperate determination.

"Jack!" she exclaimed, running after him and turning her cell on. He stopped and turned, clearly unhappy to be doing so. "Here, take this," she said, turning the flashlight app on as she handed him her phone.

He took it, his face blank as he registered her offer, and then hugged her fiercely, saying, "Thank you so much for everything," in her ear. He bolted toward the path in the woods, her phone lighting his way.

By the time she had returned to the car, the remaining three travellers had emerged. Maggie immediately embraced her, crying and whispering "Thank you" to her, much as her husband had just done. Kathy's tears were back now, too. Suddenly Zoe was wrapping her arms around them, saying, "Let me in on this hug-cry, girls," and they giggled through their tears. Finally, Sam, overcome with emotion, joined in, wrapping his arms around them and crying, too. When they finally separated, they were wiping their eyes and laughing a little.

Zoe perked up and looked at Kathy. "Oh! After we talked to you, I called Martin. He said the police had been to see him, and he's been scouring Wolfville since then."

Maggie sniffed, still recovering, and said, "Poor guy. He sounded so wrecked."

"You know he doesn't see us often; Mom was no exception to that rule," Zoe replied, and they were all silent for a moment.

"Where's Jack?" Zoe asked, suddenly anxious.

"You didn't see? He went straight for the woods!" Kathy replied.

"Shit. I'm going, too." Zoe started off but immediately turned back. "It's fucking dark."

Kathy couldn't help but laugh. "Use your cell flashlight."

"Good call. You guys coming?"

Kathy answered first. "I'm going to stay. I promised I would, and the police aren't here yet."

Zoe nodded. "Makes sense. Maggie?"

Maggie looked thoughtful, then blank. Then she raised a finger, turned unceremoniously to her left and vomited loudly into the snow. Kathy, Zoe and Sam were momentarily frozen with shock, and then all three of them were panicking and asking Maggie if she was alright.

Maggie stood, wiping her mouth with the back of her glove. "Phew! I've been holding that in since we took off in Cuba!"

The group broke into nervous laughter, and Zoe hugged her sister-in-law.

Sam spoke up. "Maybe Maggie should hang back here while we go traipsing into the woods."

Zoe nodded quickly in agreement, then looked thoughtful for a moment.

"Don't you puke too!" Kathy exclaimed.

"Ha! No, actually I was just thinking that maybe you should stay back too, Sam. Fewer people might be better for Mom if - *when* we find her back there."

Sam looked concerned, his face shadowed further by the porch light that had automatically switched on with the increasing dark. "I don't like you going through the woods on your own," he said, his voice low. He sounded defeated, anticipating Zoe's reaction.

"Looks like I won't have to!" she said triumphantly as a police cruiser turned into the driveway.

Chapter 40 – Reinforcements

The cruiser lights still on, a hulking beast of a man exited the passenger side door and, not stopping, pointed to the back yard. "That where I need to go?"

"Yes!" answered Maggie, still somewhat breathless.

Kathy piped up, "There's a small bridge at the back and a path leading to the clearing." She threw her hands up and started jogging. "I'll show you."

Zoe bolted after them, calling "I'm coming!" and they vanished into the dark. Maggie and Sam turned to see a much smaller officer now exiting the driver's side. She approached them, her hand extended.

"Hi, everyone. I'm Detective Frost, and that was Constable Lewis. We were updated by Constable Spinny after he spoke to - you?" She turned to Maggie, then Zoe.

"Nope, that was Kathy," Maggie answered, gesturing in the direction that Kathy had just run with the other cop.

A quick nod from the detective as she continued. "I apologize for the delay; it's been an unusually busy day for us."

Mumbles of "That's OK" and "Thank you for coming" from Maggie and Sam as Kathy jogged back and rejoined them, breathing hard.

The Detective put a hand up. "And we have some news: the Wolfville Branch called us about forty minutes ago to let us know they could confirm that Mrs. Ridgewood took a taxi – here – at approximately nine-thirty this morning."

Maggie's hand flew to her mouth. Kathy put her arm around Maggie, squeezing slightly.

"That's a long time for her to be out in this," Sam said, gesturing around them at the snow.

"Agreed. Hence Constable Lewis's haste." The detective held up her hand again as Sam started talking. "Now, good folks, I know you're scared for your relative, and that's understandable. But let's remember that she appears to have been inside the house -" she gestured again, her motions sure, "- for at least part of the morning."

Sam nodded, but Maggie was not comforted. "That was hours and hours ago, Detective! And we don't know with any confidence that she's in that cabin. And even if she is, it's not heated!"

"Even then, the building itself will do a lot to protect Mrs. Ridgewood -"

"Alice," Maggie broke in.

"Sorry; Alice." The detective touched Maggie's arm and lowered her voice to a comforting monotone. Kathy was impressed with her demeanour and couldn't help but be comforted as well as she continued. "Look, I've seen people come out of worse, virtually unscathed! At least Mrs. – Alice – is wearing a coat and shoes. Seniors with dementia who tend to wander often do so without thinking to dress for the weather." She raised her eyebrows and looked at all three in turn, her hand still resting on Maggie's arm. "We don't know anything yet, folks, but panicking isn't going to help her. Let's try and stay positive, at the very least."

Kathy, slightly girl-crushing on this woman, nodded and answered first. "Yes. That's best." She looked at Maggie and Sam. "You two must be wiped out. I mean, you're supposed to be in Cuba right now!"

Maggie slumped slightly and nodded.

Detective Frost pointed at the little puddle of vomit in the snow. "Is this – er – recent?"

Maggie turned and shuffled her boots in the snow, partially covering her mess.

"She's pregnant," Sam explained.

"OK, all the more reason to get inside, put the kettle on and settle in a bit while we wait."

Once inside, Detective Frost joined Kathy in the kitchen after leaving Maggie and Sam on the couch. "I'm going to update the station, and if they're not back by the time I'm done," she paused to nod at the darkened window, "I'm going after them."

Kathy felt a surge of fear course through her. It was almost completely dark now. She allowed herself the thought that had been nagging at her since the arrival of Maggie and the others: *they'd be back by now if they hadn't found* something *back there.*

Chapter 41 – Max and Charis

At the speed they were carrying, Charis and Max burst into the clearing quite suddenly, and Charis stopped abruptly. Max, whose mind was whirling, slammed into her and they both fell hard into the snow.

A mortified Max sprang up and helped her to stand, apologizing profusely. But as soon as she was back up, Charis walked on, slowly now, her gaze fixed on the small building just ahead. "This is it," she whispered, stopping to look back at Max.

He just nodded as he absentmindedly wiped the snow from his pants, his eyes fixed on the cabin.

Charis pressed a finger to her lips and gestured at a set of tracks in the snow. He studied it, a rising excitement in his belly. They were weird. He could see the small prints of Alice's shoes in the snow; those were obvious. But there was a strange pattern of marks around the whole line of prints which led, predictably, straight to the cabin.

Charis, noticing his confusion, positioned herself behind Max, trying to see what he was scowling at. She took another step closer, squatting to observe the markings around them. On both sides of the foot holes, all the way to the cabin, were lighter, swishing marks in the snow. She looked back at Max, pointing at them. "Her nightgown?"

Max inhaled deeply and nodded. "I think I know what that's from, too." He was pointing to another mark on the right side of the rest, a fairly straight line in the snow, punctuated at each step by a deeper plunge.

"Shit," Charis muttered as she realized what Alice had dragged successfully to her destination.

The axe.

She rubbed her hands together and took a second to figure out how to phrase what she needed to say next.

Max made a move toward the small building, but Charis held her hands out. "Wait," she whispered.

He did, too tired to protest or even ask why.

"You can't -" She paused, trying to form her words in a way he'd agree with, rather than balk at. She could be blunt at times. It had often proved ineffective.

"Don't you dare tell me - I can't go in there?" It had started as a statement and then petered out into a question.

"Shhh!" Her hands motioned up and down in an effort to quiet him. "Max. You have to trust me."

He took a step back and looked hard at her.

"Please," she added.

"You'd better be right."

"I am," she whispered, her face smoothing in relief as she backed away from him and then toward their destination.

As she turned around and continued, careful now to tread *beside* Alice's trail in the snow rather than over it, Max allowed himself a moment to breathe. Aside from Charis's progress through the snow, he could hear the frozen branches swaying creakily behind him and the cold air soughing through the pines. His chest still heaved as he caught his breath, and he felt uncomfortably damp with sweat inside his heavy jacket. The sunset sky was beautiful, but menacing, too, as they were plunged increasingly into darkness.

Charis, having reached the cabin, now waved at him to get his attention. Apparently, she'd modified her plan. She pointed to him, then to the snow beside her, then put her finger to her mouth again. He nodded, understanding that she wanted him close, but quiet, and began to walk toward the cabin as she approached the door.

She was more than a little nervous. So many "what-if's" and "how-should-I's" threatened to shatter her confidence, and the least pressing of them occurred to her now: should she open the door or knock? It wasn't Alice's reaction that concerned her; it was Rose's.

The entire time she'd been travelling toward this moment from when she'd gotten the call from Max this morning, Charis had been painfully aware that she could no longer connect to the ghost attached to Alice and Maggie. The ghost she now knew to be Rose Maplestone had become familiar to her. And the inability to connect would make sense if Rose's every ounce of energy was focused on controlling Alice. There was no way to share this with Max – or anyone! – without having to answer a zillion questions, so she'd kept it to herself, inwardly molding her decisions around it.

At the sound of Max's approach, she put a hand up for him to stop, which he did. She made a mental note to be extra nice to this poor guy when this was all over.

The distraction had made her decision for her, and it was now or never.

She tried to turn the knob, simultaneously pushing the door in her sudden haste, and was perplexed to find the knob frozen solid, not giving a millimetre. However, the door scraped open into the cabin, and she stumbled inward. *See? she thought, psychics can be surpr* -

The scream cut her thought off, and she found herself crouching, her hands protectively covering her ears. She heard Max move outside and held one hand out to him. His grunt of frustration was barely audible.

Would it go on forever? She replaced her hand on her ear and looked to the end of the little cabin. There was Alice, stooped over a makeshift wood counter beneath a dingy window. Her left hand appeared stuck somehow to the wood surface, and the right hand gripped the axe at the end of the wide arc of her arm above her head. Her head was turned toward Charis, her eyes fixed steadily on her, and her mouth was stretched down as she screamed. A lone candle was lit in the corner of the counter, and its flame elongated the shadows on and around the old woman grotesquely.

"Alice!" Charis shouted. "Alice, please stop!"

"No, *you* stop," answered Alice, but now Charis was able to identify why the scream had sounded so strange. There were two voices coming from Alice's mouth.

"Alice -"

"*No!*" screeched the figure at the end of the cabin, her mouth drawing up at the corners in a bone-chilling, gaping smile as the rest of her mouth hung down, a bit of spittle on her lower lip reflecting the candlelight.

Charis, remaining in her crouch so as not to appear threatening, tried to answer calmly, but her voice broke as she replied, "No? not Alice?"

"Noooot Aliiiiiice," the woman replied with her double voice, drawing out the vowels until Charis thought she would go mad. The corners of the woman's mouth were still smiling, seemingly frozen in place, even as the rest of the mouth worked itself around her words.

Charis made an effort not to scream. *Get your shit together!* she shouted inwardly. *You've seen – well, you haven't seen* this *before, but –* Her internal pep talk ended there as the stooped woman made as if to lunge at her, her arms remaining in their awkward positions, one flat to her elbow on the counter and the other brandishing the axe above her head, as she mock-stepped in Charis's direction with a yell. A double yell.

Charis screamed despite herself, squeezing her eyes shut, her hands splayed in front of her in a subconscious effort to protect herself.

Somehow, the resulting double laughter that filled the little room was far more terrifying than any scream that had come before.

Charis opened her eyes and studied the figure.

Then something happened; two things, actually. Alice's eyes fluttered and started to roll back in her head. *She's going to pass out!* Charis thought, excitedly. *That could end this now!* But the flash of hope was dashed immediately when Alice's legs buckled and straightened beneath her and her eyes opened wide, the fear behind them obvious.

"Alice!" Charis called, hoping to reach the woman so she could regain full control of her body. In those few seconds, Charis had witnessed both the souls inhabiting the body in front of her and realized that Rose's hold on Alice's body was not complete. Alice was still in there, as exhausted and terrified as she was.

"No Alice!" the mouth screamed again, its corners having seemingly been knocked out of their eerie upcurve by the near-faint and sudden jolt of its body.

"OK! OK – no Alice!" Charis said, slowly rising now and signalling again to Max to stay put. That poor man.

"Only Rose!" she cried, the double voices quieter now.

"OK. Rose. I'm sorry. I've seen you. Remember? You showed me some things?" Charis tried to sound as casual as possible as she noted the tremor in the arm holding the axe and realized that what she had taken for shadows around Alice's mouth had indeed been a darkening of the skin, and while it was too dark to discern the colour, she knew that it was blue.

Alice was fading.

The woman squinted at her then shook her head in apparent confusion. "I have to get my baby." She focused again on the left forearm on the counter and planting her feet.

Charis jumped. "No!"

Alice/Rose jerked at Charis's shout and even stumbled a bit. Charis's thoughts raced. She could motion Max in now; they could overpower her, and Rose's tenuous hold on Alice's failing body would be severed.

She very nearly did it.

But then it wouldn't be over. It would keep happening again and again until it was resolved.

"Rose!" Charis shouted, an idea sparking in her desperate mind.

Rose looked her way again, through Alice's eyes, but said nothing. The right arm wavered but remained poised above her head.

"Rose," she said calmly now, conspiratorially, "I know where you can find your baby."

The woman gasped, that tremulous right arm suddenly falling to her side, and Charis tensed, imagining the head of the axe burying itself in the flesh of Alice's leg. She breathed out in unabashed relief when it merely swung heavily beside her calf.

Rose pointed the axe at Charis and shook it. "Who do you think you are?" she asked with lowered dual voices that reached inside Charis and squeezed her heart.

Rose's gaze didn't waver as she looked at Charis silently. Charis thought that if she reached out toward that axe, she might be able to touch the cold metal of the business end.

"It's alright! I'm a friend. I want to help you."

"*You* want to help *Alice*!"

"Yes! Yes, I want to help Alice, too! I want to help both of you, Rose!"

Charis stepped forward.

"No!" the woman shrieked and swung the axe above her head again, turning her head to find her target, still solidly on the counter.

"No!" Charis screamed again, but it was too late. It was as though the woman was powerless to stop the path of the heavy-headed tool. It dug itself rather pathetically into the surface of the counter, several inches from its intended destination.

Alice's body wouldn't be useful to this ghost for very much longer. And likely not useful to her own ghost, either.

Charis took another step forward as the other woman struggled pitifully to extract the axe from the counter. Interestingly, her left arm remained where it was, dutifully awaiting its fate.

That must take a lot of energy to hold, thought Charis. Then, still trying to be calm but with an obvious edge to her voice, she tried again. "Rose, Alice doesn't have your baby."

"What?" It was so quiet it would have been calming if it hadn't been said with two voices.

"Remember, Rose? Even when you did this the first time, you didn't find your baby."

The woman paused her efforts and looked at Charis. "That's because - that's because he stopped me."

"Your husband?" Charis ventured, fearfully traversing the shaky ground of their conversation.

Rose shook Alice's head now and then hung it low, her hair draped over her face. Charis thought she saw the light glint off a tear falling to the ground.

"No, not *him.* My boy. I had to stop because it scared him."

"Yes. You stopped because you were a good mother."

She sniffled and nodded but said nothing more.

"You can be a good mother to your baby, too. She's waiting for you."

Alice's face twisted in Rose's agony. "No. I can't find her. My beautiful girl!" She cried harder, her voice breaking and howling alternately, and Charis was shocked to realize the two voices were separating themselves.

"I can help you find her. You just have to let me." Charis ventured another step, and, for the first time since she'd entered the cabin, the woman opposite her straightened, her left arm hanging easily at her side.

What Charis hadn't noticed was that she had stepped completely out of view of the increasingly desperate Max, who was fighting his urge to rush into the cabin. The voices had gotten so low he couldn't tell what was happening, and when Charis stepped out of his view, his resolve broke. Bleating a plaintive *"Alice!"* he burst through the door.

Rose screamed in fear and ripped the axe from the counter with an apparent surge of strength. She brandished it above her head again with a primal scream of effort, and Charis stumbled backward and fell helplessly to the hard floor, pain shooting through her hip bones and lower back.

Rose/Alice looked briefly toward Charis, then back at Max. *"Get away!"* she howled at him, crying pathetically between her screams. Max, confused and simultaneously transfixed by the alternating screaming and crying, each transforming the helpless body from standing (when screaming) to collapsing forward into a trembling mess (when crying), stumbled backward himself, only avoiding falling by banging into the wall behind him.

Charis watched the two inhabitants of Alice's body fight for control of it and, gathering all the strength she had left, screamed, *"Aliiiiiiiice!"* again.

Unknown to them, Jack, in his crazed journey toward the cabin, paused as the sound of his mother's name reverberated through the cold air. It sounded so far away. *"Mom!"* he shouted in answer.

Which slowed the pace of Constable Lewis and Zoe, who had just entered the woods.

While the three were reacting to Charis's desperate plea to Alice, Max was, too.

Adrenaline surged through him like wildfire, and he leapt forward, not thinking. Just acting, finally.

Observing the approach of the man whom Rose saw as her husband, madness indeed in his eyes, Rose/Alice raised the axe above her head once more, screaming, *"You won't take her away from me again!"*

Without a pause, she placed her left arm back on the counter and brought the axe down, and Charis screamed again as she saw the brutal strength behind it now.

Max reached for the axe with both hands, mid-leap. He missed his target, but as he fell, his outstretched fingers found her legs and grabbed on tightly.

The axe, having first been jarred by the impact of Max and then further thrown off-course as Alice started to fall, found three inches of wood and half an inch of forearm flesh.

It remained in the counter as Alice's body collapsed like a doll's onto Max, who instinctively released her legs and managed to catch her mid-fall, her head bouncing solidly off his solar plexus and winding him.

"Alice!" Charis exclaimed and crawled across to them, wincing at the continued pain in her back.

She sat back on her feet as she reached them and leaned down to see Max, whose head was resting on the floor as he struggled to regain his breath. "Max! Are you OK?"

"Yes," he croaked. "Is she?"

Charis touched the soft cheek of the unconscious woman still lying on Max's chest. Getting no response, she anxiously placed her head on the woman's chest, listening for her heart.

It was there, beating fast and strong, and Charis whooped with unbidden glee. Max raised his head as Charis turned her attention to Alice's left arm. Her groan at what she saw told him he needed to get up.

Gingerly moving Alice off his chest and sitting up to move the bag off his back and open it, Max glanced at Alice's arm, only to find her wound to be covered (and not gently, judging by the indents around Charis's fingers) by Charis's hand. Mid-forearm, it had already spilled more precious blood than he'd hoped, but he held onto the comforting thought that at least it was her forearm rather than her wrist or her hand. It may have been only flesh that had been damaged, rather than bone. The fact that she'd so easily slid away from the axe fuelled his hope.

He took a blanket from the bag and placed it beneath Alice's head, then found the pair of socks they'd packed, all the way at the bottom. Moving quickly and wordlessly, he stretched the length of one sock around Alice's arm, tying it between her elbow and Charis's hand.

He paused as he studied her hand again, then looked at Charis.

"I don't want to move," she said, her fear showing all over her face.

"It's OK," he said. "Wait." He sprang up and ripped off his coat, then removed his t-shirt in one smooth movement.

Charis merely watched him, trusting that he had a plan.

Max tore at the t-shirt with his teeth, then from the resulting hole ripped it into thick strips. He threw his coat back on and knelt beside the women. Readying the first strip, he said, "Let go." Charis yanked her hand out of the way, and Max quickly wound the strip of fabric around the arm and over the wound once, twice, then tied it securely. He watched it for two seconds, repeated the process with a second strip, then said, "Grab the other blanket from the bag."

Charis jumped to get the blanket. Once she'd handed it to Max, she went back for the flashlight she'd spotted. They'd need it. She looked fervently out the door, and her stomach dropped at the darkness that had fallen. She glanced at her watch; it was nearing six o'clock. She watched as Max cocooned Alice's limp frame in the blanket, working fast and quietly. She was impressed. When he was done, Max made to lift her, but Charis stopped him. "Wait!"

Max sat back. Alice had opened her eyes. Charis knelt beside her, smoothing her hair and saying, "It's OK, Alice. We've got you."

The old woman tried to talk, then, failing, cleared her throat. "Can you still help me find her?"

Charis felt the hairs on the back of her neck stand up. "Rose? Is that you?"

"All I ever wanted was to find her. To get her back."

Charis took a sharp breath in as she realized she was hearing one voice. Just one.

"You can be with her now," Charis whispered. "All you have to do is – let go."

"But what if I let go and she's not there? And then I've lost her forever."

"You'll never find her here, Rose. You're supposed to be with her now. She died, and -" she stroked Alice's hair again and couldn't help but say, "Oh, you're so cold."

"My baby," cried Rose, tears welling in Alice's eyes again.

"I know you're in pain. I can't imagine what losing your child must have been like. But *she* is no longer in pain, Rose, and you don't have to be, either. You died, too, do you remember? You can be together. Close your eyes."

She looked afraid for a moment, almost panicked. But then she closed Alice's eyes, slowly.

"Rose, do you feel a pull? Something pulling you to somewhere else?"

"Always. I always feel it. Sometimes, when I'm tired, I nearly slip toward it. But it will take me away from her. I can't go!"

"Oh, sweetheart. You must have suffered terribly in life."

Alice's face contracted with Rose's pain as the tears flowed.

"Rose. Your baby is there. All your loved ones are there. They are pulling you."

She opened her eyes, looking disbelievingly at Charis. "How do I know you're right?"

"I know it's hard to trust. But I promise. I promise with all the love and sincerity you didn't get when you had a body of your own. She is there."

Alice's eyes flashed – hope? – before they closed again. "Hold my hand," she said, the request given so quietly it was barely there at all.

For a moment, Charis panicked. Max had swaddled Alice, her hands effectively bound to her sides. Hoping it would be enough, she found the lump of Alice's hand through the blanket and gripped it clumsily. "Go to her," she whispered into Alice's ear.

And she was gone.

Charis had felt her go just as surely as she felt the presence of Max behind her and Alice, unconscious, beneath her. She swung around to Max, who was frozen in place, the paths of his tears marking his face. "Take her, quickly!"

Max jumped up immediately and crouched to lift Alice's swaddled, unconscious body. "That was the most amazing thing I've ever seen." He looked at Charis as she flicked the flashlight on.

She nodded. "Let's just make sure Rose isn't the only one where she's supposed to be, shall we?" Charis stood and exited the cabin, Max on her heels, the little candle still flickering in the corner.

They moved as quickly as they could in the deep snow, following the tracks from their approach, and then faster when they reached the path in the woods.

Max wasn't thinking; for perhaps the only time in his life, his mind was blank as he routed all his energy into his straining arms and legs. She wasn't heavy, but he had spent all of his daily allowance of adrenaline well before now. He was going on sheer panic and determination.

Charis navigated with care, keeping tabs on Max behind her and speeding up or slowing down according to how closely he followed her. The flashlight bobbed in her hand but effectively lit their way through the quiet wood.

A stray thought entered Max's mind. A warning: he would collapse soon. "Shit," he grunted, finally acknowledging the warm numbness that had come over his legs and was working at his arms.

Charis instantly slowed, a spike of panic reaching her heart. He wouldn't make it. "Max? Stay with me, Max. We're going more slowly now." She cheered him on, but he made no reply, his feet shuffling behind her. She moved to her left, knowing Alice's head was on that side, and manoeuvred herself into position beside Max, bracing her right arm around his waist and her left beneath his, taking as much weight as she could. The effect on her own already flagging strength was staggering. They slowed again, only managing to walk awkwardly. The path truly wasn't wide enough for them to be comfortable as they were, but Charis knew that if she hadn't helped, both Alice and Max would be on the ground.

The heat resulting from Max's efforts was palpable through his jacket, and his breath rasped in his throat. Desperation coursed through them both, but neither had the strength to voice it.

But then Charis squeezed his waist and pulled him to a stop. "Wait!" she managed, breathing fast and heavy.

Max stopped, his knees buckling at the reprieve, focusing solely on staying upright. And then he heard it, too. Footsteps coming toward them.

"Hello?" they both shouted into the dark, their voices hoarse, but stronger together.

Like Alice and Rose, Charis thought before she could stop herself.

"Max!" came the reply, loud but sounding as desperate as they felt.

"Jack!"

Charis nearly collapsed in relief. The flashlight, still awkwardly grasped in her left hand, shone shakily ahead of them, and they both merely breathed as they stared ahead, waiting for Jack to appear. When he did, and he took her from them, they both fell to their knees on the cold, hard ground and sobbed.

Chapter 42 – Jack

Jack's heart hammered painfully in his chest. He cried, "Mom!" again as he took the blanket-wound body of his mother from Max and the petite woman before him. "Oh, my God!" he exclaimed, her weight and expressionless face striking fear into his heart.

From below him now, where Charis and Max had simultaneously collapsed in a heap of tearful exhaustion and relief, Max croaked, "She's alive. She has a wound on her left forearm."

Jack put his lips to his mother's forehead, searching for warmth and, thank God, finding it. "Are you two OK?" he demanded, every muscle in his body poised in readiness to turn around and keep running, this time with his mother safe in his arms.

"Yes," breathed Charis. "Go!"

That was all he needed. He went.

Securely cradled in his strong arms, the next part of Alice's unconscious journey back home was markedly quicker and more stable. Her son's construction worker's arms, combined with his love for her, ensured that. It was only several minutes into his cellphone-lit sprint that he started to feel tired.

"Shit!" he muttered, in an effort to snap himself out of it and focus on his goal. He thought only of his anxious family waiting for them back at the house. He thought of dialling 911 but couldn't manage the dexterity it required.

He was mercifully unaware that he was slowing, his physique failing to match his determination. It was only when he saw a light bobbing toward him that he acknowledged his diminished pace.

"Jack?" He heard Zoe's voice, and his heart sank. She wouldn't be able to carry their mother. She could help, though. That would have to do.

Before he could call out to his sister, another voice cut through the air: "Mr. Ridgewood, this is Constable Lewis. Can you hear me?"

"Yes," he called, his arms like noodles as he slowed further. "I'm here! Please hurry."

Two people finally rushed toward him from where the path straightened out toward the house. He saw that now and was glad; he hadn't done so badly, after all. He took a moment to kiss Alice's forehead again, comforted by the increased warmth he felt there.

A moment was all he had, for a hulking mammoth of a cop was taking Alice out of his arms with the ease of picking up a sack of bread. Zoe reached him next and barrelled into him, squeezing him with all her might as she cried.

"She's OK," he said, and put his arms around Zoe with some effort; they felt a hundred pounds heavier. Each.

"Thank God," Zoe breathed and stepped back, studying him in the light of her own phone. "Are you OK?"

"Yes." He looked at the cop. "Constable Lewis?"

"Yes, sir."

"Please get my mother to the house while I call for an ambulance."

"No need," Lewis replied as he jogged away from them. "It was only about ten minutes behind us."

Jack and Zoe had begun walking the rest of the way, their arms around each other, when Jack remembered the puddle of Max and Charis he'd left behind.

"Max!" he called back down the trail, as loudly as he could manage.

Seconds later, they heard a faint "We're coming."

Jack and Zoe didn't wait.

Chapter 43 – Maggie

Maggie moved about the room, humming and gathering Jack's dirty work clothes. A mixture of emotions spun through her as she went about this mundane task. So much had happened, so much had been threatened, and yet here she was, doing laundry.

And pregnant.

Her stomach did a somersault at the thought. Today was the ultrasound. She was only doing laundry to keep herself busy until Jack returned from work to drive them both to the appointment. They were planning on seeing Alice afterward, who, after recovering in intensive care over the past weekend, had been admitted to the psych ward for observation.

But things for Alice were hopeful. Zoe's report from her visit earlier in the week was made with much relief. Alice's wound had not broken any bones in her arm. Surgery had been needed to repair muscle, tendon and tissue, but it had gone smoothly. She was recovering well and taking antibiotics to stave off possible infection; given her condition, the doctors agreed she could use the added protection.

Her hypothermia was – strange. The doctors couldn't explain it; she'd been exposed to the elements for more than 10 hours, and had exhibited the majority of symptoms for what they called "advanced hypothermia" – loss of consciousness, pale/blueish skin, slowed breathing – but one thing didn't add up: her heart rate. From the moment Charis had placed her head on Alice's chest to listen for her heart, to the ambulance ride vitals, to her transfer vitals when she was moved to the psych ward three days later, Alice's heart had beaten strong, true and at a healthy pace, even for a woman her age without hypothermia!

The doctors were at a loss.

The family was just grateful.

Charis had spent Friday night at the Ridgewood house before flying home on Saturday. After she and Max had given their account of what had happened, the family had showered her not only with more than enough money to cover both flights but with love and gratitude as well. She, too, had mentioned her surprise and delight when she'd listened to Alice's heart that first time, saying that it *should* have been slow, even weak.

But then, there'd been the strong presence of Rose until Charis had helped her move on. Charis was sure the ghost had fortified Alice in some way. Though Rose's actions had seemed malevolent, they'd come from a soul tortured by the pain of loss and lingering too long between planes. One who'd suffered great torment in life and, in her effort to fix it after she died, had twisted it up into a desperate and dangerous thing – something that drove her and clouded her vision, effectively rooting her in her own private hell.

The family had understood, touched by Charis's explanation, though Max and Jack could not shake their anger entirely. Max had been there but hadn't seen everything Charis had. He'd only heard the screams and seen the bloody end of the confrontation. He hadn't seen the desperate fear of Rose shining through Alice's eyes as she made the terrifying decision to let go. And they still didn't have all the pieces to the puzzle. It was hard to understand the wrath of the spirit when they couldn't fully understand from whence it came. Alice – Alice might know. They had all agreed to let Alice tell her story in her own time, but since then, she'd made great strides in recovering, and Zoe's visit to her on the psych ward had been very reassuring. In fact, Zoe had reported that a very happy and peaceful Alice had received her on that day. She'd said she couldn't remember ever seeing her mother so content.

Even more surprising, Zoe said that Martin had called her to talk about everything that had happened *and* had visited Alice on the weekend.

"Big changes from such a scary time," Zoe had said, and they'd agreed, both overwhelmed and happy at Zoe's news.

Maggie only wished Alice had shed more light on what had happened. Zoe had reported the bits and pieces that did come through – the gradual taking over of her body, the cold she'd felt, and strange ideas about her hand and how it could get Rose her baby back.

It was valuable information, but only raised more questions for Maggie. Max had brought up the paperwork Walter had on how Rose had been found in front of their house before being admitted to the psych ward herself. He vowed to check up on the old cop that day and ask him for details once again. Hopefully, he'd be more successful this time.

Maggie shook her head at all that had gone on.

Max and Kathy had departed Friday night after the group had reviewed the events together. Max was clearly exhausted yet bolstered by the gratitude of the family when Charis had lauded his quick actions to save Alice after she'd collapsed in the cabin.

Something else had quieted Max. When Maggie had pressed him as they got ready to leave, he'd shaken his head, saying, "I just can't stop thinking about what would have happened if I hadn't burst in there when I did. Charis had been so sure that I shouldn't make myself known, and now I understand why." Visions of Alice/Rose's reaction when he appeared flitted through his mind. "I'll never doubt that woman again."

Maggie had embraced him, saying, "Charis herself said you were a hero in there, Max. I believe in my heart that it happened the way it was supposed to."

Max had snickered. "That's so cliché," he said, a little smile on his face, and Maggie released him, having buoyed him up again.

It had always been her role, and she felt honoured to fulfill it.

Charis's departure the following day had been emotional. This woman was still such a stranger to Maggie, but she felt as though she'd known her forever. She was so grateful to her and no longer unsure of her abilities, only glad of them. She also really *liked* Charis and felt their connection wouldn't end with her departure.

Maggie laughed out loud now as she remembered the group taking turns to give their statements to Constable Lewis, who took extra time to speak to Charis, Max and Jack about everything they had experienced during the search for and rescue of Alice. Detective Frost had gone back to the station, promising to update Walter as soon as he was well enough.

Jack's statement was the shortest; it had covered only the middle section of the desperate run through the woods.

Max and Charis had spoken to Constable Lewis in the living room for nearly an hour as the rest of the family drank tea and hot chocolate at the kitchen table. On their walk back to the house, they had agreed to be completely open about their experiences. (After all, Walter had been aware of all of the circumstances surrounding the house and the people in it; they weren't about to start hiding things now.)

Lewis had listened with interest, writing notes and asking questions as they went. When they were finished, he shrugged. "I know how easy it would have been for both of you just to tell me that

359

you'd found an elderly, senile woman in a cabin in the middle of the woods. And while we would have been satisfied with that, especially considering we got her back alive, it would have left a lot of unanswered questions. So, thank you both for being so frank."

Relieved, Max had reached out his hand to Lewis, who shook it with both of his own. "Thank you," he said.

"Good job tonight, Mr. East. Without your quick work, we might not have such a happy ending to this story."

Emotionally and physically exhausted, tears welled in Max's eyes as he nodded gratefully to the cop then went to find the comforting embrace of his wife.

Charis, who'd never imagined being so openly received after telling such a tale, remained on the couch, gazing on the constable with a new light in her eyes.

Lewis sat back down and turned to her. "So. You're a psychic."

Maggie had watched as the two continued to chat, each obviously dazzled by the other. Before driving off in her rental the next day, Charis had taken both of Maggie's hands and said, "Constable Lewis – Fred, actually. Fred is his name, isn't that adorable? Anyway, he has family in Ottawa!" Her eyes sparkled. Maggie had laughed and hugged her, elated at this little unexpected gift after such a difficult time.

She left the full basket beside the basement door. (Rose might have been at rest, but Maggie was still hesitant to go into that basement alone, given the recent, additional horror stories Max had recounted to them about what he and Walter had experienced.) Despite her lingering resistance to the basement, though, she'd have been the first to admit that the house had felt entirely different since the events of the past week. It felt – *lighter*. It felt as if they were finally free to make it their own.

Hearing the familiar sounds of Jack's truck pulling in, Maggie did a skip-hop to the front door. She'd been impatient to have the ultrasound; after dreaming of a baby for so long, she was determined to enjoy every second of this – even the sprints to the bathroom (or the quick turns to double over and puke in the snow in front of her family). While she'd been in Cuba, she, with Zoe's help and Jack's support, had determined to put her anxieties to the side for the remainder of the pregnancy. Sam had even remarked to her, in a rare moment of the two of them being alone in each other's company, that "Nothing in this world is guaranteed, but we all have a choice whether to flounder in the negative or prosper in the positive."

Maggie had been touched at the beautiful words from the usually quiet Sam. And, knowing some details of his difficult past, had taken them to heart.

When she opened the door, she smiled excitedly into Jack's eyes. She was met with echoed excitement as he held out his hand to her. "Ready?"

"Dude, I've been ready for this for *years!*" she said, taking his hand as they made their way to the truck.

Jack laughed. "Me too, babe."

Maggie thought of Sam's words over and over on the way to the hospital in Kentville and in the waiting room, whenever a worry threatened her composure. She found Jack glancing at her often, obviously making sure she was OK. He was trying hard, too, to just focus on the positive. Today, he'd get to see his baby on the ultrasound screen. *That* was wonderful, no matter what.

And that is what they did see. One baby – one, beautiful, 19-week-old baby, moving and waving. Heart beating miraculously. The visual confirmation was all the two needed to relax. The ultrasound tech was patient and offered a running description of the process. They watched in awe as their baby's head, stomach and leg bones were measured and recorded, and they thrilled at the proclamation, "This baby looks great!" She handed them some printout pictures of what they'd seen and left to fetch the doctor.

Jack, having had to ask questions at each new thing he'd seen on the screen and who was mildly frustrated when the women had exclaimed over a hand in front of the mouth or a particularly vigorous kick (having only perceived a confusing jumble of blurry shapes and movement), asked Maggie to explain the pictures to him in detail. She did, giggling. Then she met his eyes.

"Jack, this is amazing!"

"I know," he answered, smiling.

"No, I mean of course, all of it's amazing! But I figured something out while we were watching him move and kick in there."

"What?"

"I've been feeling him move!"

"What? Really?"

"Yeah. I've been writing it off as gas or indigestion," she laughed, "but every time we saw him move on the screen, I realized I was feeling those familiar little flutters at the same time!"

He hugged her, thrilled. "That *is* amazing! And -" he stepped back and looked at her, "why are you saying, 'him'?"

"No reason at all," she answered, her eyes wide. "I just don't like calling our baby 'it'."

"You didn't see any identifying markers, then?" he asked, mildly concerned that he'd missed something in his ineptitude at ultrasound reading.

"No!" she answered. "No, I honestly haven't the slightest clue. In fact, I've made a point of not thinking about it, as your mom has a bit of anxiety when it comes to boy pregnancies, you know?"

Jack nodded as the doctor came in briskly and introduced himself. Maggie wondered whether all ultrasound experiences were this nice or whether high-risk caregivers were trained to be more effective in their bedside manner. Judging by the stories Zoe had told her, she decided on the latter.

Repeating the tech's measurements quickly and confirming the numbers she'd recorded, he turned to them and announced, "Looks like an approximate due date of May 25th; does that sound right compared with what your family doctor told you?

"Yes," answered Maggie. "He said with my irregular ovulation, it was difficult to pinpoint, but he thought mid to late May, based on my dates.

The doctor nodded. "Good! And I'm sure he talked to you a bit about your interesting uterus?"

Maggie laughed. "Well, that's a positive spin on it!"

The doctor smiled. "No reason not to be; it's only mild and, in your case, shouldn't alter the course of your pregnancy or cause any concern unless you have a lot of trouble with incontinence or the opposite – emptying your bladder."

"Pfft, no problem there!" she exclaimed, and they all laughed.

"Even women who do experience discomfort, difficulty finding baby's heartbeat, severe urinary incontinence or difficulty with urination tend to see a lessening of symptoms during the late second trimester as the uterus expands with the baby. You don't need to think of it as a problem."

Maggie nodded and asked, "I did hear that it would be harder to feel the baby move, though?"

The doctor shrugged. "It depends on the woman and on her specific tilt. But that should also resolve as baby grows and the uterus takes up more space. Do you think you've felt the baby move?"

"Yes," she said, smiling.

"Good, then. Especially for a first pregnancy."

Maggie smiled at Jack, and he squeezed her hand. "All good news," he said quietly.

The doctor turned back to the screen and placed the wand on Maggie's abdomen again. "So far, so good! Now, let me just see here if I can get a look in between the legs. We'll record the sex, just for reference, but it's up to you whether you'd like to know. Oh, there it is! You were right," he nodded to the tech, then looked at Maggie for her decision.

It had happened so fast that she was caught completely off-guard. All she'd cared about until this point had been the viability of the pregnancy itself. She looked at Jack, who nodded, his eyes bright in the dimly-lit room.

"Yeah, we'd love to know!" she answered, finally, and the doctor smiled and pointed at the screen.

"I can say with nearly 100% certainty that that's a penis… and here's the scrotum. You've got a boy."

Jack actually jumped in the air, saying, "Woo!" and Maggie, despite herself, broke into happy tears.

"Well, that's good news, then, all of it," the doctor said and rose to leave. "See you in two weeks?"

"Yes, and thank you," they both said as the doctor and the tech left the room. Maggie and Jack hugged. "We're having a boy!" said Maggie.

"I know! I didn't even have a preference, but just knowing a little more about who – he – is, is really cool," answered Jack, his hands on the little protrusion of her abdomen.

They remained elated as they walked out of high-risk and took the elevator to the psych ward on the fifth floor. They only felt the sobering effect of the floor, with its strange noises and closed doors, when the elevator closed behind them and they turned their focus to the visit they'd have with Alice.

Following the signs to the front desk, they registered and were allowed through the inner security doors.

"Do we tell her?" Maggie asked, looking up at Jack for the decision. It was his mother, after all, and she'd just been through a rough time, to say the least.

"Absolutely. This is good news, Magpie."

He sounded so sure that she felt her anxieties melting away.

Finding Alice by the window in the open "Congregation Room", Maggie's stomach did a flip. She hoped fervently she wouldn't throw up.

Alice turned at their approach, and the smile that lit up her face brought relieved tears to both Maggie and Jack's eyes. They hadn't visited her in Intensive Care; Zoe had warned them of the strict visiting hours and the militant enforcement of rest and quiet, so they'd waited, with some difficulty, until today. They embraced her as she sat in her wheelchair, still recovering from the past week's adventures.

"Mom, you look wonderful," Jack said as he squatted in front of Alice. She leaned forward and grasped his hands. "Jackie, I feel better than I have in years."

Jack smiled, and a tear escaped onto his cheek. Maggie was so touched she had to turn around and distract herself by finding two chairs to drag over. Sitting, they both revelled in her bright smile.

"How are you feeling?" asked Maggie.

"Oh, you know. Still some blank spots, and confusion here and there, as before, I guess, but otherwise I feel so happy," she answered, her face sincere.

Jack glanced around. "How long are they going to keep you in here?"

"Not too long, I'm sure. "I think they're just making arrangements with the home."

Maggie made a mental note to find someone to discuss this with.

"Are you sure you're comfortable going back there, Mom?" Jack asked.

"Why yes, of course. It wasn't their fault, son; it was Rose who made me go. And she told me just how to do it. I don't think I would have gotten out without her."

Maggie squirmed, unsure of how to proceed. She didn't want to overwhelm Alice, but she had so many questions for her. "Why do you think Rose finally left, Alice?" she asked, tentatively.

Alice looked a bit blank as she searched for the answer. "I don't think I remember exactly *how* it happened, but somebody finally helped her find her baby."

Maggie sat back in her seat. "So, she did have another baby besides the son?"

"Oh yes, but had her far too soon. He killed her, you see." She shook her head, tears in her eyes. "Terrible business."

Jack reached out and took his mother's hand. "You don't have to talk about this right now if you don't want to, Mom."

Maggie nodded in agreement, sorry she'd taken it that far.

"No, no! It's alright now! At least they're together. And it's good we know about the baby; her husband made sure it was never officially recorded. It made Rose so sad. It was as if she had never existed – the baby," she clarified, and Maggie's hand covered her mouth as she struggled not to cry even harder.

"Oh, love. It's all OK now. That lovely girl, the one who helped - well, woman, but I mean she was petite, you know? She was so good to Rose. But it isn't finished yet."

Maggie's skin went cold. "What?"

"Well, we've helped Rose, but we haven't helped her baby, now, have we?"

"What do you mean?" Jack asked.

Alice looked out the window and then around the room, seemingly searching for something.

"Are you alright? Is there something I can get for you?" asked Maggie, getting ready to rise from her chair.

"Hm?" Alice seemed a bit surprised at the question. She put the fingers of her bandaged arm to her temple. "Oh, I'm sorry. I do feel so much better, I really do, but I still get tired so fast. I was just going to ask them to put a hot water bottle in my bed for my feet."

"I'll go find someone, Mom. You want to nap?"

"Oh, thank you, Jack. Yes, that would be nice."

Jack disappeared into the hallway, and Maggie placed her hand on Alice's.

Alice smiled at her. "What was I saying, dear?"

"It's OK, Alice. Let's get you all snuggled into bed. Sounds wonderful," answered Maggie, stifling a yawn.

"Poor thing, you're tired too, and it's no wonder! How are you feeling?"

Maggie perked up, her words suddenly spilling out. "Oh! I just had the ultrasound! I'll wait 'til Jack's back to tell you, but we found out the sex. The baby is healthy, Alice. He looked beautiful, moving all around -"

Alice had gasped. "He?" she asked.

"Oh, shit!" Maggie exclaimed before she could stop herself. "I said I'd wait for Jack -"

Jack came back in, then. "They're getting your bed ready for you, Mom, and they say you'll be back in your room in Wolfville tomorrow morning."

"Oh, good," Alice answered, a bit absently, looking again out the window.

"You talked to them?" Maggie asked him quietly.

Jack nodded, "Yep. I'll fill you in after." Jack wheeled Alice out of the room, Maggie in tow. As they walked toward her room, Alice asked Jack innocently if they'd had the ultrasound of the baby yet. Maggie gratefully squeezed her shoulder and inwardly remarked on Alice's improved presence of mind.

They tucked Alice carefully into her bed after hugs all around at the announcement (again) of the baby's gender. Alice met Maggie's eyes and said, pointedly, "Your baby boy is very lucky to have you."

They kissed her goodbye and were leaving the room when Alice spoke up once more. "Don't forget to find her when the snow melts. She deserves that. She shouldn't be buried where she is."

Jack and Maggie exchanged a look. "OK, Mom. We love you."

They walked off the ward, holding hands and not speaking. They kept silent until they stepped out of the elevator on the main floor and were walking toward the exit.

"We need to speak to Walter," said Jack.

"Yeah. I mean, I was thinking Charis, but Walter, too. I know Max checked up on him on Saturday, but he wasn't able to get any details about – well, anything, really. Walter was sleepy and confused and a bit pissed that he'd missed everything, to be honest. Max says he believes his wife wants him to help figure all of this out."

369

"His wife?" Jack asked.

"Yeah – his dead wife. She died just two years ago, I think."

Jack stopped in his tracks. *"Another ghost?"*

Maggie laughed a bit, then nodded solemnly. "Strange, isn't it? And now this about it not being over -" she gestured back toward the hospital.

Jack hugged her. "Don't worry. We'll do this final step when the snow melts, as Mom said."

Maggie smiled. "OK," and then, as a flicker of remembrance lit up her eyes, "Oh! I almost forgot! Max *did* get something out of Walter; he actually found the Maplestone son!"

"Really? After all this time -"

"I know. He's been going by his father's Russian name, I guess."

"Wonder what'll happen with the property now?" Jack looked thoughtful at this new bit of news. "You know, he'd be the perfect person to help us with finding – well, with what Mom was talking about."

Maggie stood on her toes and kissed his cheek. "I love you, you know."

"I know. I love you too – you and my *baby boy*, woohoo!" he shouted, smiling.

Maggie laughed and looked around, only mildly embarrassed at his endearing show of excitement. "I'm starving."

Jack looked thoughtful. "Let's got to that Italian place in Wolfville!"

Maggie paused, frowning. "It's OK to put all this stuff aside for a while, right? Forget about ghosts long enough to enjoy -" she looked down as she touched her belly, "- this?"

Jack took her hands and kissed her forehead. "Not only is it OK; I insist on it!"

"I was hoping you'd say that," she smiled.

"We're having a baby!" Jack whispered, eyes twinkling.

She nodded as they turned toward the car, but part of her still thought of another baby - lost, buried and nearly forgotten. Would have been, if it weren't for the ghost who loved her.

And maybe her brother, too.

The End